"THE OLDEST OF WOMEN WILL BE ALWAYS THERE!"

THE INVASION OF

FRANCE IN 1814

TRANSLATED FROM THE FRENCH OF

ERCKMANN-CHATRIAN

ILLUSTRATED

NEW YORK
CHARLES SCRIBNER'S SONS
1903

CONTENTS

CHAP.   PAGE

     I. The Old Shoemaker and his Daughter,   . 1

    II. The Shoemaker's Visitor, ... 17

   III. At Phalsbourg, ... 29

   IV. Madame Lefèvre, ... 46

    V. The Depot, ... 55

   VI. Among the Mountaineers, .   .   . 77

  VII. Rising of the Partisans, .   .   . 90

 VIII. The Leader, ... 100

   IX. The Conscript, ... 109

    X. Robin's Vision, ... 122

   XI. A Reconnoissance, ... 132

  XII. The Landlord of the "Pineapple," . 139

 XIII. Round the Watchfires, .   .   . 159

 XIV. "Forward! Forward!".   .   . 169

  XV. The Battle Renewed, .   .   . 183

 XVI. Painful Scenes, ... 200

 XVII. Round the Festive Board, .   . 211

XVIII. The Cave of Luitprandt, .   . 219

 XIX. Gaspard's Letter, ... 230

  XX. The Surprise, ... 241

 XXI. "All is Lost," 266

 XXII. On the Falkenstein, .   .   . 280

XXIII. Marc Dives's Mission, .   .   . 286

XXIV. A Flag of Truce, ... 294

 XXV. "Battle of the Rocks," .   .   . 305

XXVI. Conclusion, ... 321

LIST OF ILLUSTRATIONS

"The Oldest of Women will be Always There!"
Frontispiece

FACING
PAGE

There was a General Shout of "Long Live France!"   96

Doctor Lorquin, ... 106

Louise Throwing her Arms Around Gaspard's Neck, 120

The Lunatic, Waving his Sceptre, Made Them a
    Discourse, ... 128

Big Dubreuil; the Friend of the Allies, . . . 172

As they Climbed Up they were Clubbed with Muskets, 180

Yégof Saluted each Phantom with Sparkling Eyes, 226

Many of Them will Never again See their Friends, 270

There Go Up in Smoke Forty Years of Toil and
    Trouble, ... 284

For Three Days Provisions had Completely Failed, 308

"Let us Overwhelm Them, as at Blutfeld!" . . 318

INTRODUCTORY NOTE

THE invasion of France by the allied armies after
the battle of Leipsic had proved the German campaign even more disastrous than that of Russia the
year before, was not only essentially the death-blow
to the power of Napoleon, but was the first real taste
France had had for many years of an experience she
had so often previously meted out to her neighbors.
In spite of all she had suffered from the conscription
and from exhaustion of men and treasure in offen-
sive war—or at least war waged outside her own
territory—the great Invasion meant for her something far more terrible than any reverses she had
yet undergone. Napoleon was not only not invincible, it appeared, he was not even able to defend
the frontiers he had found firmly established on his
accession to power. The allies had announced that
they were warring not against France but against
the French Emperor—" against the preponderance
that Napoleon had too long exercised beyond the
limits of his empire." Everywhere in France except

in the official world of Paris, the once enchanted name of Napoleon had become recognized as a synonym of national disaster.

Nevertheless nothing—except, perhaps, the similar circumstances of the Prussian invasion in 1870 —has ever so well attested the fundamental and absorbing patriotism of the French people as their heroic resistance to this invasion and their instinctive and universal refusal to separate in this crisis the cause of their Emperor from their own. The presence of a foreign foe on whatever pretext within their boundaries sufficed to arouse them *en masse.* No such enthusiasm had been known since the days of the Republic's and the Consulate's victories as was awakened, in the thick of national disaster and amid the ruin of all ambitious hopes, by the thought of an enemy within the borders of *la patrie.* And in " The Invasion " of MM. Erckmann-Chatrian this enthusiasm and devotion find a chronicle which is most realistically impressive. So soon as the peasants of the outlying villages of the eastern frontier learn of the impending descent of the Cossacks and Germans, without thought of their own comfort and safety—which it is, however, impartially pointed out they know would hardly be better secured by submission—they organize for resistance. They blockade the highways and defend the mountain passes. Women and children aid in the work. While the siege of Phalsbourg goes on the heights are occupied by sturdy peasants who oppose for a while an effective obstacle to the passage of the invaders. The worst hardships, the most perilous adventures, are accepted by them with the heroic courage of regulars. Outlaws and smugglers work and fight hand to hand with the respected worthies of the neighborhood. They watch their farms burn from their outlook on the hill-tops, they suffer the pangs of starvation when their supplies are intercepted by the enemy, they fight to desperation when their position is finally turned by the treachery of a crazy German they have long harbored—and whose vagaries give, by the way, a most romantic color to the narrative—and they are finally slain or captured just as Paris capitulates and peace is made. None of the National Novels is more graphic or more significant historically than "The Invasion."

THE INVASION OF FRANCE IN 1814

CHAPTER I

THE OLD SHOEMAKER AND HIS DAUGHTER

IF you would wish to know the history of the great invasion of 1814, such as it was related to me by the old hunter Frantz du Hengst, you must transport yourself to the village of Charmes, in the Vosges. About thirty small houses, covered with shingles and dark-green houseleeks, stand in rows along the banks of the Sarre: you can see the gables carpeted with ivy and withered honeysuckles, for winter is approaching; the beehives closed with corks of straw, the small gardens, the palings, the hedges which separate them one from the other.

To the left, on a high mountain, arise the ruins of the ancient château of Falkenstein, destroyed two hundred years ago by the Swedes. It is now only a mass of stones and brambles; an old " timber-way," with its worn-out steps, ascends to it through the pine-trees. To the right, on the side of the hill, one can perceive the farm of Bois-de-Chênes—a large building, with granaries, stables, and sheds, the flat roof loaded with great stones, in order to resist the north wind. A few cows are grazing in the heather, a few goats on the rocks.

Everything is calm and silent.

Some children, in gray stuff trousers, their heads and feet bare, are warming themselves around their little fires on the outskirts of the woods; the spiral lines of blue smoke fade away in the air, great white clouds remain immovable above the valley; behind these clouds arise the arid peaks of the Grosmann and Donon.

You must know that the end house of the village, whose square roof is pierced by two loophole windows, and whose low door opens on the muddy street, belonged, in 1813, to Jean-Claude Hullin, one of the old volunteers of '92, but now a shoemaker in the village of Charmes, and who was held in much consideration by the mountaineers. Hullin was a short stout man, with gray eyes, large lips, a short nose, and thick eyebrows. He was of a jovial, kind disposition, and did not know how to refuse anything to his daughter Louise, a child whom he had picked up among some miserable gypsies—farriers and tin-sellers—without house or dwelling-place, who go from village to village mending pots and pans, melting the ladles, and patching up cracked utensils. He considered her as his own daughter, and never seemed to remember she came of a strange race.

Besides this natural affection, the good old fellow possessed others still: he loved above all his cousin, the old mistress of the farm of Bois-de-Chênes, Catherine Lefèvre, and her son Gaspard, who had been carried off that year by the conscription—a handsome young fellow, the " fiancé " of Louise, and whose return was expected by all the family at the end of the campaign.

Hullin recalled always with enthusiasm his campaigns of the Sambre-et-Meuse, of Italy and of Egypt. He often thought of them, and sometimes in the evening, when the work was over, he would go to the sawmills of Valtin, that dark manufactory formed of trunks of trees still bearing their bark, and which you can perceive down there at the end of the valley. He sat down among the wood-cutters and charcoal-gatherers, and sledges, in front of the great fire; and while the heavy wheel turned, the dam thundered and the saws grinded, he, his elbow on his knee, and his pipe in his mouth, would speak to them of Hoche, of Kleber, and finally of General Bonaparte, whom he had seen hundreds

of times, and whose thin face, piercing eyes, and
eagle profile, he would depict as though he were
present.

Such was Jean-Claude Hullin.

He was one of the old Gallic stock, fond of extraordinary adventures and heroic enterprises, but
constant to his work, out of a sentiment of duty,
from New Year's day until Saint Sylvester's.

As for Louise, the child of the tramp, she was
a slender creature, with long delicate hands, eyes
of such a soft deep blue that they seemed to penetrate to the depths of your soul, skin of a snowy
whiteness, hair of a pale straw-color, like silk in
texture, and drooping shoulders like those of a vir-
gin praying. Her ingenuous smile, pensive forehead—in fact, her whole appearance—recalled the
old *Lied* of the Minnesinger Erhart, when he said:
" I have seen a ray of light pass by: my eyes are
still dazzled by it. Was it a moonbeam piercing
the foliage? Was it a smile from the dawn in the
forests? No, it was the beautiful Edith, my love,
who passed by. I have seen her, and my eyes are
still dazzled."

Louise only cared for fields, gardens, and flowers. In spring-time, the first notes of the sky-
lark made her shed tears of delight. She went to
see the budding hawthorn and blue cornflowers be-

hind the hedges on the hill-sides; she watched for
the return of the swallows, from the little windows
of the garret. She was always the true child of the
homeless vagrants, only less wild. Hullin forgave
her everything; he understood her nature, and
would sometimes say, laughingly:—" My poor
Louise, with the booty that thou bringest us,—thy
fine sheaves of flowers and golden wheat-ears—we
should die of hunger in three days! "

Then she would smile so tenderly at him and
embrace him so willingly, that he would go on
with his work, saying:—" Bah! why need I grumble? She is right: she loves the sunshine. Gaspard will work for two—he will have the happiness
of four. I do not pity him: on the contrary. One
can find plenty of women who work, and that does
not improve their beauty; but loving woman!
what luck to have found one—what luck! "

Thus reasoned the good old fellow; and days,
weeks, and months wore away in the expectation
of Gaspard's return.

Madame Lefèvre, an extremely energetic woman, partook of Hullin's ideas on the subject of
Louise.

" As for me," she said, " I only want a daughter
who loves us; I do not wish her to have anything
to do with my household affairs. So long as she

is contented! Thou wilt not bother me—is it not so, Louise?"

And then they would embrace each other. But Gaspard did not return, and for two months they had had no tidings of him.

On that same day, toward the middle of December, 1813, between three and four o'clock in the afternoon, Hullin, bending over his bench, was finishing a pair of nailed shoes for the wood-cutter Rochart. Louise had just put an earthenware porringer down on the little iron stove, which sang and crackled in a plaintive manner, while the old clock counted the seconds in its monotonous tic-tac. Outside, all along the street, could be perceived small pools of water, covered with a coating of thin white ice, announcing the approach of intense cold. At times the sound of great wooden shoes, running along the hardened road, could be heard, and a felt hat, a cape, or a woollen cap would pass by: then the noise would cease, and the plaintive hissing of the green wood in the flames, the humming of Louise's spinning-wheel, and the boiling of the porridge-pot again prevailed. This had gone on for about two hours, when Hullin, glancing accidentally through the little window-panes, stopped his work, and remained with his eyes wide open, staring, as though absorbed by some unusual spectacle.

In fact, at the corner of the street, in front of the " Trois Pigeons," there advanced, in the midst of a crowd of whistling, jumping, and shouting boys, who called out " The King of Diamonds! The King of Diamonds! "—There advanced, I say, one of the strangest personages imaginable. Picture to yourself a red-headed, red-bearded man, with a grave face, gloomy expression, straight nose, the eyebrows meeting on the forehead, a circle of tin on the head, a gray dogskin floating over the back, its forepaws tied around the neck; the chest covered with little copper crosses, the legs clothed with a sort of gray cloth trousers fastened above the ankle, and the feet bare. A great raven, with black wings glossed over with white, was perched on his shoulder. From his imposing gait one would have taken him for one of the ancient Merovingian kings, such as are represented by the images of Montbé- liard; he held in the left hand a short thick stick in the shape of a sceptre, and with the right he made ostentatious gestures, raising his finger toward heaven, and apostrophizing his retinue.

All the doors opened on his passage; behind every pane appeared inquisitive faces. Some few old women on the outer stairs of their houses, called out to the madman, who would not deign to turn his head; others went down into the streets and tried to prevent him passing; but he, lifting his head and raising his eyebrows, with one word and a sign, forced them to make way.

"Hullo!" said Hullin, "here is Yégof. I did not expect to have seen him again this winter. It is not one of his customs. What on earth can bring him back in such weather?"

And Louise, laying down her distaff, hurried away to contemplate "The King of Diamonds." It was a great event, the arrival of Yégof the mad-man at the commencement of winter: some rejoiced over it, hoping to keep him and make him relate his glory and fortunes in the inns; others, and especially the women, were filled with a sort of vague uneasiness, for madmen, as all know, have ideas from another world: they know the past and the future—they are inspired by God: the only thing is to know how to understand them—their words bearing always two meanings: one for the ordinary run of people, the other for more refined and delicate souls, and the wise. This madman besides, more than another, had truly some sublime and extraordinary thoughts. None knew from whence he came, nor where he went, nor what he wanted; for Yégof wandered about the country like some troubled spirit. He spoke of extinct races, and pretended that he was Emperor of Australasia, of Polynesia, and of other lands besides. Great books could have been written on his palaces, castles, and strongholds—of which he knew the number, the situation, the architecture—and whose beauty, riches, and grandeur, he would celebrate in a simple and modest manner. He spoke of his stables, of his hunts, of his crown-officers, ministers, counsellors, of the heads of his provinces; he never made any mistakes as to their names or different merits; but he bitterly bewailed having been dethroned by the accursed race: and the old midwife, Sapience Coquelin, every time that she heard him groan over this subject, would cry bitterly, and others also did the same. Then he would raise his arms to heaven and cry out,—" O women, women! remember, remember! The hour approaches—the spirits of darkness flee! the old race—the masters of your masters—advance like the waves of the sea! "

And every spring he was in the habit of making a survey of all the old owls' nests, the ancient castles, and all the ruins which crown the Vosges in the depths of their forests, at Nideck, Géroldseck, Lutzelbourg, and Turkestein, saying that he was going to visit his territories, talking of re-establishing the past splendor of his states, and of putting all mutinous people into slavery, with the aid of his cousin the " Grand Gôlo."

Jean-Claude Hullin made light of these things, from not having a soul elevated enough to enter into the invisible spheres; but Louise was much troubled by them—above all, when the raven flapped its wings and gave its hoarse cry.

Yégof, then, descended the street, without stopping anywhere; and Louise, all excitement, seeing that he looked toward their little house, said aloud, —" Papa Jean-Claude, I believe he is coming our way."

"It is quite possible," replied Hullin. "The poor devil must be in need of a pair of good lined shoes for the great cold, and if he were to ask me, I should hardly be able to refuse them to him."

"Oh, how kind you are!" said the young girl, embracing him affectionately.

"Yes, yes! thou art flattering me," said he, laughing, "because I do what thou wishest. Who will pay me for my wood and work? It will not be Yégof!"

Louise kissed him again, and Hullin, looking lovingly at her, murmured,—" This payment is worth the other."

Yégof was then about fifteen yards from their door: the tumult still kept increasing; the boys hung on to the tatters of his coat, crying out, " Diamond! Club! Spade!" Suddenly he turned, raised his sceptre, and called out in a dignified though furious manner,—" Go back, accursed race! Go back, deafen me no longer, or I will loose my bloodhounds against you! "

This menace only made the shouts of laughter and hisses redouble; but as at that moment Hullin appeared on the threshold with a long strap in his hand, and distinguishing five or six of the most obstinate among them, he warned them that that evening he would go and pull their ears during their supper—a feat which he had already performed several times with the consent of the parents, the whole band dispersed in great consternation. Then, going toward the madman,—" Enter, Yégof," said the shoemaker, " come and warm thyself by the fire."

" I do not call myself Yégof," replied the unhappy man, looking offended. " I call myself Luitprandt, King of Australasia and Polynesia."

" Yes, yes, I know," said Jean-Claude—" I know! Thou hast already told me all that. But what does it matter that thou callest thyself Yégof, or Luitprandt? come in all the same. It is cold; try to warm thyself."

" I come in," replied the madman; " but it is for a much more serious affair: it is for a state affair—to form an indissoluble alliance between the Germans and the Triboques."

"Well, we will talk of that."

Yégof, stooping under the door, entered as though in a reverie, and saluted Louise by bowing and lowering his sceptre; but the raven would not come in. Opening his great wings, he made a circuit around the house, and came and fastened himself onto the window-panes to break them.

"Hans," shouted the madman, "take care! I am coming!"

But the bird did not detach its sharp claws from the casement, and never ceased fluttering its great wings so long as its master remained in the cottage. Louise did not take her eyes off it: she was afraid. As for Yégof, he sat down in the old leathern arm-chair behind the stove, his legs stretched out as though on a throne; and gazing around him in a triumphant manner, he cried out,—"I come direct from Jérome, to conclude an alliance with thee, Hullin. Thou art not ignorant that I have deigned to cast my eyes on thy daughter, and I come to ask her of thee in marriage."

At this proposition Louise blushed to the roots of her hair, and Hullin burst into a loud laugh.

"Thou laughest!" cried the madman, in a hollow voice. "Well! thou art wrong to laugh. This alliance may alone save thee from the impending ruin of thyself, thy house, and all thy belongings.

At this moment my armies are advancing. They are countless—they cover the earth. What can you do against me? You will be vanquished, annihilated, or reduced to slavery, as you have already been for centuries: for I, Luitprandt, King of Australasia and of Polynesia—I have decided that everything shall be as it once was. Remember!"— here the madman raised his finger solemnly—" remember what has passed! You have been beaten! And we, the old northern races—we have put our yokes upon you. We have burdened you with the largest stones for building our strong castles and our subterraneous prisons; we have harnessed you to our ploughs; you have been before us as the straw before the hurricane. Remember, remember, Triboque, and tremble!"

" I remember very well," said Hullin, still laughing; " but we had our revenge. Thou knowest?"

" Yes, yes," interrupted Yégof, frowning; " but that time has gone by. My warriors are more numerous than the leaves in the forests; and your blood flows like the water of the brooks. Thou, I know thee—I knew thee a thousand years ago!"

" Bah! " said Hullin.

" Yes, it was this hand—dost thou hear?—this hand that has vanquished thee, when, for the first time, we entered your forests. It has made thy head bow beneath the yoke—it will make it bend again! Because you are brave, you believe yourselves masters of this country and of all France forever. Well, you are wrong! We have spoiled you, and we will spoil you again. We will restore Alsace and Lorraine to Germany, Brittany and Normandy to the men from the North, with Flanders and the South to Spain. We will make France into a little kingdom around Paris—a very little kingdom—with a descendant of the ancient race at your head. And you will no longer agitate yourselves—you will be very tranquil. Ha, ha, ha!" Yégof began to laugh.

Hullin, who had no knowledge of history, was astonished that he should know so many names.

"Bah! stop that, Yégof," said he; "and come, take a little soup to warm thy inside."

"I do not ask thee for soup; I ask thee for this girl in marriage—the most beautiful on my estates. Give her to me willingly, and I raise thee to the steps of my throne: else my armies shall take her by force, and thou shalt not have the merit of giving her to me."

While thus speaking, the unhappy creature regarded Louise with an air of profound admiration.

"How beautiful she is! I destine her to the

greatest honors. Rejoice, young girl, rejoice! Thou shalt be queen of Australasia."

"Listen, Yégof," said Hullin. "I am very much flattered by thy demand: it shows that thou canst appreciate beauty. It is well. But my daughter is already affianced to Gaspard Lefèvre."

"And I," said the madman, greatly irritated— "I will not hear of such a thing!" Then rising up, —"Hullin," said he, in solemn tones, "it is my first demand. I will renew it yet twice again—dost thou hear—twice! And if thou wilt persist in thy obstinacy—misfortune, misfortune on thee and thy race!"

"What! thou wilt not take any soup?"

"No, no! I will accept nothing from thee so long as thou hast not consented. Nothing, nothing!" And then marching toward the door, much to the satisfaction of Louise, who was intent on the raven, fluttering its wings against the window-panes, he said, raising his sceptre,—"Twice again!" and departed.

Hullin went off into a shout of laughter. "Poor devil!" he exclaimed. "In spite of himself, his nose turned toward the porringer. He has nothing in his inside—his teeth chatter with hunger. Well! his madness is stronger than either cold or hunger."

"Oh, how he frightened me!" said Louise.

"Come, come, my child, calm thyself. He is gone. He thinks thou art pretty, fool though he is; do not let that terrify thee."

But although the madman had left, Louise still trembled, and felt herself blushing when she thought of how he had looked at her.

Yégof had taken the road to Valtin. He could still be seen, his raven on his shoulder, walking slowly along and making curious gestures, although no one was near him. The night was drawing on, and soon the tall figure of "The King of Diamonds" disappeared in the gray shadows of the winter twilight.

CHAPTER II

In the evening of that same day, after their supper, Louise, having taken her spinning-wheel, was gone for a little diversion to the Mother Rochart's where all the good women and young girls of the neighborhood used to assemble till near midnight. They spent their time in relating old legends, talking of the rain, of the weather, of marriages, baptisms, of the departure or return of the conscripts, and what not, that enabled them to pass the hours agreeably.

Hullin remained alone before his little copper lamp, nailing the shoes of the old wood-cutter. He no longer thought of the madman Yégof. His hammer rose and fell, driving the great nails into the thick wooden shoes quite mechanically, by force of habit. In the meantime thousands of ideas came into his head; he was thoughtful without knowing why. Now it was Gaspard, who gave no signs of being alive; then it was the campaign, which was

2   17

being indefinitely prolonged.   The lamp threw its
yellowish light around the smoky little room.   Outside, not a sound.   The fire began to die away.
Jean-Claude rose to put on a fagot, then sat down
again, muttering,—"Bah! this cannot last; we
shall receive a letter one of these days."

The old clock began to strike nine; and as Hullin was recommencing his work, the door opened and
Catherine Lefèvre, the mistress of Bois-de-Chênes,
appeared on the threshold, to the great stupefaction
of the shoemaker, for it was not her custom to arrive
at such a time.

Catherine Lefèvre might have been sixty years
old, but she was as upright and strong as at thirty.
Her clear gray eyes and beaked nose resembled those
of a bird of prey; the corners of her mouth turned
down, and made her look somewhat gloomy and
sad; two or three locks of gray hair fell over her
forehead; a brown striped hood reached from her
head, over her shoulders and down to her elbows.
Her physiognomy announced a steadfast, tenacious
character, with something indescribably grand and
mournful about it, which inspired both respect
and fear.

"Can it be you, Catherine?" said Hullin, in
astonishment.

"Yes, it is I," replied the old dame, calmly.

"I am come to talk with you, Jean-Claude. . . . Louise is away?"

"She has gone for a little amusement to Madeleine Rochart's."

"It is well."

Then Catherine pushed back her hood from her head, and sat down at the end of the bench. Hullin looked fixedly at her: he perceived something extraordinary and mysterious about her which fascinated him.

"What has happened, then?" said he, putting down his hammer.

Instead of answering this question, she turned toward the door, and seemed to be listening; then hearing no sound, her serious expression came back.

"Yégof the madman spent last night at the farm," said she.

"He came to see me this afternoon," rejoined Hullin, without attaching any importance to this fact, which was totally indifferent to him.

"Yes," replied the old dame, in a low voice, "he spent the night with us; and yesterday evening, about this time, in the kitchen, before us all, this madman related terrible things!"

Then she relapsed into silence, and the corners of her mouth seemed to turn down more than ever.

"Terrible things!" murmured the shoemaker, excessively astonished: for he had never seen Catherine Lefèvre in such a condition before. "But what then? say, what?"

"Dreams I have had!"

"Dreams? You certainly want to make fun of me!"

"No!"

Then, after a short pause, she slowly continued —"Yesterday evening, all our people were assembled in the kitchen around the large fireplace after supper; the table still remained covered with empty dishes, plates, and spoons. Yégof had partaken of it with us, and had amused us with the history of his treasures, castles, and provinces. It might have been toward nine o'clock: the madman was sitting at one end of the blazing fire; old Duchêne, my ploughboy, was mending Bruno's saddle; the herdsman, Robin, was plaiting a basket; Annette arranged her pans on the shelves: and I had brought my wheel nearer the fire to finish spinning a distaff-ful before going to bed. Out of doors, the dogs were barking at the moon; the cold was very great. We were all there, talking of the coming winter. Duchêne said it would be very severe, for he had seen several flocks of wild-geese. And Yégof's raven, on the edge of the mantel-piece, its head buried in its ruffled feathers, seemed to sleep; but now and then it would elongate its neck and watch us, listen a moment and then cover itself again in its plumes."

She remained silent a moment, as though to collect her ideas; her eyelids drooped, her great beaked nose seemed to bend down on to her lips, and a strange pallor came over her face.

"What the devil is coming next?" thought Hullin.

The old woman continued: "Yégof near the fire, with his tin crown, and his short stick on his knees, was dreaming of something. He looked at the great black chimney, the stone mantel-piece, which is carved with different figures and trees, and the smoke which went up in great clouds around the sides of bacon: when suddenly he struck with the end of his stick on to the tiles and called out, as though in a dream—' Yes, yes, I have seen that long ago—long ago!' And as we all looked at him speechless—' In those times,' he went on to say, ' the pine-forests were forests of oak. The Nideck, the Dagsberg, Falkenstein, Géroldseck, all those old ruined castles did not exist. In those times the bison could be hunted in the depths of the woods, the salmon caught in the Sarre, and you, the fair men, were buried in snow six months of the year.

You lived on milk and cheese, for you had many
flocks and herds on the Hengst, the Schnéeberg,
the Grosmann, the Donon. In the summer you
hunted: you came down to the Rhine, the Moselle,
the Meuse. I can recall it all! '

"And wonderful to relate, Jean-Claude, as the
madman spoke, I seemed to see also these countries
of years gone by, and to remember them as I should
a dream. I had let fall my distaff, and Duchêne,
Robin, Jeanne—in fact, everybody—listened.
'Yes, it was long ago,' he continued. 'In those
days you were already building these great chim-
neys; and all around, at a distance of two or three
hundred yards, you planted palisades fifteen feet
high, and with the points hardened by the fire.
And inside them you kept your big dogs with their
hanging cheeks, who barked day and night.'

"We could see what he said, Jean-Claude; we
could see it all. But he paid no heed to us: he regarded the figures on the chimney-piece with his
mouth open; but, in an instant, having stooped his
head and seeing how attentive we all were, he
laughed with a wild, mad laughter, and cried out:
—'In those days you believed yourselves the lords
of the country, O fair men, with your blue eyes
and white skins, fed on milk and cheese, and only
tasting blood in the autumn, at the great hunts:

you believed yourselves the masters of the plains
and mountains, when we, the red men, with the
green eyes, out of the sea—we who drank always
blood and only liked battles—one fine morning we
arrived with our axes and spears, and ascended the
Sarre under the shadows of the old oaks. Ah! it
was a cruel war, which lasted weeks and months.
And the old woman—there—' said he, pointing at
me, with a singular smile, 'the Margareth of the
clan of Kilberix, that old woman with her beaked
nose, in her palisades, in the midst of her dogs and
warriors—she fought like a wolf. But when five
moons had passed, hunger arrived. The doors of
the palisades opened for flight, and we, in ambush
in the stream—we massacred all!—all—except the
children and the beautiful young girls. The old
woman, alone, defended herself to the last with her
teeth and nails; and I, Luitprandt, clove her head
in two; and I took her father, the aged man and
blind, to chain him at the door of my castle like a
dog!'

"Then, Hullin," continued the old woman,
"the madman began to chant a long song—the
lamentation of the old man chained to his doorway.
Wait till I can recall it, Jean-Claude. It was
mournful—mournful as a *Miserere*. No, I cannot
remember it; but I seem still to hear it. It made

our blood curdle; and, as he laughed without ceasing, at last all our servants gave a terrible cry, rage seized them. Duchêne sprang on the madman to strangle him; but he, with more strength than one could suppose he possessed, threw him back, and raising his stick furiously, said to us:—'On your knees, slaves—on your knees! My armies are advancing! Do you hear? The earth trembles with them. These castles, the Nideck, the Haut-Barr, the Dagsberg, the Turkestein, you shall build them up again! On your knees!'

"I never saw a more fearful face than Yégof's at that moment; but, seeing for the second time my servants rising against him, I was obliged to defend him myself. 'It is a madman,' I said to them. 'Are you not ashamed to believe in the words of a madman?' They stopped on my account; but I could not close my eyes that night. The words of that wretched man kept recurring to me. I seemed to hear the chant of the old prisoner, the barking of our dogs, and the sounds of battle. For years I have never felt so uneasy. That is why I came to see you, Jean-Claude. What do you think of it?"

"I?" exclaimed the shoemaker, in whose ruddy face both irony and pity were visible. "If I did not know you so well, Catherine, I should say you were deranged:—you, Duchêne, Robin, and the rest of you. All that has about the same effect on me as one of Geneviève de Brabant's tales—made up to terrify little children, and which shows us how foolish our ancestors were."

"You do not comprehend these things," said she, in a calm, grave voice; "you have never had any of those ideas."

"Then you believe all that Yégof has said to you?"

"Yes, I believe it."

"What, you, Catherine?—you, a sensible woman? If it were the mother of Rochart I should say nothing; but you!"

He rose as though annoyed, took off his apron, shrugged his shoulders, then sat down again quickly, and called out:—"This madman, do you know what he is? I will tell you. He is most assuredly one of those German school-masters who stuff their brains with 'Old Mother Goose' tales, and then gravely relate them to others. By dint of studying, dreaming, ruminating, their wits get out of order; they have visions, many-sided ideas, and take their dreams for realities. I have always looked upon Yégof as one of those poor wretches. He knows lots of names, he speaks of Brittany and Australasia, of Polynesia and the Nideck, and then of

Jéroldseck, of the Turkestein, of the Rhine—in act of everything at hazard; and it ends by having he appearance of something when it is nothing. In ordinary times you would think as I do, Catherine; but you are troubled at not receiving any tidings from Gaspard. These rumors of war and of invasion that are going about torment and unsettle you. You cannot sleep; and what a poor madman says, you regard as Bible truths."

"No, Hullin; it is not that. If you yourself had heard Yégof——"

"Get along!" exclaimed the good old fellow. "If I had, I should have laughed at him as I did just now. Do you know that he came to ask Louise of me in marriage, to make her queen of Australasia?"

Catherine Lefèvre could not restrain a smile; but, regaining almost at once her serious expression —"All your reasonings, Jean-Claude," said she, "cannot convince me; but, I confess it, the silence of Gasper frightens me. I know my son: he would certainly have written to me. Why have his letters never reached me? The war is going on badly, Hullin—we have all the world against us. They don't want our revolution—you know it as well as I do. So long as we were masters, and won victory after victory, they looked kindly on us; but since our Russian misfortunes, things wear a bad aspect."

"Là, Là, Catherine, how you get carried away. You see everything gloomily."

"Yes, I see everything gloomily, and I am right. What makes me so uneasy is, that we never get any news from the outer world; we live here as in a savage country: one knows of nothing that goes on. The Austrians and the Cossacks could be upon us at any time, and we should be taken by surprise."

Hullin observed the old dame, whose expression was very animated; and even he began to be influenced by the same fears.

"Listen, Catherine," said he, suddenly. "When you speak in a reasonable manner, it is not I who would say anything against it. All you now tell me is possible. I do not believe in it; but one might as well make sure. I had intended to go to Phalsbourg in a week, to buy sheepskins for trimming some shoes: I will go to-morrow. At Phalsbourg, a garrison and post town, there must be some reliable news. Will you believe those I shall bring you on my return from that place?"

"Yes."

"Good; it is then arranged. I shall leave to-morrow early. There are five leagues in all. I shall return about six o'clock. You will see, Catherine, that all your dismal ideas have no sense in them."

"I hope so," she replied, rising. "I hope so. You have somewhat reassured me, Hullin. Now I will go to the farm, and may I sleep better than I did last night. Good-night, Jean-Claude."

CHAPTER III

THE next day at dawn, Hullin, wearing his blue cloth Sunday breeches, his large brown velvet jacket and red waistcoat with brass buttons, and a broad beaver mountaineer's hat turned up like a cockade above his ruddy face—started on his way to Phalsbourg, a stout stick in his hand.

Phalsbourg is a small fortress, half-way on the imperial road from Strasbourg to Paris; it dominates Saverne, the defiles of Haut-Barr, Roche-Platte, Bonne-Fontaine, and of the Graufthâl. Its bastions, outposts, and demilunes are cut out in zigzags on a rocky plain: from afar, the walls look as though they might be cleared at a jump; but on coming closer one perceives the moat, a hundred feet wide, thirty deep, and the dark ramparts hewn in the face of the rock. That makes one stop suddenly. Besides, with the exception of the church, the town-hall, the two gateways of France and Germany, in shape of mitres, and the peaks of the two

29

powder-magazines, all the rest is hidden behind the
fortifications.   Such is Phalsbourg, which is not
without a certain imposing effect, especially when
one crosses its bridges and piers, under its thick
gates, garnished with iron-spiked portcullis.   In
the interior, the houses are distributed in regular
quarters; they are low, in straight lines, built of
freestone: everything bears a military aspect.

Hullin, owing to his robust constitution and jovial disposition, never had any fears for the future,
and considered all rumors of retreat, rout, and invasion, which circulated in the country, as so many
lies propagated by dishonest individuals; so that
one may judge of his stupefaction when, on leaving
the mountains and from the outskirts of the woods,
he saw the whole surroundings of the town laid as
bare as a pontoon: not a garden, not an orchard,
not a promenade, or a tree, or even a shrub—all
was destroyed within cannon-range.   A few poor
creatures were picking up the last remnants of their
little houses, and carrying them into the town.
Nothing was to be seen on the horizon but the line
of ramparts standing out clearly above the hidden
roads.   It had the effect of a thunder-bolt on Jean-
Claude.

For some moments he could neither articulate a
word nor make a step forward.

"Oh, ho!" said he, at last, "this is bad—this is very bad. They expect the enemy."

Then his warlike instincts prevailed; a dark flush came over his brown cheeks. "It is those rascally Austrians, Prussians, and Russians, and all the other wretches picked up out of the dregs of Europe, who are the cause of this," cried he, waving his stick. "But beware! we will make them pay for the damages!"

He was possessed with one of those white rages such as honest people feel when they are driven to extremities. Woe to him who annoyed Hullin just then!

Twenty minutes later he entered the town, at the rear of a long file of carriages, each harnessed to five or six horses, pulling, with much trouble, enormous trunks of trees, destined to construct block-houses on the *place-d'armes*. Among the conductors, the peasants, and neighing, stamping horses, marched gravely a mounted *gendarme* —Father Kels—who did not seem to hear anything, and said, in a rough voice, "Courage, courage, my friends! We will make two more journeys before evening. You will have deserved well of your country!"

Jean-Claude crossed the bridge.

A new spectacle opened before him in the town.

There reigned the ardor of defence: all the doors
were open; men, women, and children came and
ran, helping to transport the powder and projectiles.
They stopped in groups of three, four, six, to make
themselves acquainted with the news.

"Hé neighbor!"

"What then?"

"A courier has just arrived in great speed. He
entered by the French gate."

"Then he has come to announce the National
Guard from Nancy."

"Or, perhaps, a convoy from Metz."

"You are right. We want sixteen-pounders,
and shot also. The stoves are to be broken up to
make some."

A few worthy tradespeople in their shirt-sleeves,
standing on tables along the pavement, were busy-
ing themselves with barricading their windows with
large pieces of wood and mattresses; others rolled
up to their doors tubs of water. This enthusiasm
reanimated Hullin.

"Excellent!" said he; "everybody is making
holiday here. The allies will be well received."

In front of the College, the squeaky voice of the
Sergeant-de-ville Harmentier was proclaiming:—

"Let it be known that the casemates are to be
opened: therefore everybody may take a mattress

there, and two blankets each. And the commissa-
ries of this place are going to commence their
rounds of inspection, to ascertain that each inhabi-
tant possesses food for three months in advance,
which he must certify.—This day, 20th December,
1813.—JEAN PIERRE MEUNIER, *Governor.*"

All this Hullin saw and heard in less than a
minute, for the whole town was in the greatest excitement. Strange, serious, and comic scenes succeeded each other without interruption.

Near the narrow street leading to the Arsenal,
a few National Guards were drawing a twenty-four
pounder. These honest fellows had a very steep
ascent to climb; they could do no more. " Ho!
all together! Mille tonnerres! Once again!
Forward! " They all shouted at once, pushing the
wheels, and the great cannon, stretching out its long
neck over its immense carriage, above their heads,
rolled slowly along, making the pavement tremble.

Hullin, quite rejoiced, was no longer the same
man. His soldier-like instincts, the remembrance
of the bivouac, of the marches, of the firing, and of
the battles—all returned. His eyes sparkled, his
heart beat faster, and already thoughts of defence,
of entrenchments, of death-struggles came and went
in his head.

" Faith! " said he, " all goes well! I have made

enough shoes in my life, and since the occasion to take up the musket presents itself, well, so much the better: we will show the Prussians and Austrians that we have not forgotten to charge at the double."

Thus reasoned the good man, carried away by his warlike instincts; but his joy did not last long.

Before the church, on the *place-d'armes*, were standing fifteen or twenty carts, full of wounded, arrived from Leipzig and Hanau. These unhappy creatures, pale, ghastly, heavy-eyed, some whose limbs were already amputated, others with their wounds still untouched, tranquilly awaited death. Near them, a few worn-out jades were eating their meagre allowance, while the conductors, poor wretches, who had been brought into requisition in Alsace, wrapped in their old mantles, slept notwithstanding the cold—their great hats turned down over their faces and their arms folded—on the steps of the church. One shuddered to see these sad groups of men, with their gray hoods, heaped up on the bloody straw—one carrying his broken arm on his knees; another with his head bandaged in an old handkerchief; a third, already dead, being used as a seat for the living, his black hands hanging down the ladder. Hullin, in front of this mournful spectacle, stopped rooted to the ground.

He could not lift his eyes from it. Great human suffering has this strange power of fascination over us: we look to see men perish, how they regard death: the best among us are not exempt from this frightful curiosity. It seems as though eternity is going to deliver up its secret!

There, then, near the shafts of the first cart, to the right of the file, were crouched two carbineers in little sky-blue vests, veritable giants, whose powerful natures gave way under the clutch of pain: like two caryatides crushed by the weight of some heavy mass. One, with great red mustaches and ashy cheeks, looked at you out of his sunken eyes, as though from the depths of some fearful nightmare; the other, bent double, with blue hands, and shoulder torn by shot, sank more and more; then would raise himself with a jerk, talking softly as though dreaming. Behind lay stretched, two and two, some infantry soldiers, the greater number struck by ball, with a leg or an arm broken. They seemed to support their fate with more firmness than the giants. These poor creatures said nothing: a few only, the youngest, furiously demanded water and bread; and in the next cart, a plaintive voice —the voice of a conscript—called, " My mother! my mother! " while the older men smiled gloomily, as though to say: " Yes, yes, she will come, thy mother! " Perhaps they did not think of anything all the time.

Now and then a shudder would pass along the whole of them. Then several wounded could be seen half lifting themselves, with deep groans, and falling back as if death had gone its rounds at that moment.

And again everything relapsed into silence. While Hullin was watching, and feeling sick to his heart's core, a shopkeeper in the vicinity, Sôme the baker, came out of his house carrying a large basin of soup. Then you should have seen all these spectres move, their eyes sparkle, their nostrils dilate; they seemed born again. The unhappy fellows were dying of hunger!

Good Father Sôme, with tears in his eyes, approached, saying, " I am coming, my children. A little patience! It is I, you know me! "

But hardly was he near the first cart, when the great carbineer with the ashy cheeks, reviving, plunged his arm up to the elbow in the boiling basin, seized the meat, and hid it under his vest. It was done with the rapidity of lightning. Savage yells arose on all sides: those men, if they had had strength to move, would have devoured their comrade. He, his arms pressed tightly to his chest, the teeth on his prey, and glaring round him, appeared to hear nothing. At these cries an old soldier, a sergeant, rushed out of the nearest inn. He was an old hand; he understood at once what it was about, and, without useless reflections, he tore away the meat from the wild beast, saying to him, " Thou dost not deserve any! It must be divided into parts. We will cut ten rations! "

" We are only eight! " said one of the wounded, very calm to all appearance, but with eyes gleaming out of their bronze mask.

" How, eight? "

" You can see, sergeant, that those two are dying fast: it would be so much food lost! "

The old sergeant looked.

" Right," said he; " eight rations! "

Hullin could bear it no longer. He went over to the innkeeper Wittmann's opposite, as white as death ; Wittmann was also a fur and leather merchant. Seeing him enter, " Hé ! is it you, Master Jean-Claude? " he exclaimed. " You arrive sooner than usual ; I did not expect you till next week." Then seeing how he staggered—" But say, you are ill? "

" I have just seen the wounded."

" Ah, yes ! the first time, it shocks you ; but if you had seen fifteen thousand pass, as we have, you would not think anything more about it."

"A glass of wine, quick?" said Hullin, who felt badly. "Oh, mankind, mankind! And to think that we are brothers!"

"Yes, brothers until it touches your purse," replied Wittmann. "Come, drink! that will set you right."

"And you have seen fifteen thousand go by?" rejoined the shoemaker.

"At the least, for two months, without speaking of those who have remained in Alsace and the other side of the Rhine; for, you comprehend, they cannot find carts enough for all, and then many are not worth the trouble of being carried away."

"Yes, I comprehend! But why are they there, those poor creatures?" Why do they not go into the hospital?"

"The hospital! What is one hospital, ten hospitals, for fifty thousand wounded? Every hospital, from Mayence and Coblentz as far as Phalsbourg, is crowded. And, besides, that terrible fever, typhus, you see, Hullin, kills more than the bullet. All the villages of the plain twenty leagues round are infected with it; they die everywhere like flies. Luckily the town has been in a state of siege these three days; the gates will be closed, and no more will enter. I have lost, for my part, my Uncle Christian and my Aunt Lisbeth, as healthy, solid people as you and I, Master Jean-Claude. At last the cold has arrived ; last night there was a white frost."

" And the wounded remained on the pavements all night? "

" No, they came from Saverne this morning ; in an hour or two, when the horses are rested, they will leave for Sarrebourg."

At that moment, the old sergeant, who had re-established order in the carts, came in rubbing his hands.

" Hé! hé! " said he, " it freshens, Papa Witt-mann. You did well to light the fire in the stove. A little glass of cognac to drive away the fog. Hum! hum ! "

His small half-closed eyes, his beaked nose, the cheek-bones being separated from it by two flour-ishing wrinkles, which were lost to sight in a long reddish imperial—everything looked gay in his face, and told of a jovial, kind disposition. It was a regular military face, scorched, burnt by the open air, full of frankness, but also of a cheery slyness ; his great shako, his blue-gray cloak, the shoulder-belt, the epaulette, seemed to partake of his indi-viduality. One could not have represented him without them. He walked up and down the room, continuing to rub his hands, while Wittmann

poured him a glass of brandy.   Hullin, seated near
the window, had at once noticed the number of his
regiment—6th Light Infantry.   Gaspard, the son
of Madame Lefèvre, served in this regiment.   Jean-
Claude could now obtain some tidings of the lover of
Louise ; but, as he was going to speak, his heart
beat loud.   If Gaspard was dead ; if he had perished like so many others !

The worthy shoemaker felt nearly suffocated ; he
kept silent.   " Better to know nothing," thought
he.   However, a few minutes later, he could do so
no longer.   " Sergeant," said he, in a hoarse voice,
" you are in the 6th Light Infantry ? "

" Yes, my citizen," said the other, turning round
in the middle of the room.

" Do you know one called Gaspard Lefèvre ? "

" Gaspard Lefèvre, of the 2d division of the 1st ?
Parbleu, if I know him !   It is I who taught him his
drill.   A brave soldier !   hardened against fatigue.
If we had a hundred thousand of that stamp——"

" Then he lives ?   he is well ? "

" Yes, citizen.   Eight days ago I left the regiment at Fredericsthal to escort this convoy of wounded.   You understand, it is hot there—one cannot
answer for anything.   From one moment to the
other, each of us may have his business settled for
him.   But eight days ago, at Fredericsthal—the

15th December—Gaspard Lefèvre still answered to the roll-call."

Jean-Claude breathed. "But then, sergeant, have the goodness to tell me why Gaspard has not written to his village for two months?"

The old soldier smiled, and blinked his little eyes. "Ah! now, citizen, do you then believe that one has nothing else to do on the march but to write?"

"No. I have served; I was in the campaigns of Sambre-et-Meuse, of Egypt and Italy, but that did not prevent me from giving some news of myself."

"One instant, comrade," interrupted the sergeant. "I have passed through Egypt and Italy also; the campaign we are finishing is altogether different."

"It has then been very severe?"

"Severe! one must have one's soul driven into every part of one's members, so as not to leave one's bones there. All was against us : sickness, traitors, peasants, townsfolk, our allies—in fact all! From our company, which was complete when we quitted Phalsbourg, the 21st of last January, only thirty-four men remain. I believe Gaspard Lefèvre is the only conscript left. Those poor conscripts! they fought well; but they were not accustomed to endure hardships : they melted like butter in an

oven." So saying, the old sergeant approached the
counter and drank his glass off at one draught. " To
your health, my citizen. Are you perchance the
father of Gaspard? "

" No, I am a relation."

" Well, you can pride yourselves on being stoutly
built in your family. What a man at twenty ! He
has gone through everything—he has, while the
others fell away in dozens."

" But," rejoined Hullin, after an instant's silence, " I cannot see anything so very different in
this last campaign ; for we also had sickness and
traitors."

" Anything different ! " exclaimed the sergeant.
" Everything was different ! Formerly, if you
have gone through the war in Germany, you ought
to remember that, after one or two victories, it was
over : the people received you well ; one drank the
little white wines, and ate sauerkraut and ham with
the townsfolk ; one danced with the buxom wives.
The husbands and grandpapas laughed heartily, and
when the regiment left, everybody cried. But this
time, after Lutzen and Bautzen, instead of feeling
kindly, the people regarded us with diabolical faces;
we could get nothing out of them but by force ; one
could have fancied one's self in Spain or Vendée.
I do not know what stuff they had in their heads

against us. Better had we only been French, had
we not had Saxons and other allies, who only awaited the moment to spring at our throats : we should
then have pulled through all the same, one against
five ! But the allies—don't talk to me of the allies ! Why, at Leipzig, the 18th of October last,
in the hottest part of the battle, our allies turned
against us and shot at us from behind ; those were
our good friends the Saxons. A week later, our former friends the Bavarians came and threw themselves across our retreat : we had to pass over them
at Hanau. The day after, near Frankfort, another
column of good friends presented themselves, and
we had to crush them. The more one kills, the
more they come ! Here we are now this side of the
Rhine. Well, there are decidedly more of these
good friends marching from Moscow. Ah ! if we
could have foreseen it after Austerlitz, Jena, Fried-
land, Wagram ! "

Hullin had become very thoughtful. " And now
how do we stand, sergeant? "

" We have had to repass the Rhine, and all our
strongholds on the other side are blockaded. The 10th
of November last the Prince of Neufchâtel reviewed
the regiment at Bleckheim. The 3d battalion had
been amalgamated with the 2d, and the ' cadre '
received orders to be in readiness to leave for the

depot. Cadres are not wanting, but men. As for twenty years we have been bled on all sides, it is not astonishing. All Europe is down upon us. The Emperor is at Paris ; he is laying down a plan of the campaign. If we may only have breathing time till the spring——"

Just then Wittmann, who was standing by the window, said,—" Here is the governor come from inspecting the clearings around the town."

It was the commandant, Jean-Pierre Meunier, wearing a three-cornered hat, and a tricolor scarf around his waist, who crossed over the square.

" Ah," said the sergeant, " I must get him to sign my papers. Pardon, citizen ; I must leave you."

" Do so, sergeant ; and thank you. If you meet Gaspard, tell him that Jean-Claude Hullin embraces him, and that they expect tidings from him in the village."

" Good—good. I will not fail to do so."

The sergeant went out, and Hullin finished his wine in a reverie.

" Father Wittmann," said he, after a pause, " what of my parcel? "

" It is ready, Master Jean-Claude." Then, looking into the kitchen, " Grédel ! Grédel ! bring Hullin's parcel."

A little woman appeared, and put down on the table a roll of sheepskins. Jean-Claude passed his stick through it, and lifted it over his shoulder.

" What, you are going to leave us so soon? "

" Yes, Wittmann. The days are short, and the roads difficult through the forests after six o'clock. I must get back early."

" Then a safe journey to you, Master Jean-Claude."

Hullin left, and crossed the square, turning away his face from the convoy, which still remained before the church.

The innkeeper from his window watched him hurrying away, and thought to himself, " How white he looked on entering ; he could hardly keep upright. It is queer that such a sturdy man, and an old soldier too, should not have energy enough for a cat. As for me, I would see fifty regiments go by on those carts without minding it any more than I did my first pipe."

CHAPTER IV

MADAME LEFÈVRE

WHILE Hullin was learning the disaster of our armies, and was walking slowly, his head bent, and an anxious expression on his face, toward the village of Charmes, everything went on as usual at the farm of Bois-de-Chênes. No one thought of Yégof's wonderful stories, or of the war : old Duchêne led his oxen to their drinking-place, the herdsman Robin turned over their litter ; Annette and Jeanne skimmed their curdled milk. Only Catherine Lèfèvre was silent and gloomy—thinking of days gone by—all the while superintending with an impassible face the occupations of her domestics. She was too old and too serious to forget from one day to another what had so much troubled her. When night came on, after the evening's repast, she entered the great room, where her servants could hear her drawing the large register-book from the closet and putting it on the table, to sum up her accounts, as she was in the habit of doing.

46

They soon began to load the cart with corn, vege-
tables, and poultry : for the next day there was a
market at Sarrebourg, and Duchêne had to start
early.

Picture to yourself the great kitchen, and all these
worthy folks hurrying to finish their work before
going to rest : the black kettle, full of beetroot and
potatoes destined for the cattle, boiling on an immense pinewood fire ; the plates, dishes, and soup-
tureens shining like suns on the shelves ; the bunch-
es of garlic and of reddish-brown onions hung up in
rows to the beams of the ceiling, among the hams
and flitches of bacon ; Jeannie, in her blue cap and
little red petticoat, stirring up the contents of the
kettle with a big wooden spoon ; the wicker cages,
with the cackling fowls and great cock, who pushed
his head through the bars and looked at the flames
with a wondering eye and raised crest ; the bull-dog
Michel, with his flat head and hanging jowl, in
search of some forgotten dish ; Dubourg coming
down the creaking staircase to the left, his back bent
with a sack on his shoulder ; while outside, in the
dark night, old Duchêne, upright on the cart, lifted
his lantern and called out, " That makes the fif-
teenth, Dubourg ; two more." One could see also,
hanging against the wall, an old hare, brought by the
hunter Heinrich to be sold at the market, and a fine

grouse, with its purple and green plumage, dimmed eye, and a drop of blood at the end of its beak.

It was about half-past seven when the sound of footsteps was heard at the entrance to the yard. The bull-dog went toward the door growling. He listened, sniffed the night air, then went back quietly, and began licking his dish again.

"It is some one belonging to the farm," said Annette. "Michel does not move."

Nearly at the same time, old Duchêne from outside called,—"Good-night, Master Jean-Claude. Is it you?"

"Yes. I come from Phalsbourg; and I am going to rest myself a minute before going down to the village. Is Catherine here?

And then the good man came forward to the light, his hat pushed off his face, and his roll of sheepskins on his back.

"Good-night, my children," said he; "good-night! Always at work!"

"Yes, Monsieur Hullin, as you see," replied Jeanne, laughing. "If one had nothing to do, life would be very wearisome."

"True, my pretty girl, true. It is only work which gives you your roses and brilliant eyes."

Jeanne was going to answer, when the door of the great room opened, and Catherine Lefèvre advanced, looking piercingly at Hullin, as though to guess beforehand what news he brought.

" Well, Jean-Claude, you have returned."

" Yes, Catherine ; with good tidings and bad."

They entered the large room—a high and spacious apartment wainscoted with wood to the ceiling, with its oak closets and their shining clasps, its iron stove opening into the kitchen, its old clock counting the seconds in its walnut-wood case, and the leathern arm-chair, worn and used by ten generations of aged men. Jean-Claude never went into this room without its bringing back to his remembrance Catherine's grandfather, whom he seemed still to see, with his white head, sitting behind the oven in the dark.

" Well? " demanded the old dame, offering a chair to the old shoemaker, who was just putting his pack down on the table.

" Well, from Gaspard the tidings are good ; the boy is in good health. He has had hardships. All the better : it will be the making of him. But for the rest, Catherine, it is bad. The war ! the war ! "

He shook his head, and the old woman, her lips pressed, sat down facing him, upright in the arm-chair, her eyes attentively fastened on him.

" So things look badly—decidedly—we shall have the war among us? "

4

" Yes, Catherine, from day to day we may expect to see the allies in our mountains."

" I thought so.   I was sure of it ; but speak, Jean-Claude."

Hullin, then, his elbows on his knees, his red ears between his hands, and lowering his voice, began to relate all he had seen: the clearing of everything around the town, the placing of batteries on the ramparts, the proclamation of the state of siege, the cart-loads of wounded on the great square, his meeting with the old sergeant at Wittmann's, and the story of the campaign.   From time to time he paused, and the old mistress of the farm blinked her eyes slowly, as though to impress more deeply the various circumstances on her mind.   When Jean-Claude told about the wounded, the good woman murmured softly—" Gaspard has then escaped it all! "

Then, at the end of this mournful tale, there was a long silence, and both looked at each other without pronouncing a word.

How many reflections, how many bitter feelings filled their souls !

After some seconds, Catherine recovering from these terrible thoughts—" You see, Jean-Claude," said she, in a serious tone, " Yégof was not wrong."

" Certainly, certainly, he was not wrong," replied

Hullin ; " but what does that prove? A madman, who goes from village to village, who descends into Alsace, and from thence to Lorraine—who wanders from right to left—it would be very astonishing if he saw nothing, and if he did not sometimes tell the truth in his madness. Everything gets muddled in his head, and others believe they understand what he does not understand himself. But what of these wild stories, Catherine? The Austrians are upon us. It only concerns us to know if we shall allow them to pass, or if we shall have courage to defend ourselves."

" To defend ourselves ! " cried the old woman, whose white cheeks trembled : " if we shall have courage to defend ourselves ! Surely it is not to me that you speak, Hullin. What ! are we not worthy of our ancestors? Did they not defend themselves? Were they not exterminated—men, women, and children? "

" Then you are for the defence, Catherine? "

" Yes, yes ; so long as there remains to me a bit of skin on my bones. Let them come ! The oldest of the women is ready ! "

Her masses of gray hair shook on her head, her pale rigid cheeks quivered, and her eyes sent forth lightnings. She was beautiful to see—beautiful, like that old Margareth of whom Yégof had spoken.

Hullin held out his hand silently, and gave an enthusiastic smile.

"Excellent," said he—"excellent ! We are always the same in this family. I know you, Catherine : you are ready now ; but be calm and listen
to me. We are going to fight, and in what way ? "

"In every way ; all are good—axes, scythes,
pitchforks."

"No doubt ; but the best are muskets and the
balls. We have muskets : every mountaineer keeps
his above his door ; unfortunately powder and balls
are scarce."

The old dame became quieter all of a sudden; she
pushed her hair back under her cap, and looked
anxiously about.

"Yes," she rejoined brusquely ; "the powder
and balls are wanting, it is true, but we shall have
some. Marc Divès, the smuggler, has some. You
shall go and see him to-morrow from me. You
shall tell him that Catherine Lefèvre will buy all his
powder and balls ; that she will pay him ; that she
will sell her cattle, her farm, land, everything—
everything—to have some. Do you understand,
Hullin ? "

"I understand. What you would do, Catherine,
is noble."

"Bah ! it is noble—it is noble ! " replied the old

dame. " It is quite simple ; I wish to revenge myself. These Austrians—these red men who have
already exterminated us—well ! I hate them, I de-
test them, from father to son. There ! you will
buy powder, and these mad ruffians shall see if we
will rebuild their castles."

Hullin then perceived that she still thought of
Yégof's tale ; but seeing how exasperated she was,
and that, besides, her idea contributed to the defence of the country, made no observation on that
subject, and said calmly,—" So, Catherine, it is settled; I am to go over to Marc Divès's to-morrow! "

" Yes ! you shall buy all his powder and lead.
Some one ought also to go the round of the mountain villages, to warn the people of what is coming,
and to arrange a signal beforehand for bringing
them together in case of attack."

" Do not fear," said Jean-Claude. " I will un-
dertake to charge myself with that."

Both rose and turned toward the door. For
about half an hour no sounds were heard in the
kitchen ; the farm-servants had gone to bed. The
old dame put down her lamp on the corner of the
hearth, and drew the bolts. Outside the cold was
intense, the air still and clear. All the peaks round,
and the pine-trees of the Jägerthal, stood out against
the sky in dark or light masses. In the distance, far

away behind the hill-side, a fox giving chase could be heard yelping in the valley of Blanru.

" Good-night, Hullin," said Catherine.

" Good-night."

Jean-Claude walked quickly away on the heath-covered slopes, and the mistress of the farm, after watching him for a second, shut her door again.

I leave you to imagine the joy of Louise when she learnt that Gaspard was safe and sound. The poor child had hardly been living for two months. Hullin took care not to show her the dark cloud which was coming over the horizon.

Through the night he could hear her prattling in her little room, talking as though congratulating herself, murmuring Gaspard's name, opening her drawers and boxes, without doubt so as to hunt up some relics in them and tell them of her love.

So the linnet drenched in the storm, will, while yet shivering, begin to sing and hop from branch to branch with the first sunbeam.

CHAPTER V

When Jean-Claude Hullin, in his shirt-sleeves, opened the shutters of his little house the next morning, he saw all the neighboring mountains— the Jägerthal, the Grosmann, the Donon—covered with snow. This first appearance of winter, coming in our sleep, is very striking to us : the old pines, the mossy rocks, adorned only the night before with verdure, and now sparkling with rime, fill our souls with an indefinable sadness. " Another year gone by," one says to one's self ; " another hard season to pass before the return of the flowers ! "   And one hastens to put on the great-coat and to light the fire.   Your sombre habitation is filled with a white light, and outside, for the first time, you hear the sparrows—the poor sparrows huddled under the thatch, their feathers ruffled—calling, " No breakfast this morning—no breakfast ! "

Hullin drew on his big iron-nailed, double-soled shoes, and over his vest a great thick cloth waistcoat.

He heard Louise walking overhead in the little garret.

" Louise," he cried, " I am going."

" What ! you are going away to-day also? "

" Yes, my child : it must be so : my affairs are not yet finished."

Then, having doffed his large hat, he went up the stair, and said, in a low tone : " Thou must not expect me back so soon, my child. I have to make some distant rounds. Do not be uneasy. If any one ask where I am, thou art to reply, ' He is with Cousin Mathias at Saverne.' "

" You will not have breakfast before leaving? "

" No : I have a crust of bread and the small flask of brandy in my pocket. Adieu, my child ! Rejoice, and dream of Gaspard."

And, without waiting for fresh questions, he took his stick and left the house, going in the direction of the hill of Bouleaux to the left of the village. In a quarter of an hour he had passed it by, and reached the path of the Trois-Fontaines, which winds round the Falkenstein along by a little wall of dry stones. The first snow, which never lasts in the damp shades of the valleys, was beginning to melt and run down the path. Hullin got on the wall to climb the ascent. On giving an accidental look toward the village, he saw a few women sweeping before their doors, a few old men wishing each other the " Good-day " while smoking their first pipes on the thresh-old of their cottages. The deep calm of life, in presence of his agitating thoughts, affected him much. He continued his way pensively, saying to himself, " How quiet everything is down there ! Nobody has any idea of anything ; yet in a few days, what clamors, what rolls of musketry, will rend the air ! "

As the first thing to be done was to procure pow-der, Catherine Lefèvre had very naturally cast her eyes on Marc Divès the smuggler, and his virtuous spouse, Hexe-Baizel.

These people lived on the other side of the Fal-kenstein, under the base of the old ruined castle. They had hollowed inside a sort of den, very com-fortable, possessing one door and two skylights, but according to certain rumors, communicating with ancient caves by a rift in the rock. The custom-house officers had never been able to discover these caves, notwithstanding numerous domiciliary visits for that purpose. Jean-Claude and Marc Divès had known each other from infancy ; they had gone nesting together after hawks and owls, and since that time had seen each other nearly every week at the saw-mills of Valtin. Hullin, therefore, believed himself sure of the smuggler, but he had some

doubts of Madame Hexe-Baizel, a most cautious person, who would not, in all probability, have the warlike instinct sufficiently developed.   " But we shall
see," he said to himself as he went along.

He had lit his pipe, and from time to time turned
round to contemplate the immense landscape, whose
limits were extending more and more.

Nothing could be grander than those wooded
mountains, rising one above the other in the pale
sky—those vast heather plains, stretching as far as
the eye could see, white with snow ; those black
ravines, shut in between the woods, with torrents
at the bottom, dashing over the greenish pebbles
polished like bronze.

And then the silence—the great silence of winter !   The soft snow falling from the top of the
loftiest pine-trees onto their lower drooping branches : the birds of prey circling in couples above the
forests, screaming out their war-cry : all this ought
to be seen for it cannot be described.

An hour after his departure from the village of
Charmes, Hullin, climbing the summit of the peak,
reached the base of the rock of the Arbousiers.   All
round this granite mass extends a sort of rugged terrace, three or four feet wide.   This narrow passage,
surrounded by the tall pines growing out from the
precipice, looks dangerous, but it is safe ; unless one

feels dizzy, there is no danger in going along it.
Overhead projects, in a vaulted arch, the rock covered with ruins.

Jean-Claude was approaching the retreat of the
smuggler. He halted a minute on the terrace, put
back his pipe into his pocket, then advanced along
the passage, which forms a half-circle, and ends on
the other side with a chasm. Quite at the farthest
extremity of it, and almost on the edge of the chasm,
he perceived the two skylight windows of the den
and the partly opened door. A great heap of manure was collected in front of it.

At the same time Hexe-Baizel appeared, tossing,
with a broom made of green furze, the manure into
the abyss. This woman was small and hard-look-
ing ; she had shaggy red hair, hollow cheeks, pointed nose, little eyes, bright like two sparks, thin lips,
very white teeth, and a florid complexion. As for
her costume, it was composed of a short dirty woollen petticoat, and a coarse but clean chemise ; her
brown, muscular arms, covered with yellow hairs,
were bare to the elbows, notwithstanding the excessive cold of the winter at this height ; and, lastly,
all she had on her feet were a pair of long shoes
hanging in shreds.

"Ha ! good-day, Hexe-Baizel," Jean-Claude
called out, good naturedly but with a tone of rail-

lery.   " You are always fair and fat, happy and
lively !   It gives me pleasure ! "

Hexe-Baizel turned sharply, like a weasel surprised on the watch ; her red hair stiffened, and her
little eyes flashed fire.   However, she calmed down
immediately, and exclaimed, in a curt voice, as
though speaking to herself, " Hullin—the shoemaker !   What does he want? "

" I am come to see my friend Marc, fair Hexe-
Baizel," replied Jean-Claude ; " we have some business to settle together."

" What business? "

" Ah, it only concerns us.   Here let me pass that
I may speak to him."

" Marc is asleep." ·

" Well, he must be awakened then ; the time is
precious."

So saying, Hullin stooped under the door, and
penetrated into a cavern, whose vault, instead of being round, was composed of irregular curves, scored
with fissures.   Close to the entrance, two feet from
the ground, the rock formed a sort of natural fireplace, on which burned a few coals and branches of
juniper.   Hexe-Baizel's culinary utensils consisted
of an iron kettle, a stone pot, two broken plates, and
three or four tin forks ; her furniture comprised a
wooden stool, a hatchet to split wood, a salt box

fastened to the rock, and her large furze broom. To
the left of this kitchen was another cavern, with a
curious door, larger at the top than at the bottom,
closing by aid of two planks and a cross-bar.

"Well, where is Marc?" said Hullin, seating
himself near the hearth.

"I have already told you that he is asleep. He
returned home late yesterday. My husband must
sleep, don't you hear?"

"I hear very well, dear Hexe-Baizel; but I have
no time to wait."

"Then go away!"

"Go away? It is easy said; only I won't go
away. I did not walk three miles, to turn back with
my hands in my pockets."

"Is it thou, Hullin?" interrupted a brusque
voice coming from the neighboring cavern.

"Yes, Marc."

"Ah! I'm coming."

The sound of straw in motion could be heard;
then the wooden barrier was withdrawn; and a
huge frame, three feet broad from one shoulder to
the other, wiry, bony, with neck and ears brick-
color, and thick brown hair, appeared in the doorway, and Marc Divès drew himself up before Hullin, yawning and stretching his long arms with a
short sigh.

At first sight, the physiognomy of Marc Divès seemed peaceable enough: his low broad forehead, bare temples, short curly hair coming down in a point almost to the eyebrows, his straight nose and long chin—above all the quiet expression in his brown eyes—would have caused him to be classed among the ruminating rather than the wilder animals ; but one would have been wrong in thinking so.   Certain rumors were prevalent in the country that Marc Divès, when attacked by the custom-house people, had never any hesitation to use his axe or carbine to decide the dispute ; to him were attributed several serious accidents which had happened to the fiscal agents ; but proofs were completely wanting. The smuggler, owing to his thorough knowledge of all the mountain defiles and by-roads from Dagsburg to Sarrbrück, and from Raon-l'Etape to Bâle in Switzerland, was always fifteen leagues from any place where a wicked action had been committed. And then he had such an ingenuous look ! and those who connected him with sinister tales generally finished badly : which clearly shows the justice with which Providence sways the world.

"Faith, Hullin," said Marc, after having left his lair, "I was thinking of thee yesterday evening, and if thou hadst not appeared, I should have gone expressly to the saw-mills of Valtin to meet

thee. Sit down! Hexe-Baizel, give a chair to Hullin!"

Then he placed himself on the hearth, his
back to the fire, in front of the open door, which
was raked by all the winds of Alsace and Switzerland.

Through this opening there was a magnificent
view : it might be compared to a picture framed in
the rock—an enormous picture, embracing the
whole valley of the Rhine, and the mountains beyond, which melted away in the mist. And then
one could breathe so freely ! and the little fire,
which glimmered in the owl's-nest, was a place to
look on, with its red light, after one had gazed into
the azure expanse.

"Marc," said Hullin, after a short pause, "may
I speak before thy wife?"

"We are as one, she and I."

"Well, Marc, I am come to buy powder and lead
of thee."

"To kill hares, is it not so?" observed the smuggler, winking.

"No, to fight against the Germans and Russians."

There was a moment's silence.

"And thou wilt want much powder and lead?"

"All that thou canst supply."

"I can supply as much as three thousand francs' worth to-day," said the smuggler.

"Then I'll take it."

"And as much more in a week," added Marc, with the same calm manner and eager look.

"I take that also."

"You will take it!" cried Hexe-Baizel. "You will take it! I should think so! But who is to pay?"

"Hold thy tongue!" said Marc, roughly, "Hullin takes it : and his word is enough for me." And holding out his large hand cordially : "Jean-Claude, here is my hand : the powder and lead are thine : but I must have my price, dost thou understand?"

"Yes, Marc : only I intend paying thee at once."

"He will pay, Hexe-Baizel, dost thou hear?"

"Eh, I am not deaf, Baizel. Go and find a bottle of 'brimbelle-wasser' for us, so that we may warm our hearts a little. What Hullin tells me rejoices me. These rascally 'kaiserlichs' will not have the easy game against us that I thought. It appears that we are going to defend ourselves, and right well."

"Yes, right well!"

"And there are people who can pay?"

" Catherine Lefèvre pays, and she it is who sends me," said Hullin.

Then Marc Divès rose, and in a solemn tone, and pointing toward the precipice, exclaimed, " She is a woman indeed—a woman as grand as that rock down there, the Oxenstein, the greatest I have ever seen in my life. I drink to her health. Drink also, Jean-Claude."

Hullin drank, then Hexe-Baizel.

" Now everything has been said," continued Divès ; " but listen, Hullin. Do not believe that it will be an easy matter to check the enemy : all the hunters, all the sawyers, all the wood-cutters and carriers on the mountains will not be too many. I come from the other side of the Rhine. They are so many—those Russians, Austrians, Bavarians, Prussians, Cossacks, and Hussars—they are so many, that the earth is black with them. The villages cannot hold them : they camp on the plains, in the valleys, on the hills, in the towns, in the open air—they are to be found everywhere."

At that moment a shrill cry was heard.

" It is a buzzard chasing something," said Marc, stopping.

But just then a shadow came over the rock. A cloud of chaffinches cleared the abyss, and hundreds of buzzards and hawks fought above them in their

5

rapid flight, uttering loud screams to terrify their prey, while the mass seemed stationary, so dense was it. The regular movement of these thousands of wings produced, in the silence, a sound like that of dead leaves blown in the wind.

" That is the departure of the chaffinches of the Ardennes," said Hullin.

" Yes, it is the last passage : the beech-nuts are buried under the snow, and the seeds also. Well, then, look ! there are more men over there than birds in this pass. All the same, Jean-Claude, we will get over them, so long as every one bears a hand in it ! Hexe-Baizel, light the lantern : I am going to show Hullin our supplies of powder and lead."

Hexe-Baizel made a face at this proposition. " For twenty years," said she, " no one has gone into the cave. He can surely believe our word. We believe, for our part, that he will pay us. I will not light the lantern—no, indeed ! "

Marc, without saying anything, put out his hand and caught up a cudgel from the pile of wood ; thereupon the old woman darted into the nearest hole like a weasel, and, two seconds later, came out with a big horn lantern, which Divès quietly lit at the fire on the hearth.

" Baizel," said he, replacing the stick in its corner, " thou must know that Jean-Claude is an old

friend of my childhood, and that I confide much
more in him than in thee, old wench; for wert thou
not afraid of being hanged the same day as myself,
I should long ago have been swinging to a rope's
end. Come, Hullin, follow me."

They went out, and the smuggler, turning to the
left, walked straight toward the chasm, which pro-
jected over the Valtin two hundred feet in the air.
He pushed aside the branches of a little oak, which
had its roots down below, put forth his leg, and disappeared as though pitched into the abyss.. Jean-
Claude shuddered, but directly after he saw, against
the side of the rock, the head of Divès, who called to
him,—" Hullin, put out thy hand to the left—
there is a hole. Stretch thy leg out boldly—thou
wilt feel a step, and then turn around."

Master Jean-Claude obeyed, with some trepida-
tion. He could feel the hole in the rock, he found
the step, and turning slightly, was face to face with
his comrade in a sort of arched niche, evidently abut-
ting on a sally-port in times past. At the end of the
niche there was a low vault.

" How the devil didst thou discover that? " exclaimed Hullin, much astonished.

" In seeking after nests thirty-five years ago. I
was one day on the rock, and I had often observed
flying from there a horned-owl and its mate, two

splendid birds : their heads were the size of my fists, and the wings six feet broad. I could hear their young calling, and I said to myself, ' They are near the cavern, at the end of the terrace. If I could get round a little beyond the chasm I should have them ! By dint of looking and bending over, I perceived at last a corner of the step above the precipice. There was a strong holly-bush at one side. I caught hold of it, put out my leg, and, faith, I found myself here. What a fight, Hullin ! The old birds wanted to tear out my eyes. Luckily, it was broad daylight. They went at me like cocks, opened their beaks and hissed, but the sun dazzled them. I kicked them. Finally, they fell on to the top of an old pine-tree down there, and all the jays in the country, the thrushes, chaffinches and tom-tits, flew about them till nightfall, plucking out their feathers. Thou canst not imagine, Jean-Claude, the quantity of bones, rat-skins, leverets, and carrion of all sorts that they had heaped up in this niche. It was pestilential. I threw it all into the Jäger-thal, and I discovered this passage. But I must also tell thee that there were two young ones. I twisted their necks and poked them into my bag. After-ward, I quietly entered, and thou shalt see what I found. Come ! ''

They slipped under the narrow archway, formed

of enormous red stones, where the light threw only a flickering glimmer.

Thirty paces farther on, a vast circular cave, low in the middle, and formed in the rock itself, appeared to Hullin. About fifty little casks were arranged at the bottom in shape of pyramids, and, at the sides, a large number of ingots of lead and bales of tobacco, which filled the air with its smell. Marc deposited his lantern at the entrance of the vault, and regarded his hiding-place with gratification and a smile upon his lips.

" That is what I discovered," said he ; " the cave was empty, only in the centre of it was the carcass of an animal, snowy white,—no doubt some fox, dead of old age. The rascal had known of the passage before I had. He slept safely here. Who on earth would have dreamed of pursuing him? In those days, Hullin, I was twelve years old. I immediately thought that this place might one day be of use to me. I did not know then what use. But, later on, when I had begun my first attempts at smuggling—at Landau, Kehl, Bâle—with Jacob Zimmer, and during two winters all the custom-house people were after us, the idea of my old cavern began to haunt me from morning till evening. I had made the acquaintance of Hexe-Baizel, who was then one of the farm-servants at Bois-de-Chênes with Catherine's father.   She brought me twenty-five louis as marriage-portion, and we settled ourselves in the cavern of the Arbousiers."

Divès paused ; and Hullin, who had become very thoughtful, asked him,—-" This hole, then, pleases thee much, Marc?"

" Pleases me !   Why, I would not go and live in the most beautiful house in Strasbourg for two thousand pounds a year.   For twenty-three years I have here hidden my wares : sugar, coffee, powder, tobacco, brandy—everything goes in here.   I have eight horses always travelling."

" But thou hast no happiness."

" I have no happiness !   Dost thou think it is nothing to laugh at the gendarmes, excisemen, custom-house people ; to enrage them, to outdo them, to hear on all sides, ' That rascally Marc—isn't he a sharp one !   How he manages his business !   He can do as he likes with the law and its agents,' and this and that.   Hé ! hé ! hé !   I can tell thee, I can, that it is the greatest pleasure in the world. And then the people like it : they get everything half price ; one helps the poor, and keeps himself warm and well-off."

" Yes, but what dangers ! "

" Bah ! a customs'-guard would never think of crossing the chasm."

" I should suppose not," thought Hullin, remembering that he must cross the precipice again.

" At the same time thou art not altogether wrong, Jean-Claude. When I first had to enter this place with those little barrels on my back, I streamed with perspiration ; now I am accustomed to it."

" And if thy foot slipped? "

" There would be an end of me ! I would as soon die, spiked on a pine, as to cough weeks and months on a mattress."

Divès then shed the light of his lantern on the piles of kegs reaching to the top of the vault.

" It is the finest English powder," said he ; " it runs like silver grains in the hand, and fires like Old Nick. No need to use much of it—a thimbleful is enough. And here is lead, unmixed with tin. From this very evening, Hexe-Baizel shall begin casting balls. She knows all about it, thou wilt see."

They were beginning to return by the path leading to the chasm, when suddenly a confused murmur of words began to fill the air. Marc blew out his lantern, and they stopped still in the darkness.

" Some one is walking up there," the smuggler softly said. " Who on earth has been able to climb up the Falkenstein in such snow? "

They listened, holding their breath, and their

eyes fixed on the ray of bluish light which came
down through a small chink into the cavern.
Around the cleft grew a few shrubs, sparkling with
frost ; above, could be perceived the ridge of an old
wall.   While they were watching, keeping profound silence, there appeared at the foot of the wall
a large shaggy head bound round with a shining circle, a long face, then a pointed red beard,—the
whole standing out in curious relief against the
white winter sky.

"It is 'The King of Diamonds,'" observed
Marc, laughing.

"Poor devil !" said Hullin, gravely ; "he has
come to walk about his castle, his bare feet on the
ice, and a tin crown on his head !   But look ! he is
speaking : he is giving orders to his courtiers ; he
points with his sceptre to the north and to the south
—all belongs to him ; he is master of the heavens
and earth !   Poor devil ! merely to see him in
those trousers of his, with his dog-skin on his back,
makes me cold all over."

"Yes, Jean-Claude, it produces on me the effect
of a burgomaster or village mayor, who puffs himself out like a bullfinch, and blows his cheeks up,
saying, 'I am Hans Aden ; I have ten acres of fine
meadows ; I have two houses ; I have a vineyard,
an orchard, a garden, h-m ! h-m !   I have this and

that ! ' The next day a little fit lays hold of him,
and—good-evening.   Mad, mad ! who is not mad?
Let us go, Hullin ; the sight of this unfortunate
who talks to the winds, and of his raven that croaks
of famine, makes my teeth chatter."

They entered the passage, and the daylight almost
blinded Hullin.   Happily, the great height of his
companion standing in front of him, prevented his
becoming giddy.

"Lean firmly," said Marc ; "imitate me : the
right hand in the hole, the right foot on the step,
turn a bit—here we are ! "

They returned to the kitchen, where Hexe-Baizel
told them that Yégof was in the ruins of the old
Burg.

"We knew it," replied Marc : "we have just
seen him breathing the fresh air over there.   Each
man to his taste."

Just then the raven Hans, sailing above the abyss,
passed the door with a hoarse cry ; they heard the
frost crackling on the bushes, and the madman appeared upon the terrace.   He was haggard ; and
after glancing toward the hearth, cried out—"Marc
Divès, clear out quickly.   I warn thee I am tired of
this disorder.   The fortifications of my domains
ought to be free.   I cannot allow vermin to lodge
where I am ; consequently, thou must make thy ar-

rangements." Then perceiving Jean-Claude, his face brightened—" Thou here, Hullin?" said he, " Art thou at length clear-sighted enough to accept the proposals that I have condescended to make thee? Dost thou feel that an alliance such as mine, is the only resource to preserve thee from the total destruction of thy race? If it is so, I congratulate thee ; thou showest more sense than I gave thee credit for."

Hullin could not help laughing.

" No, Yégof, no ! heaven has not yet enlightened me, or I might accept the honor thou wouldst make me. Besides, Louise is not old enough to be married."

The madman became again serious and gloomy. Standing on the edge of the terrace, his back to the abyss, he seemed quite at home, and his raven, hovering from right to left, did not trouble him.

He raised his sceptre, frowned, and exclaimed :

" Then this is the second time, Hullin, that I have made my demand, and for the second time thou darest refuse me. Now, I will renew it once again —once, dost thou hear? Then the fate shall be accomplished ! "

Hullin, Marc Divès, and Hexe-Baizel herself burst into fits of laughter.

" He is a great madman," said Hexe-Baizel.

"I think thou art right there," replied the smuggler. "Poor Yégof! decidedly he is out of his wits. But never mind! Baizel, attend to me. Thou must commence melting balls of all sizes. I am going to start for Switzerland. In a week, at latest, the remainder of our ammunition will be here. Give me my boots."

Then stamping down his heels, and twisting round his neck a thick scarf of red wool, he unhooked from the wall one of those dark-green mantles such as herdsmen wear, threw it over his shoulders, put on an old worn hat, took a gourd, and shouted : "Don't forget what I have been telling thee, old woman, or beware ! Let us go, Jean-Claude ! "

Hullin followed him on the terrace without wishing good-by to Hexe-Baizel, who, for her part, did not deign even to go to the doorstep to see them depart. When they were come to the base of the rock, Marc Divès drew up and said, " Thou art going into the mountain villages, art thou not, Hullin? "

" Yes : that must first be done. I must warn the wood-cutters, charcoal-burners, and others, of what is going on."

" Without doubt. Do not forget Materne of Hengst and his two boys, Labarbe of Dagsburg, and

Jérome of St. Quirin.   Tell them that there will be
powder and balls ; that we are of the number, Catherine Lefèvre, myself, Marc Divès, and all the honest folks of the country."

" Calm thyself, Marc—I know my men."

" Then good-by for the present."

They shook hands warmly.

The smuggler took the path to the right, toward
Donon ; Hullin that to the left, toward the Sarre.

They were now at some distance from each
other, when Hullin called out to his comrade: " Hé !
Marc, inform Catherine Lefèvre, as thou passest by,
that all goes on well.   Tell her I am going into the
mountains."

The other assented by a nod, and they both continued their different ways.

CHAPTER VI

An extraordinary agitation reigned at that time all along the line of the Vosges: the tidings of the invasion which was approaching spread from village to village, and among the farm-houses and woodmen's cottages of the Hengst and the Nideck. The hawkers, wagoners, tinkers, all that floating population which is continually moving from the mountains to the plains and from the plains to the mountains, brought every day, from Alsace and the borders of the Rhine, many strange reports. "The towns," so these people said, "were being put into a state of defence; expeditions were being made to provision them with corn and meat; the roads to Metz, Nancy, Huningue, and Strasbourg were swarming with convoys. Everywhere you met powder and ammunition wagons, cavalry, infantry, artillery, going to their posts. Marshal Victor still held the route to Saverne; but the bridges of the fortresses were already raised from seven in the evening to eight in the morning."

No one thought that all this could bode any good. Nevertheless, though many were seriously afraid of war, and though the old women lifted up their hands to heaven, crying, " Jesus! Mary! Joseph!" the greater number were preparing the means of defence. Under such circumstances, Jean-Claude Hullin was well received by all.

The same day, toward five in the evening, he reached the summit of the Hengst, and halted with the patriarch of forest-hunters, old Materne. He spent the night there; for in winter the days are short and the roads difficult. Materne promised to keep watch over the defile of the Zorn, with his two sons Kasper and Frantz, and to reply to the first signal which was made from the Falkenstein.

On the following day, Jean-Claude started early for Dagsburg, so as to come to an understanding with his friend Labarbe, the wood-cutter. They visited together the nearest hamlets, reanimating the love of country in the people's hearts; and the next day Labarbe accompanied Hullin into Christ-Nickel's, the anabaptist farmer of Painbach—a sensible and respectable man, but who could not be prevailed upon to participate in their glorious enterprise. Christ-Nickel had only one reply for all their observations: " It is well, it is just, but the

Bible saith, 'Put up thy sword into its place. He who lives by the sword shall perish by the sword.'" He promised them, however, to pray for the good cause: it was all they could obtain.

They went from there to Walsch, and had some hearty shakes of the hand with Daniel Hirsch, a former marine gunner, who agreed to collect all the people of his district.

At this place Labarbe left Jean-Claude to make his way by himself.

For eight days longer he beat about the mountain, from Soldatenthal, to Léonsberg, Meienthal, Abreschwiller, Voyer, Loëttenbach, Cirey, Petit-Mont, and Saint-Sauveur; and on the ninth day he reached St. Quirin and saw the bootmaker Jérome. They visited the pass of Blanru together; after which Hullin, satisfied with what he had done, took his way to the village. He had been walking briskly for about two hours, picturing to himself the life of the camp,—the bivouac, marches and counter-marches—all that life of a soldier which he had so often regretted, and which he now saw returning with enthusiasm—when in the far distance, amidst the shades of the twilight, he perceived the hamlet of Charmes in a bluish mist, his little cottage sending forth a scarcely perceptible line of smoke, the small gardens surrounded with palisades, the stone-covered roofs, and to the left, bordering the hill, the great farm of Bois-de-Chênes, with the saw-mills of Valtin at the end of the now dark ravine.

Then suddenly, and without knowing why, his soul was filled with a great sadness.

He slackened his pace, and thought of the calm, peaceable life he was abandoning—perhaps forever; of his little room, so warm in the winter, and cheerful in spring when he opened his windows to the breath of the woods; of the tic-tac of the old timepiece, and then of Louise, his good little Louise, spinning in the silence with downcast eyes, and in the evenings singing some quaint strain with her pure penetrating voice when they were both feeling weary. These reflections laid such hold of him that the slightest objects, every instrument used in his profession,—the long shining augers, the round-handled hatchet, the mallets, the little stove, the old closet, the platters of varnished wood, the ancient figure of Saint Michael nailed to the wall, the old four-post bed at the bottom of the alcove, the stool, the trunk, the copper lamp,—all these things impressed themselves on his mind like a living picture, and the tears came into his eyes.

But it was Louise, his darling child, whom he pitied. How she would weep, and implore him to

renounce the war! And how she would hang on
his neck, saying:—" Oh! do not leave me, Papa
Jean-Claude! Oh, I will love you so much! Oh,
surely you will not abandon me! "

And the honest fellow could see the terror in
her beautiful eyes—he could feel her arms round
his neck. For a moment he fancied that he might
deceive her, make her believe anything, no matter
what, and so account for his absence to her satisfaction; but such means were not in accordance with
his character, and his sadness increased the more.

Arrived at the farm of Bois-de-Chênes, he went
in to tell Catherine Lefèvre that all was going well,
and that the mountaineers were only awaiting the
signal.

A quarter of an hour after, Master Jean-Claude
came down by the Houx road in front of his own
little house.

Before pushing open the creaking door, the
idea struck him to see what Louise was about at
that moment. He glanced into the little room
through the window: Louise was standing by the
curtains of the alcove; she seemed very animated,
arranging, folding and unfolding clothes on the
bed. Her sweet face beamed with happiness, and
her large blue eyes sparkled with a sort of enthusiasm; she even talked aloud. Hullin listened; but

6

a cart happening to pass at the time in the street, he could hear nothing. Making a firm resolve, he entered, saying quietly: "Louise, I have returned."

Immediately the young girl, joyous and skipping like a deer, ran to embrace him.

"Ah! it is you, Papa Jean-Claude! I was expecting you. Mon Dieu! mon Dieu! how long you stayed away! At length you are back."

"It was, my child," replied the honest fellow, in a more undecided tone, putting his stick behind the door and his hat on the table, "it was because——"

He could say nothing else.

"Yes, yes, you went to see our friends," said Louise, laughing: "I know all about it—Mamma Lefèvre has told me everything."

"What! thou knowest? And dost thou not mind? So much the better, so much the better! it shows thy sense. And I, who fancied thou wouldst have cried!"

"Cry! and what for, papa Jean-Claude? Oh, I am courageous; you don't know me yet—go!" She put on a resolute air, which made Hullin smile; but he did not smile long when she continued: "We are going to war—we are going to fight—we are going to pass up the mountain!"

"Hullo! we are going! we are going!" exclaimed he in astonishment.

"Certainly. Then are we not going?" said she, regretfully.

"That is to say—I must leave thee for a little time, my child."

"Leave me—oh, no! I go with thee; it is all agreed upon. Look, see! my small parcel is ready, and here is yours, which I have arranged. Don't trouble yourself, let me alone, and you will be satisfied!"

Hullin could not get over his stupefaction. "But, Louise," he exclaimed, "thou canst not think of such a thing. Consider: we must pass nights abroad, and march and run; consider the cold, the snow, the musketry! It cannot be."

"Come," said the young girl, in a tearful voice, throwing herself into his arms, "do not pain me! You are only making fun of your little Louise. You cannot forsake her!"

"But thou wilt be much safer here—thou wilt be warm—thou wilt hear from us every day."

"No, no. I will not—I must go too. The cold does not harm me. Only too long have I been shut up. I, too, must breathe a little. Are not the birds out of doors? The robins are out all the winter. Have I not known what cold was when I was quite tiny? and hunger also?"

She stamped, and, for the third time, putting her arms round Jean-Claude's neck,—" Come then, Papa Hullin," said she softly, " Mamma Lefèvre said yes. Would you be more naughty than she was? Ah, if you only knew how much I love you!"

The good man had sat down and turned away his head, so as not to yield, and did not allow himself to be embraced.

" Oh, how naughty you are to-day, Papa Jean-Claude!"

" It is for thy sake, my child."

" Well, all the worse. I will run away after you. Cold—what is cold? And if you are wounded—if you ask to see your little Louise for the last time, and she is not there—near you, to take care of you, and love you to the end—oh, you must think me very cold-hearted."

She sobbed, and Hullin could not stand it any longer.

" Is it true that Mamma Lefèvre consents?"

" Oh, yes—oh, yes—she told me so. She said to me,—' Try and make Papa Jean-Claude decide. I am willing, and quite satisfied.'"

" Well, what can I do against two of you. Thou shalt come with us; it is quite decided."

She gave a scream of delight which ran through the cottage,—" Oh, how kind you are!"

And with one rub she wiped all her tears awa
—"We are going to be off, to take to the woo
and to make war."

"Ah," said Hullin, shaking his head, "I see
now; thou art always the little gypsy. As soon t₁
to tame a swallow."

Then making her sit on his knees:—"Louise,
it is now twelve years since I found thee in the
snow: thou wast blue, poor little one. And when
we were in the cottage, near a good fire, and thou
wert slowly reviving, the first thing thou didst was
to smile at me. And since that time thy will has
always been mine. With that smile thou hast led
me wherever thou wouldst."

Then Louise began again to smile at him, and
they embraced each other. "Now we will look at
the packages," he said, sighing. "Are they well
made, I wonder?"

He approached the bed, and was surprised to
see his warmest clothes, his flannel-waistcoats, all
well brushed, folded, and packed; and Louise's bun-
dle, with her best dresses, petticoats, and stout shoes,
in nice order. At last he could not help laughing
and crying out—"O gypsy, gypsy! you are the one
for making fine bundles, and going away without
ever turning the head."

Louise smiled. "Are you satisfied?"

"I suppose I must be. But during all this piece of work, I will venture to say thou hast never thought of preparing my supper."

"Oh, it will soon be ready. I did not know you would return this evening, Papa Jean-Claude."

"That is true, my child. Bring me something —no matter what—quickly, for I am hungry. Meanwhile I shall smoke a pipe."

"Yes, that's it; smoke a pipe."

He sat down on the side of the bench and struck the tinder-box quite dreamily. Louise rushed right and left like a sprite, seeing to the fire, breaking the eggs, and turning out an omelette with surprising celerity. Never had she appeared so lively, smiling, and pretty. Hullin, his elbow on the table and his face in his hand, watched her gravely, thinking how much will, firmness, and resolution there was in this girl—as light as a fairy, yet determined as a hussar. In a few seconds she served him with the omelette on a large china plate, with bread, and the glass and bottle.

"There, Papa Jean-Claude, be hungry no longer." She observed him eating with a look of tenderness.

The flame sprang up in the stove, lighting clearly the low beams, the wooden stair in the shadow, the bed at the end of the alcove, the whole of the

abode, so often cheered by the joyous humor of the
shoemaker, the little songs of his daughter, and the
industry of both.   And all this Louise was leaving
without any hesitation: she cared only for the
woods, the snow-covered paths, and the endless
mountains, reaching from the village into Switzerland, and even beyond.   Ah, Master Jean-Claude
had reason to cry "gypsy, gypsy!"   The swallow cannot be tamed: it needs the open air, the
broad sky—continual motion.   Neither storms, nor
wind, nor rain in torrents frighten it, when the
hour of its departure is at hand.   It has only one
thought, one desire, one cry—"Let us away!   Let
us away."

The meal finished, Hullin rose and said to his
daughter, "I am tired, my child; kiss me, and let
us go to bed."

"Yes; but do not forget to awake me, Papa
Jean-Claude, if you start before daybreak."

"Do not trouble thyself.   It is understood thou
shalt come with us."   And seeing her mount the
stair and disappear in the garret: "Isn't she afraid
of stopping in the nest, that's all!" said he to himself.

The silence was great outdoors.   Eleven o'clock
had struck from the village church.   The good man
was sitting down to take off his boots, when he

caught sight of his musket suspended above the
door: he took it down, wiped it, and drew the trig-
ger. His whole soul was intent on the business in
hand.

"It is all right," he murmured: and then in a
grave tone: "It is curious. . . . The last time I
held it . . . at Marengo . . . was fourteen years
ago, and yet it seems like yesterday!"

Suddenly the hardened snow cracked under a
quick footstep. He listened: "Some one!" At
the same time two little sharp taps resounded
on the panes. He ran to the window and opened
it. The head of Marc Divès, with his broad
hat stiff with the frost, bent forward from the
darkness.

"Well, Marc, what news?"

"Hast thou warned the mountaineers—Materne,
Jérome, Labarbe?"

"Yes, all."

"It was time: the enemy has passed."

"Passed?"

"Yes, along the whole line. I have walked
fifteen leagues through the snow since this morning
to announce it to thee."

"Good; the signal must be given: a great fire
on the Falkenstein."

Hullin was very pale. He put on his boots.

Two minutes later, his large blouse on his shoulders and his stick in his hand, he softly opened the door, and with long strides followed Mark Divès on the way to the Falkenstein.

CHAPTER VII

RISING OF THE PARTISANS

From midnight till six in the morning a flame shone through the darkness on the summit of the Falkenstein, and the whole mountain was on the alert.

All the friends of Hullin, Marc Divès, and of Mother Lefèvre, their long gaiters on their legs and old muskets on their shoulders, journeyed, through the silent woods, toward the gorges of the Valtin. The thought of the enemy traversing the plains of Alsace to surprise the passes, was present to the minds of all. The tocsins of Dagsburg, Abreschwiller, Walsch, and St. Quirin, and of all the other villages, began to call the defenders of the country to arms.

Now you must picture to yourself the Jägerthal, at the foot of the old castle, in unusually snowy weather, at that early hour when the clumps of trees begin to creep out of the shadow, and when the extreme cold of night softens at the approach of day. Picture, also, to yourself the old Sawyerie, with its flat roof, its heavy wheel.burdened with icicles, the low interior dimly lit up by a pine-wood fire, whose blaze fades away in the glimmer of the coming dawn; and, around the fire, fur bonnets, caps, and black profiles, gazing one over the other, and squeezing close together like a wall; and farther on, in the woods, more fires lighting up groups of men and women squatting in the snow.

The agitation began to decrease. As the sky became grayer the people recognized each other.

" Ah, it is Cousin Daniel of Soldatenthal. You have come too? "

" Yes, as you see, Heinrich, with my wife also."

" What, Cousin Nanette! Where is she? "

" Down there, near the old oak, by Uncle Hans' fire."

They shook hands. Many could be heard yawning loudly: others threw on the fire bits of planks. The gourds went round; some retired from the circles to make room for their shivering neighbors. Meanwhile the crowd began to grow impatient.

" Ah," cried some, " we did not come here only to get our feet warmed. It is time to see and come to an understanding."

" Yes, yes! Let them hold a council, and name the chiefs."

" No; everybody is not yet arrived. See, there are more coming from Dagsburg and St. Quirin."

Indeed, the lighter it became, the more people could be seen hastening along all the mountain paths. At that time there must have been many hundreds of men in the valley—wood-cutters, charcoal-burners, raftsmen—without counting the women and children.

Nothing could be more picturesque than that gathering in the midst of the snows, in the depths of the defile, closed in as it was by tall pines losing themselves in the clouds. To the right, the valleys opening away into each other as far as the eye could reach; to the left, the ruins of the Falkenstein rising into the sky. From a distance one would have said it was a flock of cranes settled on the ice; but, nearer, these hardy men could be distinguished, with stiff beards bristling like a boar, gloomy fierce eyes, broad square shoulders, and horny hands. Some few, taller than the rest, belonged to the fiery race of red men, white-skinned, and hairy to the tips of their fingers, with strength enough to pull an oak up by the roots. Among this number was old Materne of Hengst, with his two sons Kasper and Frantz. These sturdy fellows —all three armed with little rifles from Innsprück —having blue cloth gaiters with leathern buttons

reaching above their knees, their loins girdled with
goat-skin, and their felt hats coming down low over
their necks—did not deign to approach the fire.
For an hour they had been sitting on a trunk by
the river-side, on the watch, with their feet in the
snow. From time to time the old man would say
to his sons, " What do they shiver for over there?
I never knew a milder night for the season: it is
nothing—the rivers are not even touched."

All the forest-hunters of the country passing by
came to shake hands with them, then congregated
round them and formed a circle apart. These fellows spoke little, being used to silence for whole
days and nights, for fear of frightening away their
game.

Marc Divès, standing in the middle of another
group, a head taller than any of them, spoke and
gesticulated—pointing now to one part of the
mountain, now to another. In front of him was
the old herdsman Lagarmitte, with his large gray
smock, a long bark trumpet on his shoulder, and
his dog at his feet. He listened to the smuggler,
open-mouth, and kept on bowing his head. The
others all seemed attentive: they were composed
of charcoal-burners and wood-carriers, with whom
the smuggler had daily intercourse.

Between the saw-mills and the first fire, on the

bridge over the dam, sat the bootmaker Jérome of St. Quirin—a man of from fifty to sixty years of age, with a long brown face, hollow eyes, big nose —his ears covered with a badger-skin cap—and a yellow beard reaching to his waist in a peak. His hands, enveloped in great green woollen gloves, were clasped over an immense stick of knotty ser-vice-tree. He wore a long sackcloth hood; and might easily have been taken for a hermit. At ev-ery rumor that arose, Father Jérome would slowly turn his head, and try to catch what it was, frown-ing.

Jean Labarbe, grasping his axe, remained im-movable. He was a white-faced man, with an aqui-line nose and thin lips. He exercised great influ-ence over the men of Dagsburg, owing to his reso-lution and the clearness of his ideas. When they shouted around him, "We must deliberate; we cannot stay here doing nothing," he simply content-ed himself with saying, "Let us wait: Hullin has not arrived, nor Catherine Lefèvre. There is no hurry." Everybody then was silenced, and looked impatiently toward the path from Charmes.

The sawyer Piorette—a small, brisk, thin, ener-getic man, whose black eyebrows met above his eyes —stood on the threshold of his hut, with his pipe between his teeth, contemplating the general ap-pearance of this scene.

Meanwhile, the impatience increased every moment. Some village mayors—in square-cut coats and three-cornered hats—advanced in the direction of the saw-mills, calling on their communes to come and decide what was to be done. Most fortunately, at last Catherine Lefèvre's cart appeared, and a thousand enthusiastic shouts arose on all sides:

" There they are! they come! "

Old Materne gravely mounted on a trunk and quietly descended, saying, " It is they."

Great agitation showed itself. The farthest groups gathered together in one crowd. A sort of impatient shiver passed over the mass. Scarcely has the old farmer's wife become visible, whip in hand, on her straw box with little Louise, than from all parts came cries of " Vive la France! Vive la mère Catherine! "

Hullin, who had remained behind, his broad hat pushed back, his musket slung across his shoulder, was now crossing the meadow of Eichmath, distributing vigorous shakes of the hand: " Good-day, Daniel; good-day, Colon. Good-day—good-day! "

" Ah! it is going to be warm, Hullin."

" Yes—yes; we are going to hear the chestnuts popping this winter. Good-day, my old Jérome! We have serious business on hand."

" Yes, Jean-Claude.   We must hope to pull through it by the grace of God."

Catherine, on arriving at the saw-works, tòld Labarbe to set on the ground a keg of brandy which she had brought away from the farm, and to get a jug from the sawyer's cottage.

Soon after, Hullin, coming up to the fire, met Materne and his two sons.

" You have come late," said the old hunter.

" Ah! yes.   What was to be done?   I had to descend the Falkenstein, get my gun, and start the women.   But as we are now here, let us lose no more time;   Lagarmitte, blow thy horn, so that all the men may assemble.   The first thing is to appoint the leaders."

Lagarmitte blew his long trumpet, his cheeks puffed out to his ears: then those who were still on the hill-sides or paths hastened their pace to be in time.   Soon all those brave fellows were assembled in front of the saw-works.   Hullin got up on a pile of tree-trunks, and looking seriously upon the crowd, said, amidst deep silence: " The enemy crossed the Rhine the day before yesterday: they are marching over the mountain into Lorraine: Strasbourg and Huningue are blockaded.   We may expect to see the Germans and Prussians in three or four days."

THERE WAS A GENERAL SHOUT OF "LONG LIVE FRANCE!"

There was a loud shout of " Vive la France! "

" Yes, vive la France! " continued Hullin; " for if the allies enter Paris they can do what they choose; they can re-establish statute-labor, tithes, convents, monopolies, and the gallows. If you wish to see that over again, you have only to let them pass."

It would be impossible to depict the savage fierceness of the audience at that moment.

" That is what I had to tell you," cried Hullin, quite white. " Since you are here, it can only be to fight."

" Yes, yes."

" It is well; but listen to me. I will be open with you. Among you are fathers of families. We shall be one against ten, against fifty: we must expect to perish. So let the men who have not reflected on it, who feel they have not heart to do their duty to the end, go—none will take notice of them. Each man is free."

Then he paused and looked around him. Everybody remained stationary: then with a firmer voice, he concluded thus: " No one goes away; you are all, all resolved to fight. Well, I am rejoiced to see there is not one coward among us. Now a leader must be chosen. In great dangers, the first thing is order and discipline. The leader you are

7

going to name will have the right of commanding
and being obeyed. So reflect seriously, for on that
man will hang the fate of you all."

So saying, Jean-Claude descended from the tree-
trunk, and the agitation became extreme. Every
village deliberated apart by itself—every mayor
proposed his friend—and the hours wore on. Catherine Lefèvre was burning with impatience. At
length she could no longer contain herself, and
standing up on her bench, signed that she was going to speak.

Catherine was held in great esteem. At first
only a few, then a larger number approached to
know what she wished to communicate.

" My friends," said she, " we are losing time.
What do you wish for? A trustworthy man, is it
not so? a soldier—a man who has seen service, and
who knows how to profit by our positions? Well,
why do you not choose Hullin? Can any one
find a better? If so, let him speak, and we will
decide. I propose Jean-Claude Hullin. Hé! do
you hear—over there? If this continues, the Austrians will have arrived before a leader has been
decided on."

" Yes,—yes! Hullin! " shouted Labarbe, Divès,
Jérome, and several others. " Let us see how many
are for and against him."

Then Marc Divès, clambering on to the trunks, cried out in a voice like thunder: "Those who do not want Jean-Claude Hullin for leader must lift up their hands."

Not one hand was uplifted.

"Those who want Jean-Claude Hullin for their leader must raise their hands."

Every hand was put up.

"Jean-Claude," said the smuggler, "mount up here, look—they have chosen you for their leader."

Master Jean-Claude having done so, saw he was named, and said immediately in a stern voice: "Good! you name me to be your chief. I accept! Let Materne the elder, Labarbe of Dagsburg, Jérome of St. Quirin, Marc Divès, Piorette the sawyer, and Catherine Lefèvre, come into the saw-works. We are going to take counsel. In a quarter of an hour or twenty minutes, I shall give my orders. Meanwhile, each village must put two men under the orders of Marc Divès, to fetch powder and ball from the Falkenstein."

CHAPTER VIII

THE persons indicated by Jean-Claude Hullin met together in the shed of the Sawyerie, before the great fireplace; a species of good-humor beaming on their faces.

"For twenty years have I heard speak of the Russians, Austrians, and Cossacks," said old Materne, smiling, "and I shall not be sorry to see a few within reach of my musket: it gives a change to one's ideas."

"Yes," replied Labarbe, "we shall see queer things; the little children of the mountains will be able to relate something of what their fathers and grandfathers did! And the old women, of an evening—won't they tell long tales in fifty years' time?"

"Comrades," said Hullin, "you know the whole country: you have the mountain under your eyes from Thann to Wissembourg. You know that the great roads, imperial roads—traverse Alsace and the Vosges. They both commence at Bâle: one runs along the Rhine to Strasbourg, from whence it ascends to Saverne and enters Lorraine. Huningue, Neuf-Brisach, Strasbourg, and Phals-bourg defend it. The other turns to the left and passes by Schlestadt: at Schlestadt it enters the mountain and reaches Saint-Dié, Raon-l'Etape, Baccarat, and Lunéville. The enemy will want to force these two roads first,—being the best for cavalry, artillery, and baggage,—but as they are defended, we need not trouble ourselves about them. If the allies besiege the fortresses—which would lengthen the campaign—we have nothing to fear; but it is not probable they will do so. After having summoned Huningue to surrender, Belfort, Schlestadt, Strasbourg, and Phalsbourg, on this side the Vosges—Bitsche, Lutzelstein, and Sarre-brück on the other—I imagine they will fall upon us. Now attend to me. Between Phalsbourg and Saint-Dié, there are several defiles for the infantry; but there is only one way practicable for cannon: this is the road from Strasbourg to Raon-les-Leaux by Urmatt, Mutzig, Lutzelhouse, Phra-mond, Grandfontaine. Once masters of this passage, the allies will be able to come out on Lorraine. This road passes the Donon, two leagues from here, on our right. The first thing to be done is to make

a firm stand there, in the most favorable part for
defence, that is to say, on the plateau of the mountain; to intersect it, to break down the bridges,
and to erect solid breastworks across it. A few hundreds of great trees across the road with all their
branches are worth as much as ramparts. They are
the best ambuscades: one is well sheltered behind
them and can see everything coming. Those large
trees hold like death. They must be taken away
piece by piece; bridges cannot be thrown over them:
—in fact it is the best thing to be done. All that,
comrades, must be accomplished to-morrow evening, or next day at the latest. I charge myself
with it. But it is not sufficient to occupy a position
and put it in a good state of defence: it must be
so managed that the enemy shall not be able to
turn it."

"I was just thinking of that," said Materne..
"Once in the valley of Bruche, the Germans can
march with their infantry into the hills of Haslach
and turn our left. Nothing can prevent their trying the same manœuvre on our right, if they reach
Raon-l'Etape."

"Yes, but to take these ideas out of their heads,
we have a very simple thing to do: it is to occupy
the defiles of the Zorn and the Sarre on our left,
and that of Blanru on our right. One can only

keep a defile by holding the heights; that is why
Piorette must place himself with a hundred men
on the side of Raon-les-Leaux; Jérome on the
Grosmann, with the same number, to close the
valley of the Sarre; and Labarbe, at the head of
the remainder on the great slopes to watch over
the hills of Haslach. You must choose your men
from those of the nearest villages. The women
ought not to have a long distance to carry provisions; and then the wounded will be nearer their
homes, which must also be thought of. There is
all I have to say to you just now. The chiefs of
posts must take care to send me every day on the
Donon, where I shall establish our head-quarters
this evening, a good walker, to inform me of what
happens, and to receive the countersign. We shall
also organize a reserve; but as we must make haste,
we will speak of that when you are all in position,
and there is no longer cause to fear a surprise from
the enemy."

"And I," exclaimed Marc Divès, "I shall have
nothing to do then? I am to remain with my arms
folded, watching the others fight?"

"Thou—thou art to survey the transport of ammunition. None of us know how to treat the powder as thou dost, to preserve it from fire and damp,
to melt the balls, and make cartridges."

"But it is woman's work, that is," exclaimed the smuggler. "Hexe-Baizel could do it as well as I. What! am I not even to fire once?"

"Softly, Marc," replied Hullin, laughing; "occasions will not be wanting. In the first place, the Falkenstein is the centre of our line; it is our arsenal and our retreating place in case of misfortune. The enemy will know through his spies that our convoys come from there; he will try, probably, to take them: the balls and bayonet-thrusts will come in thy way. Besides, to have thee in safety will be all the better, for thy cellars and caves must not be confided to the first comer. But if thou really wouldst like——"

"No," said the smuggler, who had been touched by Hullin's reference to his caves—"no! all things considered, I believe thou art right, Jean-Claude. I have my men—they are well armed—we will defend the Falkenstein; and if the opportunity of firing a shot should present itself, I shall be all the freer."

"Then that is a decided and well-understood business?" demanded Hullin.

"Yes, yes, it is decided."

"Well, comrades," said the worthy fellow, joyously, "let us warm ourselves with a few good glasses of wine. It is ten o'clock; let each one return to his village, and make his preparations. To-morrow morning all the defiles must be vigorously occupied."

They quitted the shed, and Hullin, in the presence of his followers, named Labarbe, Jérome, and Piorette chiefs of the defiles: then he told those of the Sarre to assemble as soon as possible near the farm of Bois-de-Chênes, with axes, mattocks, and muskets. "We shall leave at two o'clock, and encamp on the Donon across the route," said he to them. "To-morrow, at dawn, we will begin the breastworks."

He retained Materne and his two sons Frantz and Kasper, announcing to them that the battle would commence undoubtedly on the Donon, and that good shots would be wanted on that side, which gave them pleasure.

Mistress Lefèvre had never looked happier than when she got into her cart again, and, kissing Louise, said in her ear:—"All goes well. Jean-Claude is a man: he sees everything; he draws people to him. I have known him forty years, yet he surprises even me." Then turning round —"Jean-Claude," cried she, "we have a ham waiting for us down there and a few old bottles, which the Germans shall not drink."

"No, Catherine, they shall not drink them. Go on, I am coming."

But just as they were starting, and when already
: number of mountaineers were climbing the hill-
ides to regain their villages, quite in the distance,
ιn the path of Trois-Fontaines, appeared a large
hin man on a big roan cob, with a flat-brimmed
cap of rabbit-skin covering the whole back of his
neck: a great sheep-dog with a black shaggy coat
bounded along near him; and the ends of his enormous surtout flapped behind him like wings. Every
one cried out,—" It is Doctor Lorquin from the
plain—the one who attends poor people gratis. He
comes with his dog Pluto. He is a good man."

In fact he it was. He galloped on, shouting,
" Halt! stop! halt! " And his red face, sharp eyes,
red-brown beard, broad shoulders, great horse and
dog, all cleaved the air and grew upon the view.
In two seconds he had reached the foot of the mountain, crossed the meadow, and appeared at the
bridge, before the shed. Instantly, in breathless
tones, he began to say:—" Ah! the cunning rogues
who want to enter on a campaign without me; they
shall pay for it! " And tapping a small box he
carried at his crupper,—" Listen, my good fellows,
listen! I have something inside there of which
you shall give me an account: every description of
knife, large, small, round and pointed, to take from
you the balls and shot of all kinds which you are

DOCTOR LORQUIN.

going to be regaled with!" Whereupon he burst out laughing, and all those near him felt a cold shiver in all their veins.

Having delivered himself of this pleasantry, Doctor Lorquin continued in a graver tone:—"Hullin, I must pull your ears! What, when the country has to be defended, you forget me! others have to warn me. It appears to me, however, that a doctor will not be out of the way here. I must call you to account."

"Pardon me, doctor, I was wrong," said Hullin, squeezing his hand. "During the last week so many things have happened! One does not always think of everything; and besides, such a man as you are, need not be told how to fulfil his duty."

The doctor was appeased.

"All that is right and good," he cried; "but nevertheless by your fault I am too late; the good places are taken, the crosses distributed. Come, where is the general, that I may make complaints to him?"

"I am the general."

"Oh! oh! really?"

"Yes, doctor, I am the general; and I promote you to be our head surgeon."

"Chief surgeon of the partisans of the Vosges! Well, it suits me. No malice now, Jean-Claude."

Approaching the cart, the worthy man told Catherine that he relied on her for the organization of the ambulances.

"Everything shall be ready, doctor," replied the farm-mistress. "Louise and I are going to set to work this evening. Is it not so, Louise?"

"Oh, yes, Mamma Lefèvre," said she, enchanted to perceive that the campaign was going to begin. "We shall work well; we will spend the night at it even. M. Lorquin shall be well pleased with us."

"Well, then, let us go. You will dine with us, doctor?"

They trotted away. While keeping pace with them, the good doctor related to Catherine laughingly how the tidings of the general rising had reached him; the affliction of his old housekeeper, Marie, who wanted to prevent his going to be massacred by the "kaiserlichs," and the various episodes of his journey from Quibolo to the village of Charmes. Hullin, Materne, and his sons were coming on behind, their carbines on their shoulders; and thus they ascended the hill-side toward the farm of Bois-de-Chênes.

CHAPTER IX

You can imagine the animation at the farm, the bustling of the domestics, the shouts of enthusiasm, the chinking of glasses and forks, the joy depicted on all faces, when Jean-Claude, Doctor Lorquin, the Maternes, and all those who had followed the cart of Catherine Lefèvre were installed in the large room around a magnificent ham, and began to celebrate their future triumphs, glass in hand.

It was on a Tuesday, baking-day at the farm. Excitement had prevailed in the kitchen all the morning: old Duchêne, with shirt-sleeves turned up and a cotton cap on his head, was taking out of the oven numberless loaves of bread, the good odor of which pervaded the whole house. Annette received them and piled them on the hearth; Louise waited on the guests; and Catherine Lefèvre superintended everything, crying out,—" Make haste, my children—make haste! The third batch must be ready when the men from the Sarre arrive. It will make six pounds of bread for each man."

Hullin, from his seat, watched the movements of the old farm-mistress.

"What a woman!" said he; "what a woman! She forgets nothing. Could one find another such in the whole country? To the health of Catherine Lefèvre!"

"To the health of Catherine Lefèvre!" replied the others.

The glasses met together, and they began again to talk over combats, assaults, and intrenchments. Each one felt animated with an invincible confidence; every one said in himself, "All will go well!"

But heaven had in store for them yet another satisfaction on that day, especially for Louise and the Mother Lefèvre. About noon, just as a beautiful gleam of winter sunshine whitened the snow and made the frost melt on the window-panes, and the great cock, putting his head out of his coop, uttered his triumphant crow, flapping his wings —just then the watch-dog, old "Yohan," half blind and toothless, began to bark so joyously and plaintively, that everyone listened with the greatest attention. The kitchen was all excitement with the fourth batch coming out of the oven, and even Catherine Lefèvre herself stopped.

"Something is going on," said she, in a low

voice; and then added, all trembling, "Since my boy left, Yohan has never barked like that."

At the same moment, rapid steps traversed the court. Louise sprang toward the door, crying,— "It is he! It is he!" and almost immediately a hand tried to hasp. The door opened, and a soldier appeared on the threshold; but such a soldier, so worn, so bronzed, so emaciated! his gray hood, with its pewter buttons, so ragged—his high leathern gaiters so torn, that all present were astonished.

He appeared unable to advance a step farther, and slowly put the butt-end of his musket on the ground. The tip of his aquiline nose—the nose of Mother Lefèvre—shone like bronze; his red mustaches shook like one of those great lean hawks which are forced by hunger to come to the very doors of the stables in winter. He looked into the kitchen, pale beneath the brown coating of his cheeks, and with his great hollow eyes filled with tears, he seemed unable to advance or say a word.

Outside, the old dog leaped, whined, and shook his chain; in the interior, one could hear the fire blazing, so great was the silence; but soon Catherine Lefèvre, with a piercing voice, exclaimed,— "Gaspard! my child! It is thou!"

"Yes, my mother," replied the soldier, softly, as though suffocating.

And at the same moment Louise began to weep, while in the great room there arose a shout like thunder. All the friends ran out, Master Jean-Claude at their head, crying,—" Gaspard! Gaspard Lefèvre! "

. Then they saw Gaspard and his mother embracing each other. This strong, courageous woman was weeping: he did not weep; he held her pressed to his breast, his red mustaches mingling with her gray locks, and murmured,—" My mother!—my mother! Ah, how often have I thought of you! " Then, in a louder voice, he said, " Louise! Where is Louise? I saw Louise! " And Louise threw herself into his arms, and their kisses were mingled together. " Ah, thou didst not recognize me, Louise! "

" Oh, yes!—oh, yes! I knew thee, even by thy step! "

Old Duchême, with his cotton cap in his hands, stammered out by the fireplace,—" Lord! is it possible? My poor child! What does he look like? "

He had brought up Gaspard, and always fancied him, ever since his departure, fresh and ruddy in a beautiful uniform with red facings. It completely deranged his ideas to see him otherwise.

At that moment Hullin, raising his voice, said,

—" And the rest of us, Gaspard,—thy old friends —art thou not going to take notice of us ? "

Then the brave fellow turned round and ex- exclaimed with enthusiasm,—" Hullin! Doctor Lorquin! Materne! Frantz! Why, they are all here! "

And the embraces recommenced, but this time more joyously, with shouts of laughter and shaking of hands that seemed endless.

" Ah, doctor, it is you! Ah, my old father, Jean-Claude! "

They looked closely at each other, with bright, beaming faces, and went arm-in-arm up and down the great room; and Mother Catherine with the knapsack, Louise with the gun, and Duchêne with the shako, followed them, laughing and drying their cheeks and eyes—nothing had ever been seen like it before.

" Let us sit down and drink! " exclaimed Doc- tor Lorquin. " This is the bouquet of the feast."

" Ah, my poor Gaspard, how happy I am to be- hold thee safe and sound," said Hullin. " Ha, ha! Without flattery, I like thee better as thou art now than with thy great red cheeks. Parbleu! thou art a man now. Thou remindest me of the old fellows of my time, those of the Sambre and Egypt —ha, ha, ha! we had not round noses, we were not

8

sleek and fat; we looked like lean rats watching a
cheese, and our teeth were long and white! "

" Yes, yes, that does not surprise me, Papa Jean-
Claude. Come, let us sit down; we can talk more
at ease. Ah, now, why are you all at the farm? "

" What, dost thou not know? All the country
is up, from Houpe to Saint-Sauveur, to defend itself."

" Yes, the anabaptist of Painbach just mentioned
it as I passed. It is then true? "

" It is true. Everybody is in it; and I am the
general in chief."

" Excellent—excellent! That these rogues of
' kaiserlichs ' should not carry everything with a
high hand in our own country gives me pleasure.
But hand me the knife. Anyway one is happy to
find one's self at home again. Hé! Louise, come
here and sit down a little while. Look, Papa Jean-
Claude: with this girl on one side of me, the ham
on the other, and the bottle to the front, I should
not need a fortnight to pick up again; and my
comrades would not know me when I joined the
company."

Everybody was now sitting down and astonished
to see with what appetite the brave fellow ate and
drank, while regarding Louise and his mother tenderly, and replying to one and the other, without
losing a single mouthful.

The farm-people, Duchêne, Annette, Robin, and Dubourg, arranged in a half-circle, watched Gaspard in ecstasies; Louise refilled his glass; the Mother Lefèvre, seated by the stove, got up and went to his knapsack, and, on only finding two old black shirts with holes wide enough to put one's hand through, with worn-out shoes and a bit of wax for cartridges, a comb with two teeth and an empty bottle, she lifted her hands to heaven and hastening to open the linen chest, saying, "Lord, can one be astonished that so many die of sheer want!"

Doctor Lorquin, in presence of such a vigorous appetite, rubbed his hands joyfully, and murmured to himself, "What a sturdy fellow! What a digestion! What a set of teeth! He could crunch pebbles like nuts."

And even old Materne said to his sons:—"In other days, after two or three days of hunting in the high mountains in winter, I also used to feel the hunger of a wolf, and to eat a haunch of venison right off: now I am getting old, one or two pounds of meat are sufficient for me—which shows what age does."

Hullin had lit his pipe, and seemed in a reverie: evidently something worried him. After a few minutes, seeing that Gaspard's appetite was less lively, he brusquely asked, "Say, then, Gaspard, without interrupting thyself, how the devil hast thou managed to come? We believed that thou wast still on the borders of the Rhine, on the Strasbourg side."

"Ah! ah! old soldier, I comprehend," said young Lefèvre, winking. "There are so many deserters, are there not?"

"Oh! such an idea would never enter my head, and yet——"

"You would not be sorry to know that I had done nothing wrong? I cannot blame you, Papa Jean-Claude: you are right. He who is missing at the roll-call when the ' kaiserlichs ' are in France, deserves to be shot. Be composed, here is my leave."

Hullin, who possessed no false delicacy, read, ——" Leave for twenty-four hours to the grenadier Gaspard Lefèvre, of the 2d of the 1st. This day, 3d January, 1814.—GEMEAU, Head of Battalion."

"Good, good," exclaimed he. "Put that carefully in thy knapsack, thou mightest lose it."

All his good-humor had returned:—"Do you see, my children, I know what love is? There is both good and bad in it: but it is particularly bad for young soldiers who come too close to their village after a campaign. They are capable of forget-

ting themselves and of not returning unless in com·
pany of two or three gendarmes. I have seen it.
But come, since everything is in order, let us drink
a glass of 'rikevir.' What say you, Catherine?
The men of the Sarre may arrive at any moment,
and we have not an instant to lose?"

"You are right, Jean-Claude," replied the old
farm-mistress sadly. "Annette, go down and bring
three bottles from the small cellar."

The servant obeyed quickly.

"But this leave, Gaspard," continued Catherine
—"how long has it lasted?"

"I received it yesterday, at eight in the evening,
at Vasselonne, my mother. The regiment is retreating on Lorraine; I must rejoin it this evening at
Phalsbourg."

"It is well; thou hast still seven hours; thou
wilt not need more than six to reach there, although
there is much snow on the Foxthal."

The good woman came and sat down again by
her son, with a full heart. Every one was moved.
Louise, with her arm on the old tattered epaulet
of Gaspard and her cheek against his, was sobbing.
Hullin emptied the ashes from his pipe at the end
of the table, frowning, without saying anything,
but when the bottles arrived and were uncorked,
"Come, Louise," said he, "take courage! this can-

not last forever; it must end in one way or another, and I venture to affirm that it will end well. Gaspard will come back to us, and then we shall have the wedding."

He refilled the glasses, and Catherine dried her eyes, murmuring, " To think that those brigands are the cause of all this. Ah! let them come—let them come here! "

They all drank with a melancholy air; but the old " rikevir," entering the hearts of these brave people quickly enlivened them. Gaspard, stronger than he had appeared at first, began to relate the terrible battles of Bautzen, Lutzen, Leipzig, and Hanau, where the conscripts had fought like tried soldiers, winning victory after victory, till traitors began to appear.

Every one listened in silence. Louise, when he spoke of any great danger—of the passage over rivers under the enemy's fire, or the taking of a battery by the bayonet—squeezed his arm as though to defend him. Jean-Claude's eyes sparkled; the doctor demanded each time the position of the ambulance; Materne and his sons stretched out their necks and clinched their jaws; and with help of the old wine the enthusiasm increased every moment. " Ah, the rascals! ah, the brigands! But look out! it is not over yet."

Mother Lefèvre admired the courage and luck of her son in the midst of these events, which will be remembered centuries to come. But when Lagarmitte, looking solemn and grave in his long gray cloth coat, with his broad black felt on his white head, and with his bark trumpet on his shoulder, crossed the kitchen, and appeared at the entrance to the large room, saying,—" The men of the Sarre are come,"—then all this enthusiasm disappeared, and the company rose, thinking of the terrible struggle which would soon take place in the mountains.

Louise, throwing her arms round Gaspard's neck, cried, " Gaspard, do not go away! Remain with us! "

He became very pale.

" I am a soldier," said he. " I am called, Gaspard Lefèvre. I love thee a thousand times more than my own life; but a Lefèvre only knows his duty."

And he unwound her arms. Louise then, sinking on the table, began to moan aloud. Gaspard rose. Hullin stood between them, and grasping his hands tightly, with trembling lips, said: " Excellently well! Thou hast spoken like a man."

His mother came forward with a calm countenance to buckle his knapsack on his shoulders.

She did it with knitted eyebrows and pressed lips, without one sigh escaping her; but two great tears slowly ran down the wrinkles of her cheeks. And when she had done it, she turned away, and with her sleeve over her eyes, said: " It is well! Go— go, my child! thy mother blesses thee. Whatever thy fortune thou wilt yet not be lost to us. Look, Gaspard: there is thy place—there between Louise and myself—thou wilt always be there. This poor child is not old enough yet to know that to live is to suffer."

Everybody left; only Louise remained lamenting in the room. A few seconds later, as the butt end of the musket sounded on the slabs of the kitchen, and the outer door was opened, she gave a piercing shriek, and darted after him.

" Gaspard, Gaspard, look! I will be courageous; I will not cry; I will not keep thee back. Oh, no; but do not leave me in anger. Have pity on me! "

" Angry! angry with thee, my Louise! Oh, no! But to see thee so unhappy breaks my heart. Ah! if thou wert a little braver now, I should feel happier."

" Well, I am. Let us kiss each other! See, I am no longer the same. I would be like Maman Lefèvre."

They calmly gave each other a parting embrace,

LOUISE THROWING HER ARMS AROUND GASPARD'S NECK.

Hullin held the gun; Catherine motioned with her hands, as though to say, " Go, go! it is enough! " And he, suddenly seizing his musket, walked away resolutely, without looking back.

On the other side, the men of the Sarre, with their axes and hatchets, were climbing the steep ascent of the Valtin.

Five minutes later, on passing by the great oak, Gaspard turned round, lifting his hands. Catherine and Louise replied to it. Hullin advanced to meet his people. Doctor Lorquin alone remained with the women; and when Gaspard, continuing his way, had disappeared, he exclaimed, " Catherine Lefèvre, you can pride yourself on having an affectionate son. God grant him good fortune! "

And the distant voices of the new-comers could be heard laughing among themselves, as they were marching to war as gayly as to a wedding.

CHAPTER X

As Hullin, at the head of the mountaineers, was taking his measures for the defence of his country, the madman Yégof, with his tin crown, that sad spectacle of humanity shorn of its noblest attribute, intelligence—the madman Yégof, his breast exposed to the fierce wind, his feet bare, reckless of cold, like the reptile in his prison, was wandering from mountain to mountain, in the midst of the snows of winter. How comes it that the madman is able to resist the sharpest severity of the atmosphere, while an intelligent being would succumb to it? Does it arise from a more powerful concentration of life, a more rapid circulation of the blood, a state of continued fever? Or is it the effect of the extraordinary excitement of the senses, or any other unknown cause?

Science tells us nothing. She admits only material causes, without giving an account of such phenomena.

So Yégof went on at random, and night came.
The cold was redoubled, the fox gnashed his teeth
in the pursuit of an invisible prey ; the famished
buzzard fell back with empty claws among the
bushes, uttering a cry of distress.   He, with his raven on his shoulder, gesticulating, jabbering, as if
in a dream, kept walking on, from Holderloch to
Sonneberg, from Sonneberg to Blutfeld.

Now, on this particular night, the old shepherd,
Robin, of the farm of Bois-de-Chênes, was destined
to be the witness of a most strange and fearful sight.

Some days ago, having been overtaken by the first
fall of snow at the bottom of the ravine of the Blutfeld, he had left his cart there to conduct his flock
back to the farm ; but having discovered that he
had forgotten his sheepskin, and left it in a shed
there, he had on this day, when his work was done,
set out about four o'clock in the afternoon to go and
fetch it.   The Blutfeld, situated between the
Schnéeberg and the Grosmann, is a narrow gorge,
bounded by rocks.   A narrow stream of water
winds through it, under shadow of the tall shrubs,
and in its depths extends a vast pasturage, all covered with large gray stones, that lie thickly scattered
about.

This gorge is very little frequented, for there is
a wild look about the Blutfeld, especially by the

light of a winter moon.   The learned folks of these
regions, the school-master of Dagsburg, and he of
Hazlach, say that in that spot occurred the famous
battle of the Triboques against the Germans, who
wished to penetrate into Gaul, under the command
of a leader named Luitprandt.   They say that the
Triboques, from the neighboring heights, hurling
upon their enemies huge masses of rocks, crushed
them there as in a mortar, and that, on account of
this great carnage, the gorge has preserved to this
day the name of *Blutfeld.*   Fragments of broken
pots, of rusty lances, of helmets, and long swords
with cross hilts, are often found there.

At night, when the moon sheds her light upon
this field and those immense stones, all covered with
snow, when the north wind blows among the frost-
covered branches, making them rattle and clatter
like cymbals, you might fancy you heard the wild
cry of the Germans at the moment of surprise, the
shrieks of the women, the neighings of the horses,
the rumbling of the chariots in the defile ; for it
seems that these people brought with them, in their
skin-covered carriages, women, children, old men,
and all that they possessed in gold, and silver, and
movables, like the Germans setting out for America.
The Triboques never ceased to massacre them during two days, and on the third day they returned to

the Donon, the Schnéeberg, the Grosmann, the Giromani, the Hengst,—their broad shoulders stooping under the weight of their booty.

This is what is related concerning the Blutfeld, and certainly to see this gorge enclosed within the mountains like an immense trap, without any other outlet than a narrow footpath, it is easy to understand how the Germans were taken at a disadvantage and fell an easy prey to their conquerors.

Robin did not reach the spot till between seven and eight o'clock, just as the moon was rising.

The worthy fellow had descended the precipice a hundred times, but never had he beheld the place so brightly illuminated, and at the same time of so gloomy an aspect.

At a distance, his white cart, at the bottom of the abyss, looked to him exactly like one of those enormous stones, covered with snow, beneath which the Germans had been buried. It was at the entrance of the gorge, behind a thick cluster of shrubs, and beside it the little torrent ran murmuring in a slender stream, bright as steel, and sparkling like diamonds.

When he arrived there, the shepherd began to look for the key of the padlock ; then, having unlocked the shed, he crept in on his hands and knees, and found, very fortunately, not only his sheepskin, but an old hatchet, which he had quite forgotten.

But judge of his surprise when, on issuing from it, he saw the madman Yégof appear at the turn of the footpath, and come straight toward him in the bright moonlight.

The honest man imme 'iately remembered the fearful story told in the kitchen of Bois-do-Chênes, and he felt afraid ; but quite another feeling came over him when behind the fool, at fifteen or twenty paces, he beheld, stealthily approaching in their turn, five gray wolves, two big and three smaller ones.

At first he took them for dogs, but they were wolves. They followed Yégof step by step, and he did not appear to see them ; his raven hovered overhead, flitting from the full moonlight to the shadow of the rocks, and then returning ; the wolves, with flaming eyes, their sharp muzzles turned up, were sniffing the air ; the fool raised his sceptre.

The shepherd pulled-to the door of the shed as quick as lightning, but Yégof did not see him. He advanced into the gorge as into a spacious chamber, to the right and left rose the steep rocks, above which myriads of stars were shining. You might have heard a fly move ; the wolves made no noise in walking ; all was silent, and the raven had just

perched on the top of an old withered oak that grew
upon one of the rocks opposite ; his shining plumage looked still darker than usual, as he turned
his head, and seemed to be listening.

It was a strange sight.

Robin said to himself :—" The fool sees nothing,
hears nothing ; they will devour him.   If he stum-
bles, if his foot slips, it is all over with him."

But in the middle of the gorge, Yégof, having
turned round, sat down upon a stone, and the five
wolves round him, still sniffing the air, squatted on
their haunches in the snow.

And then, a really terrible sight—the fool raising his sceptre, made them a speech, calling them
each by his name.

The wolves answered him with dismal howls.

Now this is what he said to them:—" Hé, Child,
Bléd, Merweg, and thou, Sirimar, my ancient, we
are met together, then, once again !   You have returned fat.   There has been good cheer in Germany, eh? "

Then, pointing to the snow-covered gorge :—
" You remember the great battle? "

First one of the wolves began to howl slowly in a
dismal voice, then another, then all the five together.

This lasted a good ten minutes.

The raven, perched on the withered branch, did not stir.

Robin would gladly have fled. He put up his prayers, invoked all the saints, and, in particular, his own patron, for whom all the shepherds of the mountain have the highest veneration.

But the wolves still continued howling, awakening all the echoes of the Blutfeld.

At last one, the oldest of the number, was silent, then another, then all, and Yégof continued :—
" Yes, yes : that is a dismal story. Look ! there is the river down which our blood flowed in streams! No matter, Merweg, no matter ; the others have left their bones to whiten on the common, and the cold moon has seen their women tearing their hair for three days and three nights! Oh, that frightful day! Oh, the dogs! were they proud of their great victory? Let them be accursed—accursed."

The fool had cast his crown to the ground. He now picked it up, groaning as he did so.

The wolves, still crouching round, listened to him like attentive spectators. The biggest among them began to howl, and Yégof answered his complaint.

" You are hungry, Sirimar ; take comfort, take comfort ; you will not want for food much longer ;

THE LUNATIC, WAVING HIS SCEPTRE, MADE THEM A DISCOURSE.

the men of our side are coming, and the strife will begin afresh."

Then rising, and striking his sceptre on a stone, " See," said he, " behold thy bones ! "

He approached another. " And thine, Merweg, behold them ! " said he.

All the troop followed him, while he, raising himself upon a low rock, and glancing round upon the silent gorge, exclaimed :—" Our war-song is silent ! our war-song is now a groan ! The hour is near ; it will reawaken, and you will be among the warriors ; you will possess once more these valleys and these mountains. Oh ! that sound of wheels, those cries of women, those blows from crushing rocks and stones ; I hear them ; the air is full of them. Yes, yes ; they fell on us from above, and we were surrounded. And now all is dead ; hear ! all is dead ; your bones sleep, but your children are on their way, and your turn will come. Sing ! sing ! "

And this time he himself began to howl, while the wolves took up again their savage song.

These dismal howls grew more and more loud and appalling ; and the silence of the rocks around, some plunged in darkness, while others were fully revealed in the moon's rays, the solemn stillness of every tree and shrub beneath its weight of snow, the

9

distant echoes replying with a sad voice to the mournful concert, all were calculated to strike terror into the breast of the old shepherd.

But by degrees his fears grew less, for Yégof and his gloomy procession were getting farther and farther away from him, and gradually retreating toward Hazlach.

The raven, in his turn, with a hoarse cry unfurled his wings, and took his flight through the sky.

The whole scene vanished like a dream.

Robin heard for a long while after the howlings of the retreating wolves. They had completely ceased for more than twenty minutes. The silence of winter reigned on all sides, when the worthy man felt himself sufficiently recovered from his fright to come out of his hiding-place, and take his way back at full speed to the farm.

On arriving at Bois-de-Chênes, he found everybody stirring. They were preparing to kill an ox for the troops from the Donon. Hullin, Doctor Lorquin, and Louise were already set out with those from the Sarre. Catherine Lefèvre was loading her great four-horse wagon with bread, meat, and brandy. People were coming and going in all directions, and all lending a helping hand in the preparations.

Robin could not bring himself to relate to any one

all that he had seen and heard. Besides, it seemed to himself so incredible that he really dared not open his mouth about it.

When he had retired to rest in his crib in the middle of the stable, he said to himself that no doubt Yégof had, during the winter, tamed a litter of young wolves, and that he talked nonsense to them just as one talks sometimes to one's dog.

But, for all that, this strange encounter left a superstitious dread upon his mind, and even when he had arrived at a great age, the old fellow never spoke of these things without shuddering.

CHAPTER XI

HULLIN'S orders had all been carried out; the defiles of the Zorne and of the Sarre were well guarded ; while that of Blanru, the extreme point of the position, had been put into a state of defence by Jean-Claude himself and the three hundred men who composed his principal force.

We must now transport ourselves to the southern slopes of the Donon, two kilomètres from Grand-fontaine, and await further events.

Above the high-road which winds round the hill-side up to within two-thirds of the summit, was a farm, surrounded with a few acres of tilled land, the freehold of Pelsly the anabaptist : it was a large building with a flat roof, much needed, so as to prevent its being blown away by the high winds. The out-houses and pigsties were situated at the back, toward the summit of the mountain.

The partisans were encamped near : at their feet lay Grandfontaine and Framont ; in a narrow

gorge farther on, at the point where the valley takes
a turn, rose Schirmeck and its old mass of feudal
ruins ; lastly, among the undulations of the chain,
the Bruche disappears in a zigzag, under the grayish mists of Alsace.   To their left arose the arid
peak of the Donon, covered with rocks and a few
stunted pines.   Before them was the rugged road,
its shelving banks thrown down over the snow, and
great trees flung across it with all their branches.

The melting snow let the yellow soil be seen in
patches here and there, or else formed great drifts,
heaped up by the north wind.

It was a grand and severe spectacle.   Not a single
traveller, not a carriage appeared along the whole
length of the road in the valley, winding as far as
the eye can reach : it was like a desert.   The fires
scattered round the farm-house sent up their puffs
of damp smoke to the sky, and alone indicated the
position of the bivouac.

The mountaineers, seated by their kettles, with
their hats slouched over their faces, were very melancholy : three days they had been awaiting the enemy.   Among one of the groups, sitting with their
legs doubled up, bent shoulders, and pipes in their
mouths were old Materne and his two sons.

From time to time Louise appeared on the step of
the farm, then quickly re-entered, and set herself

again to her work. A great cock was scratching
up the manure with his claws, and crowing hoarsely ; two or three fowls were strutting up and down
among the bushes. All that was pleasant to look
upon ; but the chief pleasure of the partisans was
to contemplate some magnificent quarters of bacon,
with red-and-white sides, which were spitted on
greenwood sticks, the fat melting drop by drop on
to the small coals—and to fill their flasks at a small
cask of brandy placed on Catherine Lefèvre's cart.

Toward eight o'clock in the morning a man suddenly appeared between the great and little Donon;
the sentinels perceived him at once ; he descended,
waving his hat.

A few minutes later Nickel Bentz, the old forest-
keeper of the Houpe, was recognized.

The whole camp was roused ; they ran to awaken
Hullin, who had been sleeping for an hour in the
farm-house, on a great straw mattress, side by side
with Doctor Lorquin and his dog Pluto.

The three came out, accompanied by the herdsman Lagarmitte, nicknamed Trumpet, and the anabaptist Pelsly—a silent man, having his arms buried
to the elbows in the deep pockets of his gray woollen
tunic trimmed with pewter clasps, with an immense
beard, and the tassel of his cotton cap half way down
his back.

Jean-Claude seemed light-hearted. "Well, Nickel, what is going on down there?" cried he.

"At present, nothing new, Master Jean-Claude; only on the Phalsbourg side one hears something like the rumbling of a storm. Labarbe says that it is cannon, for all night we have seen flashes through the forest of Hildehouse, and since the morning gray clouds have been spreading over the plain."

"The town is attacked," said Hullin; "but what about the Lutzelstein side?"

"One can hear nothing," replied Bentz.

"Then the enemy is trying to turn the place. In any case, the allies are down there : there must be hosts of them in Alsace." And turning toward Materne, who was standing behind him, "We cannot remain any longer in uncertainty," said he; "thou, with thy two sons, go on a reconnoissance."

The old hunter's face brightened. "So be it ! I can stretch my legs a little," said he, "and see if I can't knock over one of those rascally Austrians or Cossacks."

"Stop an instant, my old fellow ! it is not now a question of knocking anybody over ; we want to see what is going on. Frantz and Kasper will remain armed ; but I know thee : thou must leave thy carbine here, thy powder-flask, and thy hunting-knife."

" What for? "

" Because thou wilt have to go into the villages, and if thou art taken in arms, thou wilt be shot directly."

" Shot? "

" Certainly.   We do not belong to the regular troops ; they do not take us prisoners ; they shoot us.   Thou wilt follow, then, the road to Schirmeck, stick in hand, and thy sons will accompany thee at a distance, in the underwood, within musket-range. If any marauders attack thee, they will come to thy rescue ; if it is a column, or a handful of troops, they must allow thee to be taken."

" They are to let me be taken ! " cried the old hunter, indignantly.   " I should like to see that."

" Yes, Materne ; it will be the best plan : for an unarmed man would be released, an armed shot. I do not need to tell thee not to sing out to the Germans that thou art come to spy upon them."

" Ah, ah ! I comprehend.   Yes, yes, that is not badly planned.   As for me, I never quit my gun, Jean-Claude, but war is war.   Hold ! there is my carbine, and my powder-flask, and my knife.   Who will lend me his blouse and his stick? "

Nickel Bentz handed him his blue blouse and his cap.   They were surrounded by an admiring crowd.

After he had changed his clothes, notwithstanding his large gray mustaches, one would have taken the old hunter for a simple peasant from the high mountains.

His two sons, proud to be of this first expedition, looked to the priming of their muskets, and fixed to the end of the barrel a boar-spear, straight and long as a sword. They felt their hunting-knives, . flung their bags upon their backs, and confident that all was in order, they glanced proudly round them.

"Ah," said Doctor Lorquin, laughing, "do not forget Master Jean-Claude's advice. Be careful. One German more or less in a hundred thousand would not make much difference in our affairs ; whereas if one or the other of you came back to us injured, you would be replaced with difficulty."

"Oh, fear nothing, doctor : we shall have our eyes open."

"My boys," replied Materne, haughtily, "are true hunters ; they know how to wait the moment and profit by it. They will only fire when I call. You can rest assured ! and now, let us start ; we must be back before night."

They departed.

"Good luck to you !" shouted Hullin, while they mounted the snow in order to avoid the breast-works.

They soon descended toward the narrow path, which turns sharply on the right of the mountain.

The partisans watched them. Their red frizzy hair, long muscular legs, their broad shoulders, and supple, quick movements,—all showed that in case of an encounter, five or six " kaiserlichs " would have little chance against such fine fellows.

In a quarter of an hour they had reached the pine-forest and disappeared.

Then Hullin quietly returned to the farm, talking to Nickel Bentz.

Doctor Lorquin walked behind, followed by Pluto, and all the others returned to their places round the bivouac fires.

CHAPTER XII

MATERNE and his two boys walked for some time
in silence. The weather had become fine ; the pale
winter sun shone over the brilliant snow without
melting it, and the ground remained firm and hard.

In the distance, along the valley, stood out, with
surprising clearness, the tops of the fir-trees, the reddish peaks of the rocks, the roofs of the hamlets, with
their icy stalactites hanging from the eaves, their
small sparkling windows, and sharp gables.

People were walking in the street of Grandfontaine. A troupe of young girls were standing round
the washing-place ; a few old men in cotton caps
were smoking their pipes on the doorsteps of the
little houses. All this little world, lying in the
depths of the blue expanse, came, and went, and
lived, without a sound or sigh reaching the ears of
the foresters.

The old hunter halted on the outskirts of the
wood, and said to his sons : " I am going down to

the village to see Dubreuil, the innkeeper of the
' Pineapple.' "

And he pointed with his stick to a long white
building, the doors and windows of which were surrounded with a yellow bordering, a pine-branch being suspended to the wall as a signboard.

" You must await me here. If there is no danger, I will come out on to the doorstep and raise my
hat ; you can then come and take a glass of wine
with me."

He immediately descended the snowy slopes to
the little gardens lying above Grandfontaine, which
took about ten minutes ; he then made his way between two furrows, reached the meadow, and crossed
the village square : his two sons, with their arms at
their feet, saw him enter the inn. A few seconds
after he reappeared on the doorstep and raised his
hat.

Fifteen minutes later they had rejoined their
father in the great room of the " Pineapple."   It
was a rather low room with a sanded floor, and heat-
ed by a large iron stove.

Excepting the innkeeper Dubreuil, the biggest
and most apoplectic landlord in the Vosges, with
immense paunch, round eyes, flat nose, a wart on his
left cheek, and a triple chin reaching over his col-
lar—with the exception of this curious individual,

seated near the stove in a leather arm-chair, Materne was alone. He had just filled the glasses. The clock was striking nine, and its wooden cock flapped its wing with a peculiar scraping sound.

"Good-day, Father Dubreuil," said the two youths in a gruff voice.

"Good-day, my brave fellows," replied the innkeeper, trying to smile.

Then, in an oily voice, he asked them, "Nothing new?"

"Faith, no!" replied Kasper; "here is winter, the time for hunting boars."

And they both, putting their carbines in the corner of the window, within reach, in case of attack, passed one leg across the bench, and sat down, facing their father, who was at the head of the table.

At the same time they drank, saying, "To our healths!" which they were always very careful to do.

"Thus," said Materne, turning to the fat man, as though taking up the threads of an interrupted conversation, "you think, Father Dubreuil, that we have nothing to fear from the wood of Baronies, and that we may hunt boar peaceably?"

"Oh, as to that, I know nothing!" exclaimed the innkeeper; "only at present the allies have not passed Mutzig. Besides, they harm no one; they receive all well-disposed people to fight against the usurper."

"The usurper? Who is he?"

"Why, Napoleon Bonaparte, the usurper, to be sure. Just look at the wall."

He pointed to a great placard stuck on the wall, near the clock.

"Look at that, and you will see that the Austrians are our true friends."

Old Materne's eyebrows nearly met, but, repressing his feelings, "Oh, ah!" said he.

"Yes, read that."

"But I do not know how to read, Monsieur Dubreuil, nor my boys either. Explain to us what it is."

Then the old innkeeper, leaning with his hands on the arms of his chair, arose, breathing like a calf, and placed himself in front of the placard, with his arms folded on his enormous paunch ; and in a majestic tone he read a proclamation from the allied sovereigns, declaring "that they made war on Napoleon personally, and not on France. Therefore everybody ought to keep quiet and not meddle in their affairs, under pain of being burnt, pillaged, and shot."

The three hunters listened, and looked at each other with a strange air.

When Dubreuil had finished, he reseated himself and said, "Now do you see?"

"And where did you get that?" demanded Kasper.

"That, my boy, is put up everywhere!"

"Well, we are pleased with that," said Materne, laying his hand on Frantz's arm, who had risen with sparkling eyes. "Dost thou want a light, Frantz? Here is my flint."

Frantz sat down again, and the old man continued, good-naturedly : "And our good friends the Germans take nothing from any one?"

"Quiet, orderly people have nothing to fear ; but as to the rascals who rise, all is taken from them. And it is just—the good ought not to suffer for the wicked. For example, instead of doing you any harm, the allies would receive you well at their head-quarters. You know the country : you would serve as guides, and you would be richly paid."

There was a slight pause. The three hunters again looked at each other : the father had spread his hands on the table, as though to recommend calm to his sons ; but even he was very pale.

The innkeeper, observing nothing, continued : "You would have much more to fear in the woods of Baronies from those brigands of Dagsburg, Sarre, and Blanru, who have all revolted, and wish to have '93 over again."

"Are you sure of that?" demanded Materne, making an effort to control himself.

"Am I sure! You have only to look out of the window and you will see them on the road to the Donon. They have surprised the anabaptist Pelsly, and bound him to the foot of his bed. They pillage, rob, break up the roads. But beware! In a few days they will see strange things. It is not with a thousand men that they will be attacked, not with ten thousand, but with millions. They will all be hung."

Materne rose.

"It is time for us to be going," said he briefly. "At two o'clock we must be at the wood, and here we are talking quietly like magpies! Au revoir, Father Dubreuil." They rushed out hastily, no longer able to contain their passion.

"Think of what I have said," cried the innkeeper to them from his chair.

Once in the open air, Materne, turning round, said, with trembling lips : "If I had not restrained myself, I should have broken the bottle on his head."

"And I," said Frantz, "should have run him through with my bayonet."

Kasper, one foot on the step, seemed about to re-enter the inn; he grasped the handle of his hunting-knife, and his face bore a terrible expression. But his father took him by the arm and dragged him off, saying : " Come, come, we will deal with him later on. To counsel me to betray the country ! Hullin told us to be on our guard : he was right."

They went down the street, looking to the right and left with haggard eyes. The people asked among themselves : What is the matter with them?

On reaching the end of the village, they halted, in front of the old cross, close to the church, and Materne in a calmer tone, pointing out the path which winds round Phramond over the heath, said to his sons: " You must take that road. I shall follow the route to Schirmeck. I shall not go too fast, so that you may have time to come up with me."

They parted, and the old hunter, with bowed head, walked on thoughtfully for a long time, asking himself by what inward strength he had been able to keep from breaking the fat innkeeper's head. He said to himself that no doubt it was from fear of compromising his sons.

While thinking over these things, Materne kept continually meeting herds of cattle, sheep and goats, which were being led into the mountain. Some came from Wisch, Urmatt, and even from Mutzig ; the poor beasts could scarcely stand.

" Where the devil are you running so fast? "

10

shouted the old hunter to the melancholy herdsmen.
" Have.you then no confidence in the proclamation
of the Austrians and Russians? "

And they angrily answered: " It is easy for you
to laugh.   Proclamations ! we know what they are
worth now.   They pillage and rob everything,
make forced contributions, carry off the horses,
cows, oxen, and carts."

" Nonsense ! impossible ! What are you talking
about? " said Materne. " You astound me! Such
worthy people, such good friends, the saviours of
France.   I cannot believe you.   Such a beautiful
proclamation as it was."

" Well, go down to Alsace, and you will see."

The poor creatures went on, shaking their heads
in extreme indignation, and he laughed slyly.

The farther Materne advanced, the number of
herds became greater.   There were not only troops
of cattle bellowing and lowing, but flocks of geese,
as far as the eye could reach, screeching and cackling, dragging themselves along the road with wings
spread and half-frozen feet: it was piteous to see.

It was worse still on approaching Schirmeck. The
people were flying in crowds, with their great wagons loaded with barrels, smoked meats, furniture,
women and children.   They were lashing their
horses almost to death on the road, and screaming in

terrified voices : " We are lost ; the Cossacks are coming."

The cry of " The Cossacks! the Cossacks ! " ran along the whole line like a puff of wind; the women turned round open-mouthed, and the children stood up on the wagons to get a better view. You never beheld anything like it before ; and Materne, angered, blushed for the terror of these people, who might have defended themselves; while selfishness and their desire to save their property, made them fly like cowards.

At the crossing of the Fond-des-Saules quite close to Schirmeck, Kasper and Frantz rejoined their father, and the three entered the " Golden Key " tavern, kept by the Widow Faltaux, on the right side of the road. The poor woman and her two daughters were watching from a window the great migration with streaming eyes and clasped hands.

In fact, the tumult increased every minute ; the cattle, wagons, and people seemed eager to get away over each other's shoulders. They no longer had any command of themselves : they were howling and striking about them in their desire to escape.

Materne pushed the door open, and seeing the women more dead than alive, white and dishevelled, he shouted, striking his stick on the ground : " What, mother, have you too gone mad? What !

you, who owe a good example to your daughters,—
have you lost courage? it is a shame."

The old woman turned round and said in a broken
voice : " Ah, my poor Materne, if you only knew—
if you only knew ! "

" Well, what then? The enemy is coming: they
won't eat you."

" No ; but they devour everything without
mercy. Old Ursula, of Schlestadt, came here yesterday evening. She says that the Austrians only
want ' Knöpfe' and ' Nudel,' the Russians
' Schnapps,' and the Bavarians ' Sauerkraut.' And
when they have stuffed all that down their throats,
they cry out with their mouths still full, ' Schocolat!
schocolat ! ' O Lord, how can we feed all these
people?"

" I know well that is difficult," said the old hunter: " you can never satisfy a jay with white cheese.
But, first of all, where are these Cossacks, these Bavarians, these Austrians? All the way from
Grandfontaine we have not met even one."

" They are in Alsace, on the Urmatt side, and
they are coming here."

" While waiting for them," said Kasper, " give
us a bottle of wine. Here is a three-crown piece :
you will hide it easier than your barrels."

One of the girls went to the cellar, and, at the

same time, several other persons entered: an alma-
nac-seller from Strasbourg, a wagoner from Sarre-
brück in a blouse, and two or three townspeople
from Mutzig, Wisch, and Schirmeck, who were flying with their herds, and were exhausted with shouting.

All sat down at the same table, before the windows overlooking the road. Wine was served them,
and each began to relate what he knew. One said
the allies were in such numbers that they had to
sleep side by side in the valley of Hirschenthal, and
they were so covered with vermin that, after their
departure, the dead leaves walked of themselves in
the woods ; another, that the Cossacks had set fire
to a village in Alsace, because they had been refused
candles for dessert after dinner ; that some of them,
especially the Calmucks, ate soap like cheese and
bacon-rind like cake ; that many drank brandy by
the pint, after having taken care to season it with
handfuls of pepper ; and that it was necessary to
hide everything from them, for nothing came amiss
to them for eating and drinking.

The wagoner said, at this point, that three days
before, a Russian corps-d'armée having passed the
night under the ramparts of .Bitsch, it had been
compelled to remain more than an hour on the ice
in the little village of Rorbach, and that the whole

of this army corps had drunk out of a warming-pan
left on the window-sill of an old woman's house ;
that this race of savages broke the ice to bathe, and
afterward crept into the brick-kilns to dry; lastly,
that they only feared Corporal Knout.

These worthy folks communicated such singular
things to each other, which they pretended to have
seen with their own eyes, or heard from trustworthy
sources, that one could with difficulty believe them.

Outside, the tumult, rolling of wagons, lowing
of herds, shouts of the drivers, and clamors of the
fugitives, continued unceasingly, and produced the
effect of a vast murmur.

Toward noon Materne and his sons were going to
leave, when a more prolonged shout than any of the
others was heard: " The Còssacks! the Cossacks! "

Then everybody rushed outside, except the hunters, who contented themselves with opening a window and looking out : they all ran away across the
fields : men, herds, wagons and all, were dispersed
like leaves in autumn.   In less than two minutes
the road was deserted, except in Schirmeck, which
was so encumbered, that it would have been impossible to walk four steps.   Materne, gazing far away
along the road, cried, " I look in vain—I can see
nothing."

" Nor do I," rejoined Kasper.

"Come, come," cried the old hunter, "I see clearly that the fear of all these people gives more strength to the enemy than he in fact possesses. It is not in such a way we shall receive the Cossacks in the mountains ; they will find who they have to deal with."

Then, shrugging his shoulders with an expression of disgust, he said : "Fear is an odious thing, and after all we have only one poor life to lose. Let us go."

They quitted the inn, and the old man having taken the road to the valley, in order to climb the summit of the Hirschberg in front of them, his sons followed him. They soon reached the outskirts of the wood, when Materne said that they must mount as high as possible, so as to see the whole plain, and bring back some positive news to the bivouac ; that all the accounts of those cowards were not worth one good look by themselves.

Kasper and Frantz agreed, and all three began to climb the slope, which forms a sort of advanced promontory commanding the plain. When they reached the peak they distinctly saw the enemy's position, three leagues distant, between Urmatt and Lutzelhouse. They formed great black lines on the snow : farther off were a few dark masses—no doubt, the artillery and baggage. Other masses surrounded the villages, and, notwithstanding the distance, the sparkling of the bayonets announced that a column had just commenced marching toward Visch.

After having contemplated this spectacle in silence for some minutes, the old man said, " We have decidedly thirty thousand men under our eyes. They are advancing in our direction ; we shall be attacked to-morrow, or the day after at the latest. It will not be a trumpery affair, my boys ; but if they are numerous we have the best of the position. And then it is always agreeable to fire into a heap ; there are no balls lost."

Having made these judicious reflections, he looked at the height of the sun, and added : " It is now two o'clock ; we know all we want. Let us return to the bivouac."

The youths slung their carbines crossways, and leaving to their left the valley of the Brocque, Schirmeck, and Framont, they climbed the steep banks of the Hengsbach, which overlook the Little Donon—two leagues distant—and came down again on the other side, without following any regular path through the snow, and only guiding themselves by the peaks in order to take a short cut.

They continued thus for about two hours : the winter sun was going down to the horizon, night was

approaching, bright and calm. They had now only
to descend, and then mount, on the other side, the
solitary gorge of Riel, forming a large circular basin
in the midst of the woods, and enclosing a bluish
pond, where the deer came sometimes to quench
their thirst.

Suddenly, as they were coming out from the underwood, not dreaming of anything, the old man,
stopping behind a thick screen of shrubs, said
" Chut ! " and lifting his hand, pointed to the little
lake, which was covered with thin clear ice.   ,

The two young fellows needed only to glance toward it to be greeted by a most strange sight. About
twenty Cossacks, with yellow shaggy beards, heads
covered with old fur caps in the shape of stove-pipes,
their lean legs draped in long rags, and their feet in
rope stirrups, were seated on their little horses, with
long floating manes and thin tails, their bodies spec-
kled yellow, black and white, like goats.   Some had
for their only weapon a long lance, others a sword,
others an axe suspended by a cord to their saddle,
and a large horse-pistol passed through their belts.
Several were looking upward with ecstasy on the
green tops of the pines, rising by stages above each
other into the clouds.   One great lanky fellow had
broken the ice with the butt-end of his lance ; and
his little horse was drinking with outstretched neck

and overhanging mane. A few having dismounted, were clearing the snow and pointing to the wood
—no doubt to indicate that it was a good place for
encamping. Their comrades on horseback were
conversing and pointing to the bottom of the valley
on their right, which descends in the form of a gap
toward Grinderwald.

Anyway it was a halt. It is impossible to describe the strange and picturesque aspect of these
fellows from a strange country, with their copper-
colored faces, long beards, black eyes, flat heads,
squat noses, and grayish tatters, on the banks of this
lake, under the lofty perpendicular rocks lifting
up their green pines to the skies.

It seemed a new world in ours,—a sort of unknown and strange game, which the three red hunters at first contemplated with intense interest. Having remained so for about five minutes, Kasper and
Frantz fixed their long bayonets at the muzzle of
their carbines, and then retired about twenty paces
into the underwood. They reached a rock, fifteen
or twenty feet high, which Materne climbed, having
no arms ; then, after a few words exchanged in
whispers, Kasper examined his priming and raised
his musket slowly to his shoulder, while his brother
stood by in readiness.

One of the Cossacks—he who was letting his

horse drink—was about two hundred paces from them. The gun went off, awakening the deep echoes of the gorge ; and the Cossack, spinning over his horse's head, plunged through the ice of the lake.

It is impossible to describe the stupor of the party at this report. They looked round them in every direction : the echo replied as though it had been a general fusillade ; while a puff of smoke rose above the clump of trees where the hunters were hiding.

Kasper had reloaded his piece in a moment ; but in the same space of time the dismounted Cossacks had bounded on their horses, and all took flight over the slope of the Hartz, one after the other, like roe-bucks, screaming wildly, " Hourah ! hourah ! "

This flight was but the work of a moment : the instant Kasper took aim for the second time, the tail of the last horse disappeared in the bushes.

The horse of the dead Cossack alone remained at the water's edge, held there by a singular circumstance : his master, whose head and part of whose body was in the water, had his foot still in the stirrup.

Materne listened from his rock, then said joyously—" They are gone ! Well, let us go and see. Frantz, remain here. Suppose any of them should return——? "

Notwithstanding this recommendation, they all three approached near the horse. Materne immediately took the bridle, saying:—" Come, old fellow, we are going to teach you to speak French."

" Let us be off," exclaimed Kasper.

" No, we must see what we have shot. Don't you see that will be good for our comrades? Dogs who have not sniffed the skin of the game are never well trained."

Whereupon they fished the Cossack out of the pool, and having placed him across the horse, began to climb the side of the Donon by such a steep path, that Materne repeated, a hundred times at least,—" The horse will never go up there." But the horse, with its long goat-like legs, passed more easily than they did ; so that the old hunter wound up by remarking—" These Cossacks have famous horses. If ever I grow old, I will keep him to go after the deer with. We have a famous horse, my boys ; with all his look of a cow, he is strong as a cart-horse."

From time to time he also made reflections on the Cossack :—" What a queer face, eh ! A round nose and a forehead like a cheese-box. There are certainly queer folks in the world ! Thou hast hit him well, Kasper ; right in the middle of the chest.

And look ! the ball came out at the back. Capital powder ! Divès always keeps good articles."

Toward six they heard the first shout of their sentinels : " Who goes there? "

" France," replied Materne, advancing.

Everybody ran to meet them. " Here is Materne ! "

Hullin himself was as curious as the rest, and could not help hastening toward them with Doctor Lorquin. The partisans were soon collected round the horse, with outstretched necks and open mouths, by the side of a large fire where the supper was cooking.

" It is a Cossack," said Hullin, squeezing Materne's hand.

" Yes, Jean-Claude ; we caught him at the pond of Riel : it was Kasper who shot him."

They stretched the corpse out near the fire. His yellow face had strange shadows on it in the firelight.

Doctor Lorquin, having looked at him, said : " It is a fine specimen of the Tartar race ; if I had time, I should put it in a lime-bath, so as to obtain a skeleton of this tribe."

He then knelt down, and opening the long tunic, —" The ball has traversed the pericardium, and has produced almost the same effect as aneurism of the heart."

The others kept silence.

Kasper, with his hand on the muzzle of his rifle, seemed quite contented with his game ; and old Materne, rubbing his hands, said : " I was sure I would bring you back something : my boys and I never return empty-handed.   There now ! "

Hullin then pulled him aside.   They entered the farm together, and after the first surprise was over, every man began to make his own personal reflections on the Cossack.

CHAPTER XIII

THAT night, which was on a Friday, the anabaptist's little farm-house never ceased for an instant to be filled with people coming in and going out.

Hullin had established his head-quarters in the large room on the ground floor, to the right of the barn, facing Framont : on the other side of the passage was the ambulance : the upper part was inhabited by the farm people.

Although the night was very still and the stars were shining in myriads, the cold was so intense that there was nearly an inch of ice on the panes.

Outside, one could hear the challenge of the sentinel, the passing of the patrols, and, on the surrounding peaks, the howling of the wolves, who followed our armies in hundreds since 1812. These wild beasts crouched on the ice, their sharp muzzles between their paws, with hunger at their entrails, calling each other, from the Grosmann to the Donon, with moaning sounds like that of the north wind.

It made more than one mountaineer grow pale.

"It is Death who calls," thought they ; " he scents the battle, he summons us ! "

The oxen lowed in the stables, and the horses gave frightful neighs.

About thirty fires blazed on the plateau ; all the anabaptist's wood was taken ; fagots were heaped one upon another. Their faces were scorched, and their backs frozen ; they warmed their backs, and the ice hung from their mustaches.

Hullin, alone, before the great pinewood table, was taking thought for all. According to the latest tidings of the evening, announcing the arrival of the Cossacks at Framont, he was convinced that the first attack would take place the next day. He had distributed cartridges, doubled the sentries, appointed patrols, and marked all the posts along the outworks. Every one knew beforehand what place he was to occupy.

Hullin had also sent orders to Piorette, Jérome of St. Quirin, and Labarbe, to send him their best marksmen.

The little dark pathway, lit by a dim lantern, was full of snow, and passing under the immovable light every instant one could see the chiefs of the ambush, with their hats pressed down to their ears, the ample sleeves of their great-coats pulled down over their wrists, with their dark eyes and beards stiffened with ice.

Pluto no longer growled at the heavy step of these men. Hullin, with his head between his hands and his elbows on the table, listened thoughtfully to all their reports:—

"Master Jean-Claude, there is a movement in the direction of Grandfontaine; and the sounds of galloping are distinguishable."

"Master Jean-Claude, the brandy is frozen."

"Master Jean-Claude, many of the men are in want of powder."

"They are in want of this: they are in want of that."

"Let some one be sent to watch Grandfontaine, and let the sentries on that side be changed every half-hour." "Let the brandy be brought to the fire." "Wait until Divès comes: he brings us ammunition. Let the remainder of the cartridges be distributed. Let those who have more than twenty give some to their comrades."

And so it went on all the night.

At five in the morning, Kasper, Materne's son, came to tell Hullin that Marc Divès, with a load of cartridges, Catherine Lefèvre on a cart, and a detachment from Labarbe, had just arrived together, and that they were already on the plateau.

11

The tidings pleased him, especially on account of the cartridges, for he had feared delay.

He immediately rose and went out with Kasper. The plateau presented a curious spectacle.

On the approach of day, clouds of mist began to rise from the valley, the fires hissed with the damp, and all around could be seen sleeping men: one stretched on his back, with his arms thrown under his hat, a blue face, and doubled-up legs; another with his cheek on his arm and his back to the fire; the greater number seated, with bent heads and their muskets slung across their shoulders. All was silent, wrapped in purple light or gray tints, just as the fire blazed or smouldered. Then, in the distance, could be discerned the profile of the sentinels, with their muskets across their arms or clubbed upon the ground, gazing into the cloud-filled abyss beneath them.

To the right, fifty paces from the last fire, could be heard the neighing of horses, and people stamping with their feet to warm themselves, and talking aloud.

"Master Jean-Claude is coming," said Kasper, going toward them.

One of the partisans having thrown a few sticks of dry wood on to the fire, there was a bright blaze; and Marc Divès's men on horseback, twelve tall fel-

lows, wrapped in their long gray cloaks, their felts
slouched back over their shoulders, with their long
mustaches either turned up or falling down to their
necks, their sabres in their grasp, stood motionless
round the load of cartridges. Farther on Catherine
Lefèvre crouched down in her cart, her hood over
her face, her feet in the straw, her back against a
large barrel. Behind her was a caldron, a grid-
iron, a fresh-killed pig, scalded all white and red,
with some strings of onions and cabbages for making soup. All stood out of the darkness for a second, and then relapsed into night.

Divès, having quitted the convoy, advanced on
his powerful horse.

"Is it you, Jean-Claude?"

"Yes, Marc."

"I have some few thousand cartridges there.
Hexe-Baizel is working day and night."

"Good!"

"Yes, old fellow. And Catherine Lefèvre
brings provisions as well; she killed yesterday."

"All right, Marc: we shall want all that. The
battle is impending."

"Yes, yes, I thought so; we came quickly.
Where is the powder to be put?"

"There, under the cart-house behind the farm.
Ah, is that you, Catherine?"

" Of course, Jean-Claude. It is dreadfully cold this morning! "

" You are always the same. Have you no fear? "

" What! should I be a woman if I were not curious? I must poke my nose everywhere."

" Yes, you always make excuses for the fine and noble things you do."

" Hullin, you are wearisome with your repetitions; let me alone with your compliments. Must not all those people eat? Can they live on air in such weather as this? And is not air fattening on a day so cold—like needles and razors. So I took my measures. Yesterday we slaughtered an ox— poor Schwartz, you know—he weighed a good nine hundred. I have brought his hind-quarters for this morning's soup."

" Catherine, it is in vain I have known you so long," cried Jean-Claude, quite touched; " you are always astonishing me. No sacrifice is too great for you, neither money, care, nor trouble."

" Ah," replied the old farm-wife, rising and springing from her cart, " you tease and worry me, Jean-Claude. I am going to warm myself."

She gave Dubourg the reins of her horse, and looking back, said, " Jean-Claude, those fires are a pleasure to behold. But where is Louise? "

" Louise spent the night cutting and sewing

bandages with Pelsly's two daughters. She is at the ambulance: over there you see, where the light is shining."

"Poor child!" said Catherine, "I will go and help her. That will warm me."

Hullin watched her retreating figure, and made a gesture, as though saying, "What a woman!"

At this moment, Divès and his people were carrying the powder into the shed, and as Jean-Claude approached the nearest fire, what was his surprise to see, among the crowd of partisans, Yégof the madman, crowned as usual, gravely seated on a stone, with his feet in the ashes, and draped in his rags as though they were a royal mantle.

Anything more strange than this figure by the fire-light could not be imagined. Yégof was the only one awake of the crowd, and might readily have been taken for some barbarian king musing in the midst of his sleeping horde.

Hullin only saw in him a madman, and laying his hand softly on his shoulder, said, ironically:

"I salute thee, Yégof! Thou art come, then, to lend us the help of thy invincible arm and of thy countless armies?"

The madman, without showing the least surprise, replied: "That depends on thee, Hullin; thy fate, and that of all these people, is in thy hands.

I have suspended my anger, and I will allow thee to pronounce sentence."

"What sentence?" demanded Jean-Claude.

The other, without replying, continued, in a low solemn voice: "Behold us two on the eve of a great battle, as we were sixteen hundred years ago. At that time, I, the chief of so many people, came among thy tribe to ask a passage."

"Sixteen hundred years ago!" said Hullin. "Zounds! Yégof, that makes us terribly old! But it is of no consequence—each to his taste."

"Yes," rejoined the madman, "but, with thy usual obstinacy, thou wouldst hear nothing. Men died on the Blutfeld—men who now call for vengeance!"

"Ah, the Blutfeld!" said Jean-Claude. "Yes, yes, an old story; I seem to have heard it before."

Yégof reddened, and his eyes sparkled.

"Thou pridest thyself on thy victory!" cried he; "but take care—take care! blood calls for blood!" And in a calmer tone, "Listen," he added. "I am not angry with thee. Thou art brave; the children of thy race might mingle with those of mine. I am anxious for an alliance with thee—thou knowest it."

"There, he is going to begin about Louise," thought Jean-Claude. And, foreseeing a formal demand, he said: " Yégof, I am sorry, but I must leave thee. I have so much to see after———"

The madman did not wait the end of this leave-taking, and rising, with his face distorted by indignation, " Thou refusest me thy daughter? " cried he, lifting his finger solemnly.

" We will talk of that later on."

" Thou refusest! "

" Yégof, thy shouts will awaken every one."

" Thou refusest, and it is for the third time! Beware! beware! "

Hullin, despairing of making him become more reasonable, walked rapidly away, but the madman furiously pursued him with these strange words:

" Huldrix, woe on thee! Thy last hour is at hand; the wolves are coming to feed upon thy carcass. All is over. I let loose the tempests of my wrath; and neither to thee nor thine shall mercy, pity, or pardon be shown. Thou hast so willed it."

And, flinging his rags over his shoulder, the poor wretch went away in the direction of the peak of Donon.

Some of the volunteers, awakened by his cries, looked up drowsily, and saw him disappearing in the darkness. They heard the fluttering of wings round the fire; then, as though it were a dream, they turned round and fell asleep again.

About an hour later, Lagarmitte sounded the *reveille;* and in a few minutes all were on their feet.

The chiefs of the ambuscade collected their men: some went toward the shed, to obtain cartridges; others filled their gourds with brandy from the cask. All this was done in good order, their chiefs being at the head of each body of men; then the several companies disappeared in the gray morning light toward the out-posts on the hill-sides.

When the sun rose, the plateau was quite deserted, and, with the exception of five or six fires which were still burning, there was no sign that the partisans were in possession of all the posts on the mountain, or in what place they had passed the night.

Hullin hurriedly ate a crust and drank a glass of wine with his friends Doctor Lorquin and Pelsly the anabaptist.

Lagarmitte was with them, for he was not allowed to leave Master Jean-Claude all day, and had to transmit his orders in case of need.

CHAPTER XIV

" FORWARD! FORWARD! "

AT seven o'clock there was no sign of any move-ment in the valley.

From time to time, Doctor Lorquin opened one of the windows in the large room and looked out. Nothing was stirring; the fires had smouldered away; all was still.

In front of the farm, on a bank, about a hun-dred feet distant, the Cossack could be seen who had been killed the previous evening by Kasper. He was white with the frost, and as hard as a stone.

In the interior, a fire had been made in the great iron stove.

Louise sat near her father, looking at him with an inexpressible affection, as though she feared never to see him again. Her red eyes showed that she had been crying.

Hullin, though firm, looked not a little moved. The doctor and the anabaptist, both grave and seri-ous, talked over the present position of affairs, and

Lagarmitte, from behind the stove, listened to them with deep interest.

"We are not only right, but it is our duty to defend ourselves," said the doctor. "Our fathers cleared these woods and cultivated them: they are our legitimate inheritance."

"No doubt," returned the anabaptist, sententiously; "but it is written, 'Thou shalt not kill. Thou shalt not shed thy brother's blood!'"

Catherine Lefèvre, who was in the act of cutting a slice of ham, evidently felt impatient at this conversation, and, turning round sharply, replied to him: "If that were true, and your religion were right, the Germans, Russians, and all these red men might take the clothes off our backs. 'Tis fine, that religion of yours; yes, fine, for it gives the rogues such an advantage! It helps them to pillage people of substance. I am sure the allies would wish for us no better religion than yours. Unfortunately, everybody does not care to live like sheep. As for me, Pelsly—and I say it without wishing to annoy you—I consider it folly to grow rich for the benefit of others. But, after all, you are honest folks; one cannot be angry with you: you have been brought up from father to son in the same notions: what the grandfather thought, the grandson thinks also. But we will defend you in spite of yourselves; and afterward we will let you tell us of the peace eternal. I am fond of discourses on peace, when I have nothing else to do, and when I am thinking after dinner: then it rejoices my heart."

After having said this, she turned round and went on carving her ham.

Pelsly opened his mouth and eyes, and Doctor Lorquin burst out laughing.

Just then the door opened, and one of the sentries who had been stationed on the edge of the plateau, cried out, " Master Jean-Claude, come and see. I believe they are mounting the hill."

" It is well, Simon; I am coming," said Hullin, rising. " Louise, kiss me. Have courage, my child. Do not fear; all will go well."

He pressed her to his breast, her eyes swollen with tears. She seemed more dead than alive.

" Above all," said the worthy man, addressing Catherine, " let no one go outside or near the windows."

Then he darted out into the road.

All those present turned pale.

When Master Jean-Claude had reached the verge of the hill, and cast his eyes over Grandfontaine and Framont, three thousand mètres below, the following sight presented itself to his eyes:

The Germans, who had arrived the evening before, a few hours after the Cossacks, and had passed the night (about five or six thousand of them) in the barns, stables, and sheds, were moving about like ants. They appeared on all sides in bodies of ten, fifteen, and twenty, buckling their knapsacks and swords, and fixing their bayonets.

Besides these, the cavalry—the Uhlans, Cossacks, Hussars—in green, blue, and gray uniforms striped with red and yellow—with their glazed linen and sheepskin caps, colbacks, and helmets— were saddling their horses and hastily rolling up their long cloaks.

Meanwhile the officers, in their great military cloaks, came down the small staircase: some were looking up at the country; others were embracing the women on the doorsteps.

Trumpeters, with their hands on their sides, were sounding the roll-call at all the corners of the streets, and the drummers tightening the cords of their instruments.

In short, through the broad expanse, one could see all their military attitudes as they were on the point of starting.

A few peasants, leaning out of their windows, were watching the scene; women were showing themselves at the loopholes of the garrets; and the

BIG DUBREUIL, THE FRIEND OF THE ALLIES.

innkeepers were filling the gourds, Corporal Knout watching them meanwhile.

Hullin's sight was keen, and nothing escaped him; besides, for years he had been accustomed to this sort of thing; but Lagarmitte, who had never seen anything like it, was stupefied: "There are great numbers of them," he exclaimed, shaking his head.

"Bah! what does that matter?" said Hullin. "In my days we exterminated three armies of them, of fifty thousand each, in six months; we were not one against four. All that thou seest there would not have been a breakfast for us. And besides, you may be sure, we shall not have to kill them all; they will run like hares. I have seen it before."

After these remarks, he resolved to inspect his men. "Come on," he said to the herdsman.

Then the two made their way behind the abatis, following a trench made two days before in the snow, which had been frozen as hard as ice: the felled trees in front of it, formed an insurmountable barrier, which extended about six hundred mètres. Below this was the broken-up road.

On coming near, Jean-Claude saw the mountaineers of Dagsburg crouching at distances of twenty paces from each other, in a sort of round nests which they had dug out for themselves.

All these fine fellows were sitting on their knapsacks, with their gourds to their right hand, their felts or foxskin caps drawn down upon their heads, and their guns between their knees. They had only to rise to have a clear view of the road fifty feet below, at the foot of a slippery descent.

Jean-Claude's arrival pleased them much.

" Ho, Master Hullin, shall we soon begin? "

" Yes, my boys, never fear; before an hour we shall be at it."

" Ah, so much the better! "

" Yes, but take care to aim at the breast: do not hurry, and show yourselves no more than you can help."

" You may rest assured, Master Jean-Claude."

He passed on; but everywhere he met with a like reception.

" Do not forget," said he, " to stop firing when Lagarmitte sounds his horn: it would be only powder lost."

Coming up to old Materne, who commanded all these men—numbering about two hundred and fifty—he found him smoking his pipe, his nose fiery red, and his beard stiffened with the cold.

" Ah, it is thou, Jean-Claude."

"Yes, I have come to shake your hand."

"In good time. But why are they so slow in coming—tell me that? Are they going to march off in another direction?"

"Don't be afraid: they need the road for their artillery and baggage. Hark! they are sounding ' to horse.' "

"Yes, I have seen already that they are preparing." Then, chuckling to himself: " Thou dost not know, Jean-Claude, what a funny thing I saw, a few minutes ago, as I was looking toward Grandfontaine."

"What was it, my old friend?"

"I saw four Germans lay hold of big Dubreuil, the friend of the allies: they stretched him on the stone bench by his door, and one great lanky fellow gave him I know not how many cuts with a stick across his back. Ha, ha, ha, he must have yelled, the old rascal! I will wager that he refused something to his good friends,—his wine of the year xi. for instance."

Hullin heard no more: for, casting his eyes accidentally down the valley, he caught sight of an infantry regiment coming up the road. Farther back in the street, cavalry were seen coming, five or six officers galloping in front of them.

"Ah, ah! there they come!" cried the old sol-

dier, whose face glowed suddenly with an expression of strange energy and enthusiasm. " At last
they have made up their minds! " Then he rushed
out of the trench, shouting: " Attention, my children! "

Passing by, he saw Riffi, the little tailor of
Charmes, bending over a long musket: the little
man had been piling up the snow to give him a
better position for aiming. Farther up, he saw
the old wood-cutter Rochart, his great shoes
trimmed with sheepskin: he had taken a gulp
at his gourd, and was rising deliberately, having
his carbine under his arm and his cotton cap over
his ears.

That was all: for in order to command the whole
of the action, he had to climb almost to the summit
of the Donon, where there is a rock.

Lagarmitte followed, striding till his long legs
looked like stilts. Ten minutes after, when they
had reached the top of the rock, half-breathless,
they perceived, fifteen hundred mètres below them,
the enemy's column, three thousand strong, with
white great-coats, leather belts, cloth gaiters, tall
shakos, and red mustaches; and in the spaces
formed by the companies, the young officers, with
flat caps, waving their swords, and shouting in shrill
voices: " Forward! forward! "

These troops were bristling with bayonets, and advancing at the charge toward the breastworks.

Old Materne, his beaked nose rising above a juniper branch and his brow erect, was also watching the arrival of the Germans; and as he was very clear-sighted, he could distinguish even faces among the crowd, and choose the man he wished to knock over.

In the centre of the column, on a large bay horse, an old officer was advancing right ahead, with a white wig, a three-cornered hat trimmed with gold, his waist encircled with a yellow scarf, and his breast decorated with ribbons. When this personage raised his head, the peak of his hat, surmounted by a tuft of black plumes, formed a vizor. He had great wrinkles along his cheeks, and looked sufficiently stern.

"There is my man!" thought the old hunter, deliberately taking aim.

He fired, and when he looked again the old officer had disappeared.

Immediately the whole hill-side became enveloped in fire all along the intrenchment; but the Germans, without replying, continued to advance toward the breastworks, their guns on their shoulders, and as steadily as though on parade.

To tell the truth, more than one brave mountaineer, father of a family, seeing this forest of bay-

12

onets coming up, and notwithstanding the excitement of battle, felt that he would have done better had he remained in his village, than to have mixed himself up in such an affair. But, as the proverb says, " The wine was drawn, and it had to be drunk."

Riffi, the little tailor, recalled the words of his wife Sapience: " Riffi, you will get yourself crippled, and it will serve you right."

He vowed a costly offering to St. Léon's Chapel should he return from the war; but at the same time he resolved to make good use of his musket.

When they were about two hundred feet from the breastworks, the Germans halted and began a rolling fire, such as had never been heard in the mountain before. It was a regular storm of shot: the balls in hundreds tore away the branches, sent bits of broken ice flying in all directions, or flattened themselves on the rocks on every side, leaping up with a strange hissing noise, and passing by like flocks of pigeons.

All this did not stop the mountaineers from continuing their fire, but it could no longer be heard. The whole hill-side was wrapped in blue smoke, which prevented their taking any aim.

About ten minutes later, there was the rolling of a drum, and all this mass of men made a rush at the breastworks, their officers shouting, "Forward!"

The earth shook with them.

Materne, springing up in the trench, with quivering lips and in a terrible voice, cried out, "To your feet! to your feet!"

It was time: for a good number of these Germans,—nearly all students in philosophy, law, and medicine, heroes of the taverns of Munich, Jena, and other places—who fought against us, because they had been promised great things after Napoleon's fall—all these intrepid fellows were climbing the icy slope, and endeavoring to jump into the intrenchment.

But they were received with the butt-end of the musket, and fell back in disorder.

It was then that the gallant conduct of the old wood-cutter Rochart was observable, knocking over, as he did, more than ten "kaiserlichs," whom he took by the shoulder and hurled down the incline. Old Materne's bayonet was red with blood; and little Riffi never ceased loading his musket and firing into the mass of Germans with great spirit. Joseph Larnette, who unluckily received a bullet in his eye; Hans Baumgarten, who had his shoulder smashed; Daniel Spitz, who lost two fingers by a sabre-cut, and many others, whose names should be honored

and revered for ages—all these never once left off
firing and reloading their guns.

Below the slope fearful cries were heard, while
above nothing but bristling bayonets and men on
horseback were to be seen.

This lasted a good quarter of an hour. No one
knew what the Germans would do, since there was
no passage; when they suddenly decided on going
away. Most of the students had fallen, and the
others—old campaigners used to honorable retreats
—no longer fought with the same steadiness.

At first they retreated slowly, then more quickly.
Their officers struck them from behind with the
flat end of their swords; the musketry-fire pursued them; and, finally, they ran away with as
much precipitation as they had been orderly in advancing.

Materne, and fifty others, rose upon the barri-
cades, the old hunter brandishing his carbine, and
bursting into hearty roars of laughter.

At the foot of the bank were heaps of wounded
dragging themselves along the ground. The trod-
den-down snow was red with blood. In the midst
of the piles of dead were two young officers, still
alive, but unable to disengage themselves from their
dead horses.

It was horrible! But men are, in fact, savages:

AS THEY CLIMBED UP THEY WERE CLUBBED WITH MUSKETS.

there was not one among the mountaineers who pitied those poor wretches; but, on the contrary, they seemed to rejoice at the sight.

Little Riffi, transported with a noble enthusiasm, just then glided out along the bank. To the left, underneath the breastworks, he had caught sight of a superb horse, which had belonged to the colonel killed by Materne, and had retired unhurt into his nook.

"Thou shalt be mine," said he to himself. "Sapience will be astonished!"

All the others envied him. He seized the horse by the bridle and sprang upon him; but judge of the general stupefaction, and of Riffi's in particular, when this noble animal began to shape his course toward the Germans in full gallop.

The little tailor lifted his hands to heaven, imploring God and all the saints.

Materne would have liked much to fire; but he dared not, the horse went so fast.

At last Riffi disappeared amid the bayonets of the enemy.

Everybody thought he had been killed. However, an hour later, he was to be seen passing along the main street of Grandfontaine, his hands tied behind him, and Corporal Knout at his back, bearing his emblem of office.

Poor Riffi! He alone did not partake of the triumph, and his comrades laughed at his misfortune, as though he had been but a " kaiserlich."

Such is the character of men; so long as they are happy themselves, the misery of others grieves them but little.

CHAPTER XV

THE mountaineers were almost beside themselves with enthusiasm: they lifted their hands and be-praised one another, as if they were the cream of mankind.

Catherine, Louise, Doctor Lorquin and all the others came out of the farm, cheering and congratulating each other, gazing at the marks of the bullets and at the bank blackened with powder; then at Joseph Larnette stretched in his hole, having his head smashed; at Baumgarten, who, with his arm hanging down, walked in great pallor toward the ambulance; and then at Daniel Spitz, who, in spite of his sabre-cut, wanted to stay and fight; but the doctor would not hear of it, and forced him to enter the farm.

Louise came up with the little cart, and poured out brandy for the combatants; while Catherine Lefèvre, standing at the edge of the sloping bank, watched the dead and wounded scattered over the

road, and led up to by long lines of blood. There
were both young and old among them, with faces
white as wax, wide-opened eyes, and outstretched
arms. Some few tried to raise themselves, but no
sooner had they done so than they fell back again;
others looked up as though they were afraid of receiving some more bullets, and dragged themselves
along the bank in order to get under shelter.

Many of them seemed resigned to their fate,
and were looking for a place to die, or else watching their retreating regiment on its way to Framont
—that regiment with which they had quitted their
homes, with which they had made a long campaign,
and which was now abandoning them! "It will
see old Germany again!" they thought. "And
when some one asks the captain or the sergeant,
'Did you know such a one—Hans, Kasper, Nickel,
of the 1st or of the 2d company?' they will reply,
'Ah! I think so. Had he not a scar on the ear,
or on the cheek? fair or dark hair? five feet six in
height? Yes, I know him. He was buried in
France, near a little village whose name I do not
remember. Some mountaineers killed him the
same day big Major Yéri-Peter was killed. He
was a fine fellow!' And then it is, 'Good-day to
you.'"

Perhaps, too, there were some of them who

dreamed of their mother, or of a pretty girl left behind them, Gretchen or Lotchen, who had given
them a ribbon, and shed hot tears when they left:
" I will await thy return, Kasper. I will only marry
thee! Yes, yes, thou wilt have to wait long! "

It was not pleasant to think of.

Madame Lefèvre, seeing this, thought of Gaspard. Hullin, who came up with Lagarmitte, cried
out in a joyous tone, " Well, my boys, you have
been under fire. Bravo! everything goes well.
The Germans will have no occasion to boast of this
day."

Then he embraced Louise, and hurried up to
Catherine.

" Are you satisfied, Catherine? There! our
success is certain. But what is the matter? You
do not smile."

" Yes, Jean-Claude, all goes well. I am satisfied. But look down at the road. What a
butchery! "

" It is only what happens in war," replied Hullin, gravely.

" Could we not go and help that little fellow
down there, who watches us with his large blue
eyes? He makes me feel so sad. Or that tall, dark
man, who is binding his leg with his handkerchief? "

" Impossible, Catherine. I am very sorry. We

should have to cut steps in the ice to get down, and
the Germans, who will be back in an hour or two,
would take advantage of them. Let us go. The
victory must be announced in all the villages—
to Labarbe, Jérome, and Piorette. Ho! Simon,
Niklo, Marchal, come here. You will have to set
out immediately, and carry the great tidings to our
comrades. Materne, keep thy eyes open, and warn
me at the slightest movement."

They approached the farm, and, as he passed,
Jean-Claude took a look at the reserve, Marc Divès
being on horseback surrounded by his men. The
smuggler complained bitterly of being left with
nothing to do, as if his honor were tarnished
thereby.

"Bah!" said Hullin, "so much the better!
Besides, thou keepest guard over our right. Look
at that flat ground down there. If we are attacked
from that point, thou wilt have to march!"

Divès made no answer; he looked both sad and
indignant, nor did his stalwart smugglers, wrapped
in their cloaks, their long swords hanging by
their sides, seem at all in a better humor ; one
might have said that they were meditating some
revenge.

Hullin, not succeeding in consoling them, entered the farm-house. Doctor Lorquin was extract-

ing the ball from Baumgarten's wound, who was making terrible cries.

Pelsly, on the doorstep, was trembling all over. Jean-Claude asked him for paper and ink, in order to transmit his orders through the mountain; but the poor anabaptist could hardly give them to him, so great was his trouble. However, he succeeded at last, and the messengers departed, proud of being charged to announce the first battle and victory.

A few mountaineers were in the large room, warming themselves at the oven and talking animatedly. Daniel Spitz had already undergone amputation of his two fingers, and sat behind the stove with his hand bound up.

Those who had been posted behind the abatis before daybreak, not having breakfasted, were now eating a crust of bread and drinking a glass of wine, shouting, gesticulating, and making great bravado meanwhile. Then they went out, looked at the intrenchments, came back to warm themselves again, and laughed fit to split their sides when they spoke of Riffi, and his wails and cries on horseback.

It was eleven o'clock. These incomings and outgoings lasted till twelve, when Marc Divès suddenly came into the room, calling out:—" Hullin! Where is Hullin?"

" Here I am."

" Well, then, come! "

The smuggler's tone had something remarkable
about it: from being a moment before furious at
having taken no part in the fight, he had now become triumphant.   Jean-Claude followed him, feeling very uneasy: and the large room was immediately deserted, everybody being convinced, from
Marc's manner, that there was something serious
the matter.

To the right of the Donon extends the ravine
of Minières, through which runs a foaming torrent
when the snows melt—descending from the summit of the mountain to the valley.

Exactly in front of the plateau defended by the
partisans, and on the other side of this ravine, at a
distance of five or six hundred mètres, projects a
sort of open terrace with rugged sides, which Hullin had considered unnecessary to occupy for the
time, wishing not to divide his forces, and seeing,
besides, that it would be easy for him to turn this
position by the pine-clumps, and to establish himself there, if the enemy showed any intention to
take it.

Now imagine the consternation of the worthy
man when, on reaching the door of the farm-house,
he saw two companies of Germans climbing this ascent, among the gardens of Grandfontaine, having

two field-pieces yoked to powerful horses, which appeared to hang over the precipice. A troop was pushing at the wheels, and in a few seconds the guns would have reached the plateau.

It was like a thunder-bolt for Jean-Claude; he turned pale, and then into a great passion with Divès.

"Couldst thou not have warned me sooner?" he cried. "Did I not command thee to watch over the ravine? Our position is turned. They will hem us in, and cut us off from the road farther on. Everything is going to the deuce."

The people present, and old Materne himself, who had come up in great haste, were startled by the glance he darted at the smuggler; who, notwithstanding his usual audacity, was quite confused, not knowing what to reply.

"Come, come, Jean-Claude," said he at last, "be calm. It is not so serious as thou sayest. We have not fought yet—we others; and besides, we have no cannons—so it will be the very thing for us."

"Yes, the very thing for us, imbecile! Thy self-love made thee wait till the last minute, did it not? Thou wert too eager to fight, and have an opportunity for boasting and making bravado; and for that thou didst not hesitate to risk all our lives.

Look! there are other troops being got ready at Framont.”

In fact, another column, much stronger than the first, was just then marching out of Framont at the charge, and advancing against the breastworks. Divès did not say a word. Hullin controlled his anger, and became suddenly calm in the presence of danger.

“ Go back to your posts,” he said briefly to tho.e around him. “ Let all be ready for the coming attack. Materne, listen! ”

The old hunter inclined his head. Meanwhile, Marc Divès had recovered his self-possession.

“ Instead of screaming like a woman,” said he, “ thou wouldst do better to give me orders to attack down there, by turning the ravine at the pine-clumps.”

“ Then do it! ” replied Jean-Claude; and in a calmer tone: “ Listen, Marc! I am very angry with thee. We were conquerors; and by thy fault the battle has to be fought over again. If thou failest in thy attack, all is lost for us.”

“ Good! good! The affair is altogether mine: I will answer for it.”

Then, springing on his horse, and throwing the end of his mantle over his shoulder, he drew his long blade with a defiant air. His men did the same.

He then turned to the reserve, composed of five
hundred mountaineers, and showing the plateau to
them with the point of his sword, said, "Look
there, my men! we must carry that position. The
men of Dagsburg must not say that they are braver
than the men of the Sarre. Forward!" And,
full of ardor, they advanced, skirting the ravine.
Hullin shouted to them—"At the point of your
bayonets!"

The big smuggler, on his great sleek roan,
turned round, laughing out of the corners of his
mustache, and waved his sword in a significant
way; then the whole body dashed into the pine-
wood.

At the same time the Germans, with their
eight-pounders, had gained the plateau, and were
putting them in position, while the column from
Framont was ascending the hill-side. Thus everything was in the same condition as before the battle,—with this difference, that the enemies' bullets
would now come into play and take the mountaineers in the rear.

One could see distinctly the two field-pieces with
their cramp-irons, levers, sponges, artillerymen,
and the officer commanding, a great lanky fellow,
with broad shoulders and fair mustaches floating in
the wind. The blue shades of the valley seeming

to diminish the distance, they looked as though you
might have touched them; but Hullin and Materne
were not to be deceived; it was a good six hundred
mètres across. No carbine could reach so far. Nevertheless, the old hunter, before returning to the
abatis, wished to have his mind set quite at rest.
He advanced as close as possible to the ravine, followed by his son Kasper and a few mountaineers;
and, leaning against a tree, he raised his gun deliberately and took aim at the tall officer with the fair
mustaches. All those about him held their breath
for fear of balking the attempt.

Materne fired, but when he laid down his
weapon to see what had occurred, no change had
taken place.

"It is astonishing how age weakens the sight,"
he said.

"Your weakened sight!" cried Kasper. "There
is not a man from the Vosges to Switzerland who
can boast of hitting his mark at two hundred mètres like you!"

The old hunter knew well it was the case, but he
did not wish to discourage the others.

"Well," he replied, "we have no time for dis-
puting. Here is the enemy again; let each do his
duty." Although these words seemed simple and
calm enough, Materne was very much troubled in

reality. On entering the trench confused sounds met his ear—the clattering of arms and the regular tramp of many feet. He looked down over the steep bank, and now saw the Germans, who this time carried long ladders with hooks at the end.

It was not a pleasant sight for the brave fellow: he made a sign to his son to approach, and said to him, in a low voice, "Kasper, that looks bad—very bad; the rascals are coming with ladders. Give me thy hand! I should like to have thee near me, and Frantz as well; but we must defend ourselves with steadiness."

At this moment a great explosion shook the abatis, and a hoarse voice was heard crying out, "Ah, my God!" Then a hundred paces distant there was a heavy sound, and a fine tree bent down slowly and fell into the abyss. It was the first cannon-ball: it had cut off old Rochart's legs. It was followed by another immediately after, which covered all the mountaineers with broken ice, and made a great rumbling. Old Materne himself had bent down under the force of the explosion, but raising himself quickly, he shouted, "Let us revenge ourselves, my children. They are before you. To conquer or die!"

Fortunately the panic of the mountaineers only lasted a second: they all understood that the slightest hesitation and they were lost. Two ladders had already been raised, notwithstanding the fusillade, and were being attached to the bank by their iron hooks. This sight made the partisans furious, and the fight became more terrible and desperate than before.

Hullin had noticed the ladders before Materne had, and his wrath against Divès increased; but as in such a case indignation is of no avail, he had sent Lagarmitte to tell Frantz Materne, who had been posted on the other side of the Donon, to come to him quickly with half his men. We may well believe the brave fellow, warned of the danger his father was in, lost not a moment. Already their large black hats could be seen climbing the hill-side amid the snows, their carbines slung across their shoulders. They came with all despatch, nevertheless Jean-Claude met them, with a haggard expression in his eyes, and shouted in a vibrating voice, " Come quicker! at that rate you will never reach us."

He was in a towering passion, and attributed all the misfortune to the smuggler.

Meanwhile Marc Divès, in about half an hour, had gone round the ravine, and, from the back of his tall horse, began to perceive the two companies of Germans, with grounded arms, about a hundred

feet behind the guns, which were being fired upon
the trench. Then, approaching the mountaineers,
he said to them, in a stifled voice, while the reports
of the cannon were re-echoed in the gorge and in
the distance the noise of battle was heard: "Comrades, you must attack the infantry with your bayonets: I and my men will be answerable for the
rest. Is it understood?"

"Yes, it is understood."

"Then, forward!"

The whole troop advanced in good order toward the outskirts of the wood, big Piercy of
Soldatenthal at their head. Nearly at the same
instant the *Wer da?* ("Who there?") of a sentinel
was heard; then two shots; a loud cry of "Vive la
France!" and the trampling of many feet in a
charge. The brave mountaineers threw themselves
like wolves on the enemy.

Divès stood up in his stirrups and watched them
with great glee. "That is well," said he.

The *mêlée* was a terrible one; the ground trembled with it. The Germans were firing no more
than the partisans: the affair was passing in silence;
the clashing of bayonets and the sound of sabre-
strokes, with here and there a rifle-shot, shouts of
anger and a great tumult: except these, one could
hear nothing else. The smugglers, with out-

stretched necks and sword in hand, sniffed the carnage and awaited the signal from their chief with
impatience.

"Now, it is our turn," said Divès, at length.
"The guns must be ours."

And out of the underwood they sprang, and their
large cloaks flying behind them like wings, they
dashed forward, bending in their saddles and pointing their swords.

"Never mind cutting! Run them through!"
cried Divès once more.

That was all he said.

In a second, the twelve vultures were down upon
the guns. Among their number were four old
Spanish dragoons and two cuirassiers of the guard,
whom a life of danger had attached to Marc: so
I leave you to imagine how they fought. Blows
from lever, rammer, and sabre, the only arms the
gunners had to hand, rained upon them like hail;
they parried them all, and every cut they made
brought down a man.

Marc Divès received two pistol-shots, of which
one singed his left cheek and the other carried away
his hat. But, at the same time, bending over his
saddle, his long arms stretched out, he transfixed
the big officer with the fair mustaches to his gun;
then raising himself deliberately, and gazing round

him with a frown, said, in a sententious manner: "We have cleared out the rubbish! the guns are ours."

To get a good idea of this terrible scene, you must imagine the crowd on the plateau of Minières. The cries, the neighings of horses, the flight of some, who threw down their arms in order to run the faster, the desperation of others;—beyond the ravine, the ladders covered with white uniforms and bristling with bayonets; the mountaineers above the escarpment defending themselves with obstinacy; the hill-sides, the road, and, above all, the space outside the breastworks, encumbered with dead and wounded;—the great numbers of the enemy, their muskets over their shoulders and their officers in the midst of them, pressing forward into action; and, finally, Materne standing on the crest of the hill, his bayonet in the air, his mouth opened wide, shouting wildly to his son Frantz, who was advancing with his troop, Master Jean-Claude at their head, to aid the mountaineers. You should have heard the fusillade, the platoon and file firing, and, above all, the distant confused shouts, intermixed with sharp wails dying away among the mountain echoes. To gain a good idea of the scene, you should imagine all these as concentrated into one moment and surveyed with a rapid glance.

But Divès was not of a contemplative turn: he lost no time in making poetical reflections on the uproar and savagery of the battle. With one look he had taken in the whole situation; so, springing from his horse, he went up to the first gun, which was still loaded, aimed it at the ladders, and fired.

Then there arose wild clamors, and the smuggler, peering through the smoke, saw that fearful havoc had been made in the enemy's ranks. He waved his hands in sign of triumph, and the mountaineers on the breastworks answered with a general hurrah.

" Now then, dismount," said he to his men, " and don't go to sleep. A cartridge, a ball, and some turf. We will sweep the road. Look out! "

The smugglers put themselves in position, and continued to fire with enthusiasm upon the white coats. The bullets rained into their ranks. At the tenth discharge there was a general *sauve-qui-peut.*

" Fire! fire! " shouted Marc.

And the partisans, now supported by Frantz's troop, regained, under Hullin's directions, the positions which they had for the moment lost.

The whole of the hill-side was soon covered with dead and wounded. It was then four in the evening; night was approaching. The last ball fell into the street of Grandfontaine, and rebounding on the angle of the pavement, knocked down the chimney of the " Red Ox."

About six hundred men perished that day: there were, of course, many mountaineers among them, but the greater number were " kaiserlichs." Had it not been for the fire of Marc Divès's cannon, all would have been lost; the partisans were not one against ten, and the enemy had already begun to gain on the trenches.

CHAPTER XVI

THE Germans, huddled together in Grandfontaine, fled in crowds in the direction of Framont, on foot and on horseback, hurrying, dragging along their ammunition-wagons, strewing the road with their knapsacks, and looking behind as though they feared to find the partisans at their heels.

In Grandfontaine they destroyed everything out of sheer revenge; they smashed in doors and windows, maltreated the people, demanded food and drink indiscriminately. Their shouts and curses, the commands of their officers, the murmurs of the townsfolk, the artillery rolling over the bridge of Framont, the shrill cries of the wounded horses, were heard as a confused murmur at the breastworks.

The hill-side was covered with arms, shakos, and dead; in fact, with all the signs of a great rout. In front was Marc Divès's cannon directed down the valley, ready to fire in case of a fresh attack.

All was finished, and finished well. Yet no shout of triumph rose from the intrenchments : the losses of the mountaineers, in this last assault, had been too great for that. There was something solemn in this silence succeeding to the uproar; all these men who had escaped the carnage, looked grave, as though astonished to see each other again. Some few called a friend, others a brother, who did not answer; and then they searched for them in the trenches, along the breastworks, or on the slopes, calling " Jacob, Philip, is it thou? "

Night came on; and the gray shadow creeping over everything, added mystery to these fearful scenes. The people came and went among the wrecks of the battle without recognizing each other.

Materne, having wiped his bayonet, called hoarsely to his boys:—" Kasper! Frantz! " and seeing them approach in the darkness, he asked, " Is that you? "

" Yes, we are here."

" Are you safe? are you wounded? "

" No."

The old hunter's voice became hoarser and more trembling still:—" Then we are all three united once more," said he, in a low tone.

And he, whom none would have thought to be

so tender, embraced his sons warmly. They could hear his chest heaving with suppressed sobs. They were both much moved, and said to each other,— "We never dreamed that he loved us so much!"

But the old man, soon recovering from his emotion, called out, "It was a hard day, though, my boys. Let us have something to drink, for I am thirsty."

Then, casting one last look on the dark slopes, and seeing that Hullin had placed sentinels at short distances apart, they proceeded toward the farm-house.

As they were picking their way carefully through the trenches, encumbered with the dead, they heard a stifled voice, which said to them, "Is it thou, Materne?"

"Ah! forgive me, my poor old Rochart," replied the hunter, bending over him, "if I touched thee. What, art thou still here?"

"Yes, I cannot get away, for I have no longer any legs to carry me."

They remained silent for a moment, when the old wood-cutter continued,—"Thou wilt tell my wife that in a bag behind the closet, there are five pieces of six. I have saved them up, in case we either of us fell ill. I no longer need them."

"That is to say—that is to say— But thou

mayst recover still, my poor old fellow. We will carry thee away."

" No; it is not worth the trouble: I cannot last more than an hour. It would only make me linger."

Materne, without answering, signed to Kasper to place his carbine with his own, so as to form a stretcher, and Frantz placed the old wood-cutter upon them, notwithstanding his moans. In this way they arrived at the farm.

All the wounded who during the combat had had strength to drag themselves to the ambulance were now assembled there; and Doctor Lorquin and his comrade Dubois, who had arrived during the day, had work enough to do. But all was far from being over yet.

As Materne, his boys, and Rochart were traversing the dark alley under the lantern, they heard to their left a cry which made their blood run cold, and the old wood-cutter, half dead, called out, " Why do you take me there? I will not go; I will not have anything done to me."

" Open the door, Frantz," said Materne, his face streaming with perspiration. " Open it! Be quick! "

Frantz having pushed open the door, they beheld in the centre of the low room with its large brown beams, Colard's son stretched out full length on a great kitchen-table, a man at each arm and a bucket beneath him. Doctor Lorquin, his shirt-sleeves turned up to his elbows, and a short saw in his hand, was cutting off the poor fellow's leg, while Dubois stood by with a large sponge. The blood trickled into the pail. Colard was as white as death.

Catherine Lefèvre was there with a roll of lint on her arm. She seemed calm; but her teeth were clinched, and she fastened her eyes on the ground as though determined to witness nothing.

" It is finished," said the doctor, turning round; and perceiving the new-comers, " Ha! it is you, Father Rochart! " he exclaimed.

" Yes, it is I; but I will not let any one touch me. I would rather die as I am."

The doctor lifted up a candle, looked at him, and made a grimace.

" It is time to see to you, my poor old fellow. You have lost much blood, and if we wait longer it will be too late."

" So much the better! I have suffered enough in my life."

" As you like. Let us pass on to another."

He cast his eyes over a long line of straw mat-tresses at the end of the room; the two last were

empty, but covered with blood. Materne and
Kasper laid the old wood-cutter down on the last,
while Dubois, approaching another wounded man,
said, " Nicolas, it is thy turn! "

Nicolas Cerf raised his pale face and his eyes
glistened with fright.

" Let him have a glass of brandy," said the
doctor.

" No, I would rather smoke my pipe."

" Where is thy pipe? "

" In my waistcoat pocket."

" Good, I have found it. And the tobacco? "

" In my trousers."

" All right. Fill his pipe, Dubois. He is a
plucky fellow; it gives one pleasure to see a man
like that. We are going to take off thy arm in a
trice."

" Is there no way of saving it, Monsieur Lorquin, to bring up my poor children? It is their
only resource."

" No; it is no use; the bone is smashed. Light
the pipe, Dubois. Now, Nicolas, smoke away."

The unhappy fellow began, though evidently
without relish.

" Is all ready? " asked the doctor.

" Yes," replied Nicolas, in a husky voice.

" Good. Attention, Dubois! Sponge away."

And he made a rapid turn in the flesh with a
great knife. Nicolas ground his teeth. The blood
spurted up, and Dubois bound up something tightly. The saw grated for two seconds, and the arm
fell heavily on the boards.

"That is what I call a well-performed operation," said Lorquin.

Nicolas was no longer smoking; the pipe had
fallen from his lips. David Schlosser, of Walsch,
who had held him, let go. They bound up the
stump with linen, and, all unaided, Nicolas went
to lie down on the straw.

"One more finished! Sponge the table well,
Dubois, and let us go on to another," said the doctor, washing his hands in a large bowl.

Each time that he said, "Let us go on to another," the wounded moved uneasily, terrified by
the screams they heard and the glittering knives
they saw. But what was to be done? Every
room in the farm, the granary, and the lofts was
full. They were thus obliged to operate under the
eyes of those who would soon in their turns come
beneath the painful knife.

The operation had taken but a few seconds.
Materne and his sons looked on for the same reason as one looks at other horrible things,—to know
what they are like. Then in the corner, under

the old china clock, they saw a heap of amputated limbs.

Nicolas's arm had already been cast among them, and a ball was now being extracted from the shoulder of a red-whiskered mountaineer of the Harberg. They opened deep gashes in his back; his flesh quivered, and the blood coursed down his powerful limbs.

The dog Pluto, behind the doctor, looked on with an attentive air, as though he understood, and from time to time stretched himself and yawned loudly.

Materne could look on no longer.

"Let us get out of this," said he.

Hardly were they outside the door, when they heard the doctor exclaim, "I have got the ball!" which must indeed have been satisfactory to the man from the Harberg.

Once outside, Materne, inhaling the cold air with delight, exclaimed: "Only think that the same might have happened to us!"

"True," said Kasper; "to get a ball in one's head is nothing; but to be cut up in that style, and then to beg one's bread for the rest of one's days!"

"Bah! I should do the same as old Rochart," said Frantz. "I should die quietly. The old fel-

low was right. When one has done one's duty,
why should one be afraid?"

Just then the hum of voices was heard on their
right.

"It is Marc Divès and Hullin," said Kasper,
listening.

"Yes; they must be just returning from throwing up breastworks behind the pine-wood, to protect the cannon," added Frantz.

They listened again; the footsteps came nearer.

"Thou must be very much bothered with these
three prisoners," said Hullin, roughly. "Since
thou returnest to the Falkenstein to-night to get
ammunition, what prevents thee from taking them
away?"

"Where are they to be put?"

"Why, in the communal prison of Abreschwiller, to be sure. We cannot keep them here."

"All right, I understand, Jean-Claude. And
if they try to escape on the way, I am to use my
sword?"

"Just so."

By this time they had reached the door, and Hullin, perceiving Materne, could not suppress a shout
of enthusiasm: "Ah! Is it thou, old fellow? I
have been searching for thee an hour. Where the
devil wert thou?"

"We have been carrying poor Rochart to the ambulance, Jean-Claude."

"Ah! it is a sad affair, isn't it?"

"Yes; it is sad."

There was a moment's pause, and the satisfaction of the worthy man again became visible.

"It is not at all lively," said he; "but what is to be done when one goes to the war? You are not hurt any of you?"

"No; we are all three safe and sound."

"So much the better. Those who are left can boast of being lucky."

"True," cried Marc Divès, laughing. "At one time I thought Materne was going to give way. Without those cannon-balls at the finish, things would have gone badly."

Materne colored, and glanced sideways at the smuggler.

"Perhaps so," said he, dryly; "but without the cannon-balls at the beginning, we should not have needed those at the end. Old Rochart, and fifty other brave men, would still have had their arms and legs, and our victory would not have been clouded."

"Bah!" interrupted Hullin, anticipating a dispute between the two brave fellows, neither of whom was remarkable for his conciliatory disposi-

14

tion. " Leave that alone. Every one has done his duty; and that is the chief thing."

Then, addressing Materne: " I have just sent a flag of truce to Framont, to bid the Germans carry away their wounded. In an hour, I dare say, they will be here. Our sentries must be warned to let them approach if they come without arms and with torches. If in any other way, let them be received with a volley."

" I will go at once," answered the old hunter.

" Materne, thou wilt afterward sup at the farm with thy boys."

" Agreed, Jean-Claude."

And he went off.

Hullin then bade Frantz and Kasper light great bivouac fires; Marc was at once to feed his horses, so that he might go without delay to procure ammunition. Seeing them hurrying away, Hullin turned into the farm.

CHAPTER XVII

ROUND THE FESTIVE BOARD

AT the end of the dark alley was the yard of the farm, into which one descended by five or six well-worn steps. On the left were the granary and the wine-press; to the right the stables and pigeon-cot, the gables of which stood out black on the dark cloudy sky; and in front of the door was the laundry.

No sound from the outside reached the yard. After so many tumultuous scenes, Hullin was impressed by the deep silence. He looked up at the piles of straw hanging from the beams of the granary roof, the ploughs and carts in the shadows of the outhouses, and an inexpressible feeling of calm and repose came over him. A cock was roosting quietly among the hens on the wall. A big cat, darting quickly by, disappeared through a hole into the cellar. Hullin thought himself in a dream.

After a few moments spent in silent contemplation, he walked slowly toward the laundry, the three

windows of which shone brightly in the darkness:
for the farm-kitchen not being large enough for
preparing food for three or four hundred men, it
was now being used for the purposes of cooking.

Master Jean-Claude heard Louise's clear voice
giving orders in a resolute tone, which astonished
him.

" Now, Katel, quick! supper-time is near. Our
people must be hungry. Since six in the morning
they have taken nothing, and have been fighting
all the time. They must not be kept waiting.
Come, bestir yourself, Lesselé; bring the salt and
pepper! "

Jean-Claude's heart leaped within him at the
sound of this voice. He could not help gazing for
a minute through the window before entering.

The kitchen was large, with low whitewashed
ceiling. A beechwood fire crackled on the hearth,
its red flames encircling the sides of an immense
kettle. The charming figure of Louise, wearing
her short petticoat so as to move unimpeded, a
bright color in her face, the short red body of her
dress leaving uncovered her round shoulders and
white neck, stood out clearly in the foreground.
She was in all the bustle of the occasion, coming
and going, tasting the soup and sauces with a knowing air, and approving and criticising everything.

"A little more salt! Lesselé, have you almost done plucking that great lean cock? At this rate we shall never have finished!"

It was delightful to see her thus busily commanding. It brought tears into Hullin's eyes.

The two daughters of the anabaptist—one tall, thin, and pale, with her large flat feet encased in round shoes, her red hair fastened up in a little black cap, her blue stuff dress falling in folds to her heels; the other fat, slowly lifting up one foot after the other, and waddling along like a duck—forming a striking contrast to Louise.

The stout Katel went panting about without saying a word, while Lesselé performed everything in her sleepy methodical way.

The worthy anabaptist himself, seated at the end of the room, with his legs crossed on a wooden chair, his cotton cap on his head, and his hands in his blouse pockets, looked on with a wondering air, addressing to them sententious exhortations from time to time: "Lesselé, Katel! be obedient, my children. Let this be for your instruction. You have not yet seen the world. You must be quicker and sharper."

"Yes, yes, you must bestir yourselves," added Louise. "Gracious! what should become of us if we stood thinking months and weeks before put-

ting a little onion into a sauce! Lesselé, you are
the tallest, unhook me that parcel of onions from
the ceiling."

The girl obeyed.

Hullin had never felt prouder in his life.

"How she makes them move about!" thought
he. "Ah! ha! ha! she is like a little hussar. I
never should have believed it."

After having watched them for five minutes, he
went into the room.

"Well done, my children!"

Louise was holding a soup-ladle at the time. She
let it fall, and threw herself into his arms, crying:
"Papa Jean-Claude, is it you? you are not wounded? Nothing is the matter with you?"

At the sound of this voice, Hullin turned pale,
and could make no reply. After a long silence,
pressing her to his heart, he said: "No, Louise, I
am quite well; I am very happy."

"Sit down, Jean-Claude," said the anabaptist,
seeing him trembling with emotion; "here, take
my chair."

Hullin sat down, and Louise, with her arms on
his shoulder, began to cry.

"What is the matter, my child?" said the
worthy man, kissing her. "Come, calm thyself.
Only a few seconds ago thou wert so courageous."

"Oh, yes, but I was only acting; I was very much afraid. I thought, 'Why does he not come?'"

She threw her arms round his neck. Then a strange idea came into her head. She took him by the hand, crying: "Papa Jean-Claude, let us dance, let us dance!"

And they made three or four turns. Hullin could not help laughing, and turning toward the grave anabaptist, said: "We are rather mad, Pelsly; do not let that astonish you."

"No, Master Hullin, it is quite natural. King David himself danced before the ark after his great victory over the Philistines."

Jean-Claude, astonished to find that he was like King David, made no reply.

"And thou, Louise," he continued, stopping, "thou wert not afraid during this last battle?"

"Oh, at first, with all the noise and the roaring of the cannons; but afterward I only thought of you and of Mamma Lefèvre."

Master Jean-Claude grew silent again.

"I knew," thought he, "that she was a brave girl. She has everything in her favor."

Louise taking him by the hand, then led him to a regiment of pans around the fire, and showed him with delight her kitchen.

"Here is the beef and roast mutton, here is General Jean-Claude's supper, and here is the soup for our wounded. Haven't we been busy! Lesselé and Katel would tell you so. And here is our bread," said she, pointing to a long row of loaves arranged on the table. "Mamma Lefèvre and I mixed up the flour."

Hullin looked on astonished.

"But that is not all," said she; "come over here."

She took off the lid of a saucepan, and the kitchen was immediately filled with a savory odor which would have rejoiced the heart of a gourmand.

Jean-Claude was deeply touched by all these proofs of attention to the wants of his men.

Just then Mother Lefèvre came in.

"Well," said she, "prepare the table; everybody is waiting over there. Come, Katel, go and lay the cloth."

The girl went running out to do so.

They all crossed the dark yard and made their way toward the large room. Doctor Lorquin, Dubois, Marc Divès, Materne, and his two boys, all very hungry, were awaiting the soup impatiently.

"How about our wounded, doctor?" said Hullin, on entering.

"They have all been attended to, Master Jean-

Claude. You have given us plenty of work to do; but the weather is favorable; there is nothing to fear from putrid fevers; things wear a pleasant aspect."

Katel, Lesselé, and Louise soon came in bearing an immense tureen of smoking soup and two sirloins of roast beef, which they deposited on the table. They all sat down without ceremony—old Materne to the right of Jean-Claude, Catherine Lefèvre to the left; and from that time the clatter of spoons and forks and the gurgling of the bottles took the place of conversation till half-past eight in the evening. The glow which might be seen from the outside upon the windows, proved that the volunteers were doing justice to Louise's cookery, which contributed greatly to the enjoyment of her guests.

At nine o'clock Marc Divès was on his way to Falkenstein with the prisoners. At ten everybody was asleep at the farm, on the plateau, and around the watchfires. The silence was only broken by the passing of the patrols and the challenge of the sentinels.

Thus terminated this great day, after the mountaineers had proved that they had not degenerated from their ancestors.

Other events, not less important, were soon to

succeed those which had already taken place: for
in this world, when one obstacle is surmounted,
others present themselves.   Human life resembles
a restless sea: one wave follows another from the
old world to the new, and nothing arrests its ever-
lasting movement.

CHAPTER XVIII

THE CAVE OF LUITPRANDT

ALL through the battle, till the close of night, the good people of Grandfontaine had observed the poor crazy Yégof standing upon the crest of the Little Donon, and, his crown on his head, with his sceptre held aloft, like a Merovingian king, shouting commands to his phantom armies. What passed through his mind when he saw the utter rout of the Germans no one can say; but at the last cannon-shot he disappeared. Where did he betake himself? On this point the people of Tiefenbach have the following story:—

At that time there lived upon the Bocksberg two singular creatures — sisters — one named "little Kateline," and the other "great Berbel." These creatures, who were almost in tatters, had taken up their abode in the "Cave of Luitprandt," so called, according to old chronicles, because the German king, before invading Alsace, had caused to be interred in that immense vault of red sandstone the

savage chiefs who had fallen in the battle of Blutfeld. The hot spring which always bubbles in the
middle of the cavern protected the eerie sisters
from the sharp colds of winter; and the wood-
cutter, Daniel Horn, of Tiefenbach, had been good
enough to fill up the largest entrance to the rock
with heaps of brushwood. By the side of the hot
spring there is another, cold as ice and clear as
crystal. Kateline, who always drank of its waters,
was scarce four foot high, thick-set and bloated;
and her cowering figure, her round eyes and enormous goître, rendered her whole appearance pecul-
iarly suggestive of a big turkey-hen in a reverie.
Every Sunday she carried into Tiefenbach a great
basket, which the people of the place filled with
boiled potatoes, crusts of bread, and occasionally,
on high days, with cakes and other remains of their
festivals;—with which she reascended breathlessly
to her rocky home, muttering, gibbering, and be-
having in the absurdest way. Meanwhile Berbel
took care to drink from the cold spring: she was
gaunt, one-eyed, scraggy as a bat, with a flat nose,
large ears, a gleaming eye, and thrived upon the
booty obtained by her sister. Seldom did she descend from the Bocksberg, except in July, at the
time of greatest heat—when she proceeded to launch
her incantations—her enchanting-wand a withered

thistle—against the crops of those who had failed
to contribute to her sister's basket. These imprecations were always believed to be followed by dire
storms, hail, and destructive vermin without stint:
whence they came to be dreaded as the plague, and
the hag herself to be regarded as a weather-witch
(*Wetterhexe*), while " little Kateline " was looked
upon as the good genius of Tiefenbach and its
neighborhood.   In such wise Berbel folded her
arms and took her ease in her cave, while her sister
went gibbering along the highways.

Unfortunately for the sisters, Yégof had for
many years established his winter-quarters in
" Luitprandt's cavern; " and it was thence he set
forth every spring on a visit to his innumerable
châteaux and feudatories, as far as Geierstein in the
Hundsrück.   Every year, therefore, toward the end
of November, after the first snows, he arrived with
his raven, to the accompaniment of piercing cries
from Wetterhexe.

" What have you to grumble at? " he would say,
while installing himself in the place of honor.
" Are you not intruders upon my domain, and
am I not truly good to permit two such useless
old hags (*Valkyries*) to stay in the Valhalla of
my fathers? "

Then Berbel, in a rage, used to overwhelm him

with abuse, while Kateline gave vent to her dissat-
isfaction in thick unintelligible utterances; but he,
regardless of both, lit his old box pipe and set himself to describe his endless peregrinations to the
ghosts of the German warriors buried in the cavern
sixteen centuries before, calling upon each of them
by name, and addressing them as personages still
living. From this it will be understood with what
disgust the arrival of the maniac came to be regarded by Kateline and Berbel; in fact for both
it was nothing less than a calamity.

Now in the year we are speaking of, Yégof, having failed to return to them at the proper time, induced the sisters to believe that he was dead and to
rejoice at the idea of seeing no more of him. But
for many days Wetterhexe had remarked an extraordinary movement going on in the neighboring
gorges, and men marching off in bodies, shouldering
their muskets, from the sides of Falkenstein and
Donon. Clearly something was taking place out
of the common. Recollecting that the year before
Yégof had informed the phantoms of the cave that
his armies, in countless hosts, were coming to in-
vade the country, the sorceress was seized with a
vague apprehension and anxiety to learn the cause
of so much agitation; but no one came up to the
cave, and Kateline having made her rounds on the

previous Sunday, could not have been induced to stir out for the gift of a kingdom.

In this state of apprehension, Wetterhexe went and came upon the side of the mountain and became hourly more restless and irritable. During the whole of that Saturday events assumed quite another aspect. From nine o'clock in the morning deep and heavy explosions began to growl like a continuous storm among the thousand echoes of the mountain; while far away in the direction of Donon, the swift lightnings swept up across the sky among the peaks; then toward night the discharges deepening in intensity filled the silent gorges with an indescribable tumult. At every report the Hengst, the Gantzlee, the Giromani, and the Grosmann cliffs seemed to echo to their lowest depths.

"What can it be?" cried Berbel. "Has the end of the world come?"

Then re-entering her lurking-place, and finding Kateline crouched in her corner and munching a potato, Berbel shook her roughly and hissed out: —"Fool! have you got no ears? Is there anything that you fear? You are good for nothing but eating, drinking, and mumbling. Oh, you idiot!"

She snatched away the potato in a rage, and then seated herself by the side of the hot spring, which

was sending up its gray fumes to the roof.   Half an
hour after, the darkness having become intense and
the cold excessive, she made a fire of brushwood,
which shed its pale gleams upon the blocks of red
sandstone and lit up the farthest corner of the cave,
where Kateline was now asleep, huddled in the straw,
with her chin upon her knees.   Without, the noisy
tumult had ceased.   Then withdrawing the brushwood curtain from the mouth of the cave, she peered
out into the darkness, and returned to crouch down
by the spring.   With her large lips compressed, her
eyes closed, and the great round wrinkles playing
upon her cheeks, she drew round her knees an old
woollen covering, and appeared to fall asleep.
Throughout the cavern there was no sound, except
that of the congealed vapor, which fell back at long
intervals into the spring with a strange splashing
noise.

   This silence lasted for about two hours; midnight was approaching, when all of a sudden a distant sound of footsteps, mingled with discordant
cries, was heard outside the cave.   Berbel listened,
and at once perceived that they were human cries.
Then she rose, trembling, and, armed with her this-
tle-wand, proceeded to the entrance of the cave;
whence, through the screen of brushwood, she saw,
at fifty paces distant, Yégof advancing toward her

in the moonlight. He was alone, but gesticulating and waving his sceptre, as if myriads of invisible beings were about him.

"Hark, ye red men!" he was shrieking, with beard sticking up on end, his hair streaming about his head, and his dog-skin upon his arm. "Hark, ye red men! Roog! Bled! Adelrik! hark! Will ye not hear me at last? Do you not see they are coming? Behold them cleaving the sky like vultures. Hark to me. Let this miserable race be annihilated! Ha, ha! it is you, Minau! it is you, Rochart . . . ha! ha!" And addressing the dead upon the Donon, he called upon them defiantly, as if they were standing before him; and then fell back a step at a time, striking the air, uttering imprecations, encouraging his phantoms, and casting about him as if in close fight. The sight of this terrible struggle against beings who were invisible caused Berbel to shudder with fright, and to fancy her hair stiffening upon her head. She sought to hide herself; but just at the moment a strange noise from behind drew her attention, and her terror may be imagined when she saw the hot spring bubbling with more than usual activity and sending out clouds of steam, which rose and broke away in separate masses toward the entrance of the cavern; and while these clouds like phantoms were slowly ad-

15

vancing in close order, Yégof appeared upon the scene, shouting hoarsely:—

"You come at last! you heard me then!"

Thus saying, he removed with an impatient effort all obstructions from the mouth of the cave: the cold air rushed down the vault and the steaming vapors rose far into the sky, writhing and glancing above the cliff, as if the slain of that day and those of the ages gone by had recommenced beyond the earth a battle that would never end.

Yégof, with face which appeared shrunken in the pale moonlight, his sceptre held high, his great beard flowing down his breast, and his eyes flaming, saluted each phantom with a wave of the hand, addressing it by name:

"Hail, Bled! Roog, hail! and you, my brave men, all hail! The hour you have been expecting for ages is at hand: the eagles are whetting their beaks and the soil is thirsting for blood. Remember Blutfeld!"

At this point Berbel's terror seemed to hold her transfixed; but soon the last volumes of gray mist disappeared out of the cavern and melted into the sky. Seeing which the crazy montagnard marched fiercely into the cave, and seating himself by the spring, with his great head between his hands, and

YÉGOF SALUTED EACH PHANTOM WITH SPARKLING EYES.

his elbows on his knees, looked down into the boiling water with a haggard stare.

Kateline was now awake and venting her guttural moans; while Wetterhexe, more dead than alive, was furtively watching the maniac from the farthest corner of the cave.

"They have all gone up from the earth!" exclaimed Yégof, suddenly. "All, all! They have gone to reanimate the courage of my youths, and inspire them with contempt of death!"

And again lifting up his face, which seemed impressed with deep anguish, he cried, fixing his wolfish eyes on Wetterhexe:—

"Oh, thou descendant of the sterile valkyries, thou who hast nurtured within thy bosom no life-breath of warriors, nor ever filled their deep goblets at the festive board, nor regaled them with the smoking flesh of the wild boar, for what purpose art thou good? To spin shrouds for the dead. Ha! take thy distaff and spin night and day; for thousands of brave men are slumbering in the snow! . . . They fought well. . . . Yes, they did all that men could do; but the time had not come, . . . now the ravens are fighting for their carcasses!"

Then in accents of uncontrollable rage, snatching the crown off his head together with handfuls of hair—"Ah, cursed race," he exclaimed, "will

you always be barring our passage? Were it not
for you we had already conquered Europe; the red
men would have been masters of the world. . . .
And I have bowed my head before the leader of
this race of curs. . . . I asked him for his daughter,
instead of seizing and carrying her away as the
wolf carries the lamb! . . . Ah! Huldrix, Huldrix!"

Then changing this rhapsody—"Listen, listen,
valkyrie!" he cried in a hoarse voice, and pointing
his finger with great solemnity.

Wetterhexe listened. A great gust of wind rose
up through the night, shaking the old forest-trees
heavy with their load of frost. Often and often
had the sorceress in the winter nights heard the
soughing of the north wind and paid it no attention,
but now she was overwhelmed with fear! And as
she stood there all trembling, a hoarse cry was heard
without; and almost at the same time the raven
Hans, sweeping beneath the rock, set himself to
describe great circles overhead, flapping his wings
with a frightened air, and uttering melancholy
cries.

Yégof became pale as death. "Vod, Vod! what
has thy son Luitprandt done for thee? Why choose
him rather than another?"

For some seconds he stood as though amazed;

then, suddenly transported by savage enthusiasm and brandishing his sceptre, he dashed out of the cavern.

Two minutes afterward, Wetterhexe, standing at the entrance of the rock, followed him with anxious eyes.

He went straight on, with neck stretched forward and long strides. You would have thought him a wild beast upon the prowl. Hans went before him, hopping from place to place.

In a moment they disappeared down the Blutfeld gorge.

CHAPTER XIX

TOWARD two o'clock the next morning, snow
began to fall. At daybreak the Germans had left
Grandfontaine, Framont, and even Schirmeck. In
the distance, on the plains of Alsace, could be seen
the black lines, which indicated their retreating
battalions.

Hullin arose early and made the round of the
bivouacs. He stopped for a few seconds on the
plateau, to look at the cannons in position, the
sleeping partisans, and the watchful sentries; then,
satisfied with his inspection, he re-entered the farm,
where Louise and Catherine were still asleep.

The gray light was spreading everywhere. A
few wounded in the next room were growing feverish; they were calling for their wives and children. Soon the hum of voices and the noise of
busy feet broke the stillness of the night. Catherine and Louise awoke. They saw Jean-Claude sitting in a corner of the window watching them, and

ashamed of having slept longer than he, they arose and approached him.

" Well? " asked Catherine.

" Well, they have left; and we are masters of the field, as I expected."

This assurance did not appear to satisfy the old dame. She looked through the window to see for herself that the Germans were retreating into Alsace; and during the whole of that day she seemed both anxious and troubled.

Between eight and nine the curé Saumaize came in from the village of Charmes. Some mountaineers then descended the slopes to pick up the dead, and dug a deep pit to the right of the farm, where partisans and " kaiserlichs," with their clothes, hats, shakos, and uniforms, were laid side by side. The curé Saumaize, a tall old man with white hair, read the prayers for the dead in that solemn, mysterious voice which seems to penetrate to the depths of one's soul, and to summon from the tomb the spirits of extinct generations to attest to the living the terrors of the grave.

All day carts and sledges continued to arrive to carry away the wounded, who demanded, with loud cries, to be allowed to see their villages once more. Doctor Lorquin, fearing to increase their irritation, was forced to consent. And toward four o'clock, Catherine and Hullin were alone in the great room: Louise had gone out to prepare the supper. Outside, large flakes of snow continued to fall, and, from time to time, a sledge might be seen silently passing along, bearing a wounded man laid in straw. Catherine, seated near the table, was folding bandages with an absent air.

"What ails you, Catherine?" demanded Hullin. "You have seemed so thoughtful since morning: and yet our affairs are going on well."

The old dame, pushing the linen slowly away from her, replied,—"Yes, Jean-Claude, I am uneasy."

"Uneasy about what? The enemy is in full retreat. Only this moment, Frantz Materne, whom I had sent to reconnoitre, and all the messengers from Piorette, Jérome, and Labarbe, told me that the Germans are returning to Mutzig. Old Materne and Kasper, having gathered up the dead, learned at Grandfontaine that nothing is to be seen in the direction of Saint-Blaize-la-Roche. All this proves that our Spanish dragoons gave the enemy a warm reception on the way to Senones, and that they fear an attack from Schirmeck. What is it, then, Catherine, that troubles you?"

And seeing that Hullin looked at her inquiringly, "You may laugh at me," said she; "but I have had a dream."

" A dream? "

" Yes, the same as at the farm of Bois-de-Chênes." And getting animated, she continued, in an almost angry tone, " You may say what you like, Jean-Claude, but a great danger menaces us. Yes, yes! you don't see any sense in all this; but it was not a dream, it was like an old tale which comes back to one: something one sees in sleep and remembers. Listen! We were as we are now, after a great victory—in some place—I don't know where—in a sort of large wooden shed, with beams across it, and palisades around. We were not, thinking of anything: all the faces I saw I knew: you were among them, Marc Divès, Duchêne, and old men already dead: my father and old Hugues Rochart of Harberg, the uncle of him who has just died: and they all had coarse gray cloth blouses, with long beards and bare necks. We had won a like victory, and were drinking out of red earthenware pots, when a cry arose: ' The enemy is coming!' And Yégof, on horseback, with his long beard and pointed crown, an axe in his hand, and with his eyes gleaming like a wolf's, appeared before me in the darkness. I rushed on him with a club, he waited for me—and from that moment I saw no more. I only felt a great pain in my neck; a cold wind passed over my face, and my head

seemed to be dangling at the end of a cord: it was
that wretched Yégof who had hung my head to
his saddle and was galloping away!"

There was a short pause; and then Jean-Claude,
rousing from his stupor, replied: "It is a dream.
I also have had dreams. Yesterday you were
agitated, Catherine, by all that tumult, that
noise."

"No," she exclaimed in a firm tone, taking up
her task again: "no, it was not that. And to tell
you the truth, during the battle, and even when
the cannons were thundering against us, I was not
afraid; I was certain beforehand that we should
not be beaten; I had seen it long ago. But now
I am afraid."

"But the Germans have evacuated Schirmeck;
the whole line of the Vosges is defended. We have
more men than we need; they are coming every
minute in great numbers."

"No matter."

Hullin shrugged his shoulders.

"Come, come! you are feverish, Catherine; try
to be calm, and think of pleasanter things. As for
all these dreams, you see, I make no more account
of them than I do of the Grand Turk, with his
pipe and blue stockings. The chief thing is to keep
a good look-out, and to have plenty of ammunition,

men, and guns: that is infinitely better than the
most rose-colored dreams."

" You are mocking me, Jean-Claude."

" No; but to hear a sensible, courageous woman
speak as you do, reminds one in spite of himself
of Yégof, who pretends to have lived sixteen hundred years ago."

" Who knows? " said the old woman, in an obstinate tone; " it is possible he may remember what
others have forgotten."

Hullin was going to relate to her his conversation of the evening before at the bivouac-fire with
the madman, thus hoping to overthrow all her
gloomy fancies; but seeing she agreed with Yégof
about the sixteen hundred years, the worthy man
said no more, but resumed his walk up and down,
with his head bent and an anxious face: " She is
mad," thought he; " one more shock and it is all
over with her! "

Catherine after a pause was going to speak, when
Louise entered like a swallow, calling out, in her
sweetest voice, " Maman Lefèvre, Maman Lefèvre,
a letter from Gaspard! "

Whereupon the old farm-wife, whose hooked
nose almost touched her lips, so angry was she to
see Hullin turning her dream into ridicule, raised
her head, the long wrinkles in her face relaxing.

She took the letter, looked at the red seal, and said to the young girl: " Embrace me, Louise: it is a good letter! " And Louise at once embraced her with joy.

Hullin came close up to them, delighted at this incident; and the postman Brainstein, his big boots dyed red with the snow, his two hands on his stick, and drooping his shoulders, stationed himself at the door with a tired look.

The old dame put on her spectacles, slowly opened the letter under the impatient eyes of Jean-Claude and Louise, and read aloud:—

. " This, my mother, is to announce to you that all goes well, and that I reached Phalsbourg on Tuesday evening just as the gates were being closed. The Cossacks were already on the Saverne road; we had to fire all night against their advanced guard. The following day, an envoy was sent demanding the surrender of the place. The commandant, Meunier, told him to go and be hanged; and three days after great showers of bombs and shells began to rain upon the town. The Russians have three batteries—one on the side of Mittelbronn, the other at the Baraques above, and the third behind the tilery of Pernette near the drinking-tank; but the red-hot shot do us the most harm: they burn down the houses, and when a fire has broken out the bombs then come in quantities and prevent the people from extinguishing it. The women and children do not leave the block-houses; the townsmen remain with us on the ramparts: they are fine fellows. Among them are some old soldiers of the Sambre-et-Meuse, Italy, and Egypt, who have not forgotten how to manage the guns. I felt sorry to see the graybeards bending over the carronades to take aim. I will answer for it that there are no balls lost with them; but all the same, when one has made the world tremble, it is hard to be obliged, in one's old days, to fight for one's home and last morsel of bread."

" Yes, it is hard," exclaimed Catherine, drying her eyes. " Only to think of it makes one's heart bleed."

Then she continued :—

" The day before yesterday, the governor decided on our making a sortie against the tile-kiln battery. You must know that these Russians break the ice of the tank, and bathe in it, in groups of from twenty to thirty; afterward drying themselves in the oven of the brick-kiln. Well! about four o'clock, as the day was closing, we went out by the Arsenal gateway, ascending the covered way, and filing along the Allée-des-Vaches, with our muskets under our arms, and marching at the double. Ten

minutes after we commenced a rolling fire on the
men that were in the tank. Then their comrades
rushed out of the brick-kilns: they had only time
to put on their cartouche-boxes, seize their muskets,
and form, all naked as they were, on the snow, like
regular savages. Notwithstanding that, the rogues
were ten times more numerous than we, and they
began a movement to the right, in the direction of
the little chapel of St. John, in order to surround
us, when the guns from the Arsenal began to send
such a storm of shot at them as I never saw before;
it carried whole files clean off. A quarter of an
hour later they retreated in a body to Quatre-Vents,
without waiting to pick up their breeches—their
officers at their head, and the hail from the fortress
bringing up the rear. Papa Jean-Claude would
have laughed at the rout immensely. At last, toward nightfall, we returned to the town, having
destroyed one of their batteries and thrown two
eight-pounders into the well of the kiln. It was
our first sortie. I am now writing to you from the
Baraques du Bois-de-Chênes, where we have been
sent to get provisions for the fortress. All this
may last months. It is said that the allies are reas-
cending the valley of Dosenheim as far as Weschem,
and that thousands of them are marching on Paris.
Oh, if the Emperor once obtained the upper hand

in Lorraine and Champagne, not one of them would
escape! But who lives will see. They are sounding the retreat on Phalsbourg. We have collected
a pretty good number of oxen, cows, and goats
about here; but shall have to fight in order to get
them in safely. Good-by, my good mother, my
dearest Louise, and Papa Jean-Claude. I embrace
you as though I held you in my arms."

At the close of the letter, Catherine Lefèvre was
overwhelmed with emotion.

"What a brave boy!" said she. "He only
knows his duty. There! thou hearest, Louise? He
embraces thee!"

Louise then throwing herself into her arms, they
embraced each other; and Catherine, notwithstanding the firmness of her character, could not keep
back two large tears from trickling down her
cheeks; then, recovering herself, "Come," said
she, "all is well! Come, Brainstein, you must eat
some meat and drink a glass of wine. And here is
a crown-piece for your journey; I would give you
the same sum every day of the week for such a
letter."

The postman, delighted with his present, followed
the old dame. Louise walked after them, and Jean-
Claude, also, being eager to interrogate Brainstein as to what he had learnt on the road, touching

the events taking place; but he could get nothing
new out of him, except that the allies were besieg-
ing Bitsche and Lutzelstein, and that they had lost
some hundreds of men in trying to force the Grauf-
thal pass.

CHAPTER XX

TOWARD ten o'clock, Catherine Lefèvre and Louise, after having wished Hullin good-night, went up to sleep in the room over the large kitchen; in which there were two feather-beds, with curtains, striped with blue and red, reaching to the ceiling.

"Come," exclaimed the old woman, climbing up to hers on a chair—" come, sleep well, my child. As for me, I am tired out, and almost asleep already."

She drew the bedclothes round her, and five minutes after was sound asleep. Louise soon followed her example.

Now this had lasted about two hours, when the old dame was awakened suddenly by a tremendous noise.

"To arms! to arms! Ho! this way quick! A thousand thunders! they are upon us!"

Five or six shots then followed each other, lighting up the dark windows.

"To arms! to arms!"

Then there was more firing, and the noise of people rushing about everywhere.

Hullin's voice, sharp and vibrating, could be heard giving orders.

Then, to the left of the farm, a great way off, there came a low dull crackling sound, from the gorges of the Grosmann.

"Louise! Louise!" cried the old farm-wife,— "dost thou hear?"

"Yes! Oh, my God! it is terrible."

Catherine sprang out of bed.

"Get up, my child," said she, "and let us dress."

The firing redoubled, and flashed like lightning upon the panes.

"Attention!" shouted Materne.

One could also hear the neighing of a horse outside, and the tramping of a great crowd in the alley, the yard, and before the farm: the house seemed shaken to its foundations.

Suddenly, the firing came from the windows of the large room on the ground-floor. The two women dressed in haste. Just at that moment, a heavy foot creaked on the stairs; the door opened, and Hullin appeared with a lantern, showing signs of great agitation.

"Make haste!" cried he; "we have not an instant to lose."

"What has happened then?" asked Catherine. The fusillade came nearer.

"Eh!" exclaimed Jean-Claude, throwing up his arms, "have I time now to explain to you?"

The old dame understood that the only thing to be done was to obey. She put on her hood and descended the staircase with Louise. By the flickering light of the shots, Catherine saw Materne, bare-necked, and his son Kasper, firing from the entrance of the alley upon the abatis, and ten others behind handing them muskets, so that they had only to aim and fire. All these men, in a throng, loading, shouldering, and firing, had a terrible aspect. Three or four dead bodies lying against the old wall added to the horror of the scene. The smoke was at the point of reaching the dwelling.

Coming down the stairs, Hullin cried, "Here they are, thank heaven!" And all the brave fellows who were there, looking up, cried out, "Courage, Mother Lefèvre!"

Whereupon the poor old lady, worn out by her emotions, began to weep and lean on Jean-Claude's shoulder; but he lifted her up like a feather, and ran along by the wall to the right. Louise followed, sobbing loudly.

Out of doors, one could only hear the whizzing of bullets and the dull heavy blows against the wall; the bricks and mortar were tumbling down, the tiles rolling about; while in front, near the abatis, and three hundred yards off, one could see the white uniforms in line, lit up by their own fire in the dark night; and, to their left, on the other side of the ravine of Minières, the mountaineers attacking them in flank.

Hullin disappeared at the corner of the farm, —where all was in darkness;—Doctor Lorquin, on horseback in front of a sledge, having a large cavalry sword in his hand and two pistols passed through his belt, with Frantz Materne and a dozen other armed men, being barely distinguishable. Hullin placed Catherine in the sledge, on some straw, and Louise by her side.

"There you are!" exclaimed the doctor. "It is well for you."

And Frantz Materne added:—"If it were not for you, Mother Lefèvre, you may well believe that not one of us would quit the plateau this night; but there is nothing to be said since you are in the case."

"No," cried the others, "there is nothing to be said!"

Just at that moment, a tall fellow, with legs long

as a heron's and a round back, came running behind
the wall and shouting, " They are coming! Fly!
fly! "

Hullin turned pale.

" It is the big knife-grinder of the Harberg! "
he exclaimed, grinding his teeth.

Frantz without saying a word put his musket to
his shoulder, aimed and fired; and Louise saw the
grinder at thirty yards in the dim light, throw up
his arms and fall face downward on the ground.
Frantz reloaded, smiling grimly.

Hullin then said: " Comrades, here is our mother
—she who has given us powder and furnished us
with food for the defence of our country; and here
is my child: save them! "

They all replied: " We will save, or die with
them."

" And do not forget to warn Divès to stay at the
Falkenstein till further orders."

" All right, Jean-Claude."

" Then forward, doctor, forward! " cried the gallant man.

" And you, Hullin? " exclaimed Catherine.

" My place is here; our position must be defended till death! "

" Papa Jean-Claude! " cried Louise, holding
out her arms to him.

But he had already turned the corner,—the doctor flicked his horse, and the sledge passed quickly along the snow. Frantz Materne and his men, with their muskets on their shoulders, marched behind; while a rolling fire of musketry was still kept up around the farm.

That was what Catherine Lefèvre and Louise saw in the space of a few minutes. No doubt something strange and terrible had happened in the night. The old farm-mistress, recalling her dream, became very thoughtful. Louise dried her eyes and looked toward the plateau, which was lighted up as by a fire. The horse bounded away under the doctor's whip, so that the mountaineers could hardly keep up. For some distance the tumult and clamor of the battle, the explosions, and whizzing of the balls among the branches, were distinctly heard; but all this grew fainter and fainter, and soon, at the descent of the path, vanished as in a dream.

The sledge had reached the opposite side of the mountain, and was flying like an arrow through the darkness. The only sounds which broke the silence were the galloping of the horse, the quick breathing of the escort, and from time to time the doctor's cry, " Here, Bruno! here then! "

A current of cold wind, coming up from the valley of the Sarre, carried upon its breeze, like a great sigh, the endless roar of the torrents and soughing of the woods. The moon was peering out from behind a cloud, and looking down on the black forests of Blanru, with their tall pines loaded with snow.

Ten minutes later the sledge had gained an angle of the woods, and Doctor Lorquin, turning round in his saddle, exclaimed,—"Now, Frantz, what have we to do? Here is the way which leads toward the hills of St. Quirin, and there is another road which descends to Blanru. Which shall we take?"

Frantz and the men of the escort came up. As they were then on the western slope of the Donon, they began to see again, high in the air, on the other side of the hill, the fusillade of the Germans, who were advancing by way of the Grosmann. First they saw the flashes, and then heard the rolling echoes in the depths of the valleys.

"The road by the hills of St. Quirin," said Frantz, "is the shortest cut to the farm of Bois-de-Chênes; it would save at least three-quarters of an hour."

"Yes," rejoined the doctor, "but we should risk being stopped by the Germans, who now occupy the defile of the Sarre. See, they are already masters of the heights; they have no doubt sent detachments to the Sarre-Rouge in order to turn the Donon."

"Let us take the Blanru road, then," said Frantz; " it is longer, but safer."

The sledge passed down the left along the woods. The partisans, gun in hand, advanced one after the other along the top of the bank, while the doctor on his horse swept along the snow in the roadway. Above, the great pine-branches met across the road, and enveloped it with their deep shadows, while the moon lit up the surrounding scenery. This road was so majestic and picturesque, that, under any other circumstances, Catherine would have been astonished at it, and Louise would not have failed to admire the garlands of icicles, looking like crystals in the pale rays of the moon; but just then they were filled with uneasiness; and, moreover, when the sledge entered the gorge, all the brightness vanished, and only the summits of the high mountains around remained visible. They had been going in this way for a quarter of an hour, when Catherine, having kept silence for some time, at last could contain herself no longer, but exclaimed: " Doctor Lorquin, now that you have us in the depths of Blanru, and can do with us what you please, will you explain to me why we have been dragged away by force? Jean-Claude carried me off, and flung me on this heap of straw—and here I am! "

" Up, Bruno," cried the doctor.

Then he gravely answered her: " This night, Dame Catherine, a great misfortune has overtaken us. You must not attribute it to Jean-Claude: it is by another's fault that we have lost the fruit of all our sacrifices! "

" Through whose fault? "

" That unlucky Labarbe's, who did not guard the defile of the Blutfeld. `He died afterward fulfilling his duty; but that does not repair the disaster; and if Piorette does not come up in time to aid Hullin, all is lost; it will be necessary to abandon the road and to fight retreating."

" What! the Blutfeld is taken? "

" Yes, Mistress Catherine. Who the deuce could ever have thought that the Germans would enter that? A defile almost impracticable for foot-passengers, enclosed by rugged rocks, where the goatherds can barely descend with their flocks. Well, they marched that way, two at a time; they turned Roche-Creuse, crushed Labarbe, and then fell upon Jérome, who defended himself like a lion till nine in the evening; but, at last, he was obliged to take refuge in the pine-woods, and leave

the pass to the 'kaiserlichs.' That is the whole
story. It is shocking. Indeed, there must be some
one among us base and vile enough to have guided
the enemy, and would deliver us over to him bound
hands and feet. Oh, the wretch!" cried Lorquin,
furiously. "I am not revengeful, but if he came
into my clutches, how I would serve him! Up,
Bruno! up, then!"

The partisans were marching along the bank like
spectres, without saying a word.

The old farm-mistress became silent in order to
collect her ideas.

"I begin to understand," said she at last. "We
were attacked to-night on both sides."

"Exactly so, Catherine. Fortunately, ten minutes before the attack, one of Marc Divès's smugglers, Zimmer, the old dragooon, had come full gallop to warn us. Had it not been for that, we would
have been lost. He fell in with our vanguard, after
having run the gauntlet of a detachment of Cossacks on the plateau of Grosmann. The poor fellow
had received a terrible sabre-thrust; and his bowels
were protruding over the saddle—was it not so,
Frantz?"

"Yes," replied the hunter, sadly.

"And what did he say?" demanded Catherine.

"He had only time to cry, 'To arms! We are

hemmed in! Jérome sends me. Labarbe is dead! The Germans have passed the Blutfeld!' "

" He was a gallant fellow," exclaimed Catherine.

" Yes, a gallant fellow," replied Frantz, with his head bent down.

Then they relapsed into silence, and for some time the sledge swept through the winding valley. Now and then they were obliged to stop, the snow was so deep—when three or four mountaineers would take the horse by the bridle—and so they continued their way.

" All the same," said Catherine, suddenly rousing up from her reverie, " Hullin might have told me."

. " But if he had mentioned these two attacks," interrupted the doctor, " you would have wanted to remain."

" And who can hinder me from doing what I like? If it pleased me to get out of the sledge this very moment, should I not be free? I had forgiven Jean-Claude, but I am sorry for it! "

" Oh, Maman Lefèvre, supposing he is killed while you are saying that! " murmured Louise.

" She is right, poor child," thought Catherine; and then quickly added, " I said I was sorry for it; but he is such a good man, that one cannot be angry

with him. I forgive him with all my heart; in .
his place I should have done the same."

Two or three hundred yards farther on they
entered the defile of Roches. The snow had ceased
falling, and the moon was shining between great
white clouds. The narrow gorge, hemmed in by
steep precipices, expanded in the distance, its sides
covered with tall pines. Nothing disturbed the
deep calm of the woods; one could have imagined
one's self far away from all human agitation. The
silence was so great that every step the horse made
in the snow could be heard, and even his sharp
quick breathing. Frantz Materne halted at times
to gaze upon the black slopes, and then hurried on
to overtake the others.

They crossed valley after valley; the sledge
mounted and descended, now to the right and then
to the left; and the partisans, with their bayonets
fixed, followed continually.

Toward three in the morning they reached the
meadow of Brimbelles, where at the present day an
old oak can still be seen bending over the valley.
To the left, in the midst of the snow-covered
heather, behind a low stone wall, stood the old house
of the guard Cuny. Three beehives were placed
on a bench, a gnarled vine hung down from the
roof and a small pine-bough was suspended over the

door by way of sign-board, for Cuny carried on the
business of innkeeper in this solitary place.

At this spot the road runs close under the meadow
wall, and as a large cloud obscured the light of the
moon, the doctor, fearing to be upset, halted beneath the oak.

" We have only one hour's journey more, Mother Lefèvre," said he; " take courage; there is no
hurry."

" Yes," said Frantz; " the heaviest part of the
road is over, and the horse may breath a while."

The small party collected round the sledge, and
the doctor got down. Some lit their pipes; but no
one spoke: they were all busy thinking of the Donon.
What was going on there? Would Jean-Claude
be able to defend the plateau till Piorette arrived?
So many dread thoughts and dismal reflections
passed through the minds of the worthy people, that
not one seemed able to speak.

They had been standing thus about five minutes, when the black cloud passed slowly away, and
the pale moonlight lit up the gorge. Suddenly, a
dark figure on horseback appeared two hundred
paces from them, in the path between the pine-
trees. By the light of the moon they quickly perceived that it was the figure of a Cossack with his
sheepskin cap, and bearing a lance under his arm.

He was advancing slowly; Frantz was already taking aim, when other Cossacks with their lances appeared behind him. They advanced deliberately
in the direction of the sledge, like people on the
search, some with their heads turned upward, others
peering into the shrubs from their saddles. They
numbered more than thirty.

Imagine the feelings of Louise and Catherine,
seated in the middle of the road. They looked on
open-mouthed. In another minute they would be
surrounded by these bandits. The mountaineers
were stupefied; it was impossible to return: they
were hemmed in on one side by the meadow wall,
on the other by the mountain-side. The old farm-
wife seized Louise by the hand, and said, in a stifled
voice, " Let us escape to the woods! "

She sprang from the sledge, leaving her shoe in
the straw.

Suddenly one of the Cossacks uttered a guttural
cry, which was repeated along the whole line.

" We are discovered! " exclaimed the doctor, as
he drew his sword.

The words had scarcely escaped his lips when
twelve musket-shots lit up the path from end to end;
a regular savage whoop answered the report of the
muskets. The Cossacks made off from the path to
the meadow in front, gave their horses the reins,

bent down in their saddles, and flew toward the guard-house like deer.

"Ha! they are off like the devil!" said the doctor.

But the worthy man was too hasty. Suddenly, when they had gone two or three hundred yards along the valley, the Cossacks again wheeled round and massed themselves firmly together ; then, with their lances in rest, and bending over their horses' heads, they rushed straight at the partisans, shouting in hoarse voices—"Hourah ! hourah !"

It was a terrible moment.

Frantz and the others sprang toward the wall, to protect the sledge.

In another second, the clashing of lances and screams of rage could alone be heard, mingled with imprecations. Under the shadow of the old oak, through the straggling moonbeams, could be seen the horses prancing with tossing manes, as they endeavored to clear the meadow wall ; while the barbarian Cossacks, with gleaming eyes and uplifted arms, struck furiously with their lances, advancing, retreating, and uttering piercing yells.

Louise, deathly pale, and Catherine, with her gray dishevelled hair, stood up in the straw.

Doctor Lorquin, in front of them, parried the strokes with his sabre, and all the time kept shout-

ing to them—" Lie down ! lie down ! " But they
did not hear him.

Louise, in the midst of the tumult and shouting,
thought only of sheltering Catherine ; and the old
dame, in the midst of her terror, had recognized Yégof, on a tall, gaunt horse—Yégof, with his tin
crown, bristling beard, long lance, and dog-skin floating from his shoulders. She saw him as distinctly
as though it were broad daylight. He stood about
ten feet distant, with sparkling eyes, brandishing his
blue lance in the darkness, and striving to reach her.
What could she do? Submit to her fate ! Thus
do the most resolute characters succumb to inevita-
ble destiny. The old dame thought her fate was
sealed. She saw all these people tearing like
wolves, thrusting and parrying in the moonlight.
She saw some fall ; and horses running, riderless
through the fields. She saw the topmost window of
the guard-house thrown open ; and old Cuny, in his
shirt-sleeves, shoulder his gun, though not daring to
fire into the crowd. All passed before her eyes with
wonderful clearness. " The madman has returned," she said to herself. " Do what they will,
he will hang my head to the side of his saddle. It
will end as I saw in my dream."

And, indeed, everything seemed to justify her
fears : the mountaineers, inferior in numbers, were

giving way. The Cossacks had cleared the wall, and were already on the footpath. A well-aimed thrust passed through the old dame's back-hair, and she felt the cold iron against her neck.

" Oh, the murderers ! " she screamed, falling back and clutching fast at the reins.

Doctor Lorquin himself had been hurled against the sledge. Frantz and the others, surrounded by twenty Cossacks, could afford them no help. Louise felt a hand on her shoulder : it was the hand of the madman, seated on his great horse.

At this fearful moment, the poor child, mad with terror, uttered a scream of distress ; then she saw something gleaming in the darkness : it was Lorquin's pistols. Quick as lightning, tearing them from the doctor's belt, she fired them off both at once, singeing Yégof's beard, and blowing out the brains of a Cossack who was bending toward her with flaming eyes. She then seized Catherine's whip, and pale as death, lashed the horse, who bounded away. The sledge flew through the bushes, swaying from right to left. Suddenly there was a shock. Catherine, Louise, the straw, and all rolled in the snow on the slopes of the ravine. The horse stopped short on its haunches, its mouth full of bloody foam. It had struck against an oak-tree.

Rapid as was the fall, Louise had seen figures

17

passing like the wind behind the underwood. She
had heard a powerful voice, that of Divès, crying
out, " Forward !   Cut them down ! "

It was like a vision—one of those confused ap-
paritions which pass before the eyes in moments of
supreme danger ; but, on rising, the young girl had
no longer any doubts.   Fighting was going on only
a few paces distant behind the cover of some trees,
and the voice of Marc was heard shouting, " Go it,
my old fellows !   Give them no quarter ! "

Then she saw a dozen Cossacks clambering up the
hill in front, like hares among the heather ; below
Yégof was crossing the valley in the moonlight with
the speed of a terrified bird on the wing.   Several
shots were sent after him, but the madman remained
unscathed, and, standing upright in his stirrups,
with his horse at full gallop, he turned, waving his
lance with bravado, and shouting " Hourah ! "
Two more shots whizzed by from the guard-house ;
a bit of rag fell from his loins, but the madman continued his course, crying " Hourah ! " in a hoarse
tone, and toiled up the path which his companions
had taken before him.

All this passed before Louise like a dream.

Then, turning round, she saw Catherine by her
side, stupefied and absorbed like herself.   They
gazed at each other for a moment, and then em-

braced with an inexpressible feeling of happiness.

"We are saved!" murmured Catherine; and they both wept. "Thou hast behaved bravely. Jean-Claude, Gaspard, and I have good reason to be proud of thee!"

Louise was deeply agitated and trembled all over. The danger being passed, her gentle nature again resumed its sway, and she could not understand whence came her courage of a few minutes before.

They were recovering from their fright and about to get into the sledge, when they saw five or six partisans with the doctor coming toward them.

"Ah! you may cry as much as you like, Louise," said Lorquin; "but, for all that, you are a regular dragoon, a real little warrior. Though you now look so gentle, we have all seen you at work. But where are my pistols?"

At that moment the shrubs were pushed aside, and Marc Divès, sword in hand, appeared.

"Ah, Mistress Catherine, these are rough adventures for you. Zounds! what luck that I happened to come up. Those villains were spoiling you right and left."

"Yes," replied she, pushing her hair under her cap again; "it was very fortunate."

"Very fortunate! I should think so. It is only

ten minutes since I arrived with my wagon at Cuny's. ' Do not go to the Donon,' said he; ' the sky has been red for an hour in that direction ; there is certainly fighting going on up there.' ' You think so?' 'Faith ! yes.' 'Then Joson must go out and reconnoitre a little and we others will drink a glass while waiting.' 'Good !' Hardly had Joson left, when I heard shouts as though five hundred devils were let loose. 'What is it, Cuny?' 'I don't know.' We pushed open the door, and saw the fray. Ha! " exclaimed the big smuggler, " we did not wait long. I jumped on my brave horse Fox, and dashed forward. What luck! "

"Ah!" said Catherine, " if we were only sure that our affairs go as well on the Donon, we might then rejoice."

"Yes, yes ! Frantz told me about that :—it is the devil—there must always be something wrong," replied Marc. " But—but why stay here with our feet in the snow? Let us hope that Piorette will not allow his comrades to be crushed, and let us go and empty our glasses, which we left half full."

Four other smugglers then arrived, saying that that rascally Yégof would probably come back, with some more brigands like himself.

"Very likely," replied Divès. " We will return to the Falkenstein, since it is Jean-Claude's or-

ders ; but we can't bring our wagon with us : it
would prevent our taking the short cuts ; and in an
hour all these bandits would be down upon us. Let
us go first to Cuny's. Catherine and Louise will not
be sorry to drink a little wine ; and the others too.
It will put their hearts in the right place again. Up,
Bruno ! "

He led his horse by the bridle. Two wounded
men had been laid in the sledge ; two others having
been killed, as well as seven or eight Cossacks
stretched with their boots wide apart in the snow,
were abandoned, and they went on toward the forester's house.

Frantz was consoling himself for not having been
on the Donon : he had finished two Cossacks, and
the sight of the inn made him feel in a good humor.
Before the door stood the small wagon full of cartridges. Cuny came out, saying : " A hearty wel-
come, Mistress Lefèvre. What a night for women!
Be seated ! What is going on up there? "

While they were hastily drinking some wine, everything had to be explained over again. The
worthy old man in a blouse and green breeches, with
his wrinkled face, bald head, and wide-open eyes,
listened with clasped hands, exclaiming: " Good
God ! Good God ! in what times are we living?
One can no longer follow the high-roads without

risk of being attacked. It is worse than the old
Swedish tales." And he shook his head.

"Come," said Divès, "time flies. We must
continue our way."

Everybody being ready, the smugglers led the
wagon, which contained some thousands of cartridges and two small kegs of brandy, about three
hundred yards off, to the middle of the valley, and
then unharnessed the horses.

"Go forward!" shouted Marc; "we will rejoin you in a few minutes."

"But what art thou going to do with the cart?"
said Frantz. "Since we have no time to take it to
the Falkenstein, it had better be left under Cuny's
shed than in the road."

"Yes, to get the poor old man hanged, when the
Cossacks arrive, for they will be here in less than an
hour. Do not trouble thyself; I have my own
idea."

Frantz rejoined the sledge, which went on its
way. In a short time they passed by the saw-works
of the Marquis and turned sharp to the right, to
reach the farm of Bois-de-Chênes, whose tall chim-
neys could be perceived three-quarters of a league
distant on the plateau. They were on the hill-side
when Marc Divès and his men overtook them, shouting:

" Halt ! Stop a bit ! Look down there ! "

And, looking down into the gorge, they saw the Cossacks capering round the wagon—about three hundred of them.

" They are coming ! Let us fly ! " cried Louise.

" Wait a bit," said the smuggler. " We have nothing to fear."

He was still speaking, when an immense sheet of flame sped out from one mountain to the other, illuminating the woods, rocks, and the little house of the forester fifteen hundred yards below ; then there was a report so terrible that the earth seemed to tremble.

While those near him gazed in bewilderment and dumb terror at each other, Marc's bursts of laughter reached their ears, in spite of the din.

" Ha, ha, ha ! " shouted he, " I was sure the rogues would stop round the wagon, to drink up my brandy. I knew the match would have just time to reach the powder ! "

" Do you think they will pursue us? "

" Their arms and legs are now hanging from the branches of the pine-trees ! Come along ! And may heaven grant the same fate to all those who have now crossed the Rhine ! "

The whole escort, the partisans, the doctor, all

had grown silent : so many terrible emotions had
filled them with endless thoughts such as do not fall
within the experience of every-day life.   They said
to themselves : " What are men that they destroy,
harass, and ruin each other in this manner?   Why
do they hate each other so?   And what spirit of evil
is it that thus excites them? "

But Divès and his men were not at all troubled
by these events : they galloped along, laughing and
boasting.

" For my part," said the big smuggler, " I never
saw such a farce before.   Ha, ha, ha ! if I lived a
thousand years, I should laugh at it still."   Then
he became more serious, and exclaimed : " All the
same, Yégof is the cause of this.   One must be
blind not to see that it was he who led the Germans
to the Blutfeld.   I shall be sorry if he has been
struck down by a piece of my wagon ; I have something better in store for him than that.   All that
I wish is that he may keep in good health till we
meet somewhere in a lonely corner of the wood.   It
is no matter whether it be in one year, ten years,
twenty years, provided only that we meet.   The
longer it is deferred, the more savage my determination becomes : the daintiest morsels are eaten cold,
like a boar's head in white wine."

He said this with an air of good-humor, but those

who knew him perceived beneath it a serious danger for Yégof.

Half an hour later, they all reached the plateau on which the farm of Bois-de-Chênes was situated.

CHAPTER XXI

"ALL IS LOST"

JEROME of St. Quirin had managed to make good his retreat to the farm, and since midnight he had occupied the plateau.

"Who goes there?" cried his sentinels as the escort approached.

"It is we, from the village of Charmes," shouted Marc, in his stentorian voice.

The sentinels approached to examine them, and then they passed on their way.

The farm was silent ; a sentry, his musket over his arm, was pacing before the granary, where about thirty partisans were asleep upon the straw. At the sight of these great dark roofs, the stables and outhouses belonging to the old building where she had spent her youth, where her father and grandfather had led their tranquil laborious lives in peace, and which she was now about to abandon, perhaps forever, Catherine felt a terrible wrenching at her heart ; but no word escaped her. Springing from the sledge, as in other days when she returned from marketing, she said : " Come, Louise, here we are at home, thank God."

Old Duchêne pushed open the door, exclaiming: " Is that you, Madame Lefèvre ? "

" Yes, it is I.   Any news from Jean-Claude ? "

" No, Madame."

They entered the large kitchen.   Some cinders were still smouldering on the hearth, and in the dark, under the broad chimney, was sitting Jérome of St. Quirin, with his big horsehair hood, his great stick between his knees, and his carbine leaning against the wall.

" Good-day, Jérome," said the old farm-wife.

" Good-day, Catherine," replied the grave chief of the Grosmann.   " Have you come from the Donon ? "

" Yes : things are going badly, my poor Jérome. The ' kaiserlichs ' were attacking the farm when we left the plateau.   Nothing but white uniforms was to be seen on every side.   They were already beginning to cross the breastworks."

" Then you think Hullin will be compelled to abandon the road ? "

" Possibly, if Piorette does not come to his assistance."

The partisans had approached near the fire. Marc

Divès bent over the cinders to light his pipe ; on rising, he exclaimed : " I ask thee one thing only, Jérome ; I know beforehand that they fought well under thy command——"

" We have done our duty," replied the shoemaker. " There are sixty men stretched on the slopes of the Grosmann who will tell you so at the last day."

" Yes ; but who, then, guided the Germans ? They could not have discovered the pass of the Blutfeld by themselves."

" Yégof the madman—Yégof," said Jérome, whose gray eyes, encircled by deep wrinkles and thick white eyebrows, seemed to sparkle in the darkness.

" Ah ! art thou certain of it? "

" Labarbe's men saw him climbing up ; he led the others."

The partisans looked at each other with indignation.

At this moment Doctor Lorquin, who had remained outside to unharness the horse, opened the door, shouting : " The battle is lost ! Here are our men from the Donon. I have just heard Lagarmitte's horn."

It is easy to imagine the emotion of the recipients of these tidings. Each thought of the relations and

friends that he might never see again ; and from
the kitchen and the granary everybody at once
rushed on to the " plateau."   At the same time
Robin and Dubourg, posted as sentinels above Bois-
de-Chênes, cried out, " Who goes there?"

" France ! " replied a voice.

Notwithstanding the distance, Louise, fancying
she could recognize her father's voice, was seized
with such a fit of trembling that Catherine was compelled to support her.

Just then the noise of many footsteps resounded
over the hardened snow, and Louise, unable to contain herself any longer, exclaimed, " Papa Jean-
Claude ! "

" I am coming," replied Hullin, " I am coming."

" My father? " exclaimed Frantz Materne, rushing to meet Jean-Claude.

" He is with us, Frantz."

" And Kasper? "

" He has received a slight scratch, but it is nothing.   Thou wilt see them both again."

Catherine   threw   herself   into   Jean-Claude's
arms.

" Oh, Jean-Claude, what joy to behold you once
more ! "

" Yes," replied the worthy man, in a suppressed

voice, " there are many who will never see their friends again."

" Frantz," said old Materne, " here, this way! "

And one could only see, on all sides, people seeking each other in the dim light, squeezing hands, and embracing. Some called for, " Niclau! Sapheri! " but many did not answer to their names.

Then the voices became hoarse, as though stifled, and relapsed into silence. The joy of some, and the consternation of others, produced a terrible sensation. Louise was in Hullin's arms, sobbing bitterly.

" Ah, Jean-Claude," said Mother Lefèvre, " you will hear strange things about that child. I will say no more now, but we have been attacked——"

" Yes, we will talk of that later ; our time is short," said Hullin. " The road to the Donon is lost, the Cossacks may be here at daylight, and we have many things to arrange." ·

He turned the corner and entered the farm, all following him. Duchêne had just thrown a fagot on the fire. All these people, with faces blackened by powder, still animated by the combat, their clothes torn by bayonet-thrusts, some blood-stained, advancing from the darkness into the light, presented a strange spectacle. Kasper, whose forehead

MANY OF THEM WILL NEVER AGAIN SEE THEIR FRIENDS

was bandaged with his handkerchief, had received
a sabre-cut ; his bayonet, buff facings, and high
blue gaiters, were stained with blood. Old Materne, thanks to his imperturbable presence of mind,
returned safe and sound from the fray. The remains of Jérome's and Hullin's troops were thus
once more united. They wore the same wild phys-
iognomies, animated by the same energy and desire
for vengeance. But Hullin's men, harassed by
fatigue, sat down right and left, on the fagots, on
the stone sink, on the low pavement of the hearth
—their heads in their hands and elbows on their
knees ; while Jérome's, who could not be convinced
of the disappearance of Hans, Joson, and Daniel,
looked about everywhere, exchanging questions,
broken by long pauses. Materne's two sons held
each other by the arm, as though afraid of losing
one another, and their father, behind them, leaning
against the wall, with his elbow on his gun, watched
them with an expression of satisfaction.

"There they are, I see them," he seemed to say :
"two famous fellows ! They have saved their
skins, both of them." If any one came to ask him
about Pierre, Jacques, or Nicolas, his son or his
brother, he would reply hap-hazard—"Yes, yes,
there are several lying down there on their backs.
What can you expect? It is war ! Your Nicolas

has done his duty. You must console yourself."
Meanwhile he thought—" Mine are out of the
scrimmage ; that is the chief thing."

Catherine and Louise were busy preparing supper. Duchêne came up from the cellar with a barrel of wine on his shoulder. He set it down, and
knocked out the bung ; and each partisan presented his flask or cup to be filled with the purple liquid
which glittered in the firelight.

" Eat and drink," said the old dame to them :
" all is not lost yet ; you will have need of your
strength again. Here, Frantz, unhook those hams
for me. Here is bread and knives. Sit down, my
children."

Frantz reached down the hams in the chimney
with his bayonet.

The benches were brought forward ; they sat
down, and notwithstanding their sorrows, they eat
with that vigorous appetite which neither present
griefs nor thoughts for the future can make a mountaineer forget. But it did not prevent a bitter sadness from filling the hearts of these brave men ; and
first one and then another would stop suddenly, letting fall his fork, and leave the table, saying—" I
have had enough ! "

While the partisans were thus engaged in re-
cruiting their strength, the chiefs were assembled

in the next room to make some last resolutions for
the defence. They sat round the table, on which
was placed a tin lamp : Doctor Lorquin, with his
dog Pluto, looking inquiringly into his master's
face ; Jérome, in the corner of the window to the
right ; Hullin to the left, very pale ; Marc Divès,
his elbow on the table and cheek in his hand, and
his back turned to the door, showed only his brown
profile and the tip of his long mustache. Materne
alone remained standing, leaning, as was his custom, against the wall behind Lorquin's chair, with
his carbine at his feet. The noise of the men in the
kitchen could be distinctly heard.

When Catherine, summoned by Jean-Claude,
entered the room, she heard a sort of groan which
made her shudder. It was Hullin who was speaking.

"All these brave lads—all these fathers of families, who fell one after the other," he cried, in a
heartrending voice, "do you think I did not feel
it? Do you think that I would not rather a thousand times have been killed myself? You do not
know what I have suffered this night! To lose
one's life is nothing ; but to bear alone the weight
of such a responsibility——"

He paused : his trembling lips, the tear which
trickled slowly down his cheek, his attitude, all

18

showed the scruples of the worthy man, in face of
one of those situations where conscience itself hesi-
tates and seeks further support.   Catherine went
and sat down quietly in the big arm-chair.   A few
seconds later Hullin continued in a calmer tone :—
"Between eleven o'clock and midnight, Zimmer
came up, shouting, 'We are turned! The Germans are coming down the Grosmann! Labarbe
is crushed! Jérome can hold out no longer!'
What was to be done!   Could I beat a retreat?
Could I abandon a position which had cost us so
much blood—the road to the Donon, the road to
Paris? If I had done so, should I not have been a
coward? But I had only three hundred men
against four thousand at Grandfontaine, and I know
not how many descending from the mountain!
Well, I decided at any cost to hold it ; it was our
duty.   I said to myself, 'Life is nothing without
honor!   We will all die ; but they shall not say
that we have yielded the high-road to France.   No,
no; they shall not say that.'"

At this moment Hullin's voice faltered, and his
eyes filled with tears, as he continued—"We held
out ; my brave children held out till two o'clock.
I saw them fall : they fell shouting, 'Vive la
France!'   I had warned Piorette in the beginning
of the action.   He came up quickly, with fifty stout

men. It was too late. The enemy poured in on
every side ; they held three parts of the plain, and
forced us back among the pine-forests on the Blanru
side ; their fire burst upon us. All I could do was
to assemble my wounded, those who could still drag
along, and put them under Piorette's escort ; a hundred of my men joined him. For myself, I only
kept fifty to occupy the Falkenstein. We had to
pass right through the Germans, who wanted to cut
off our retreat. Happily, the night was dark; had
it not been for that, not one of us would have escaped. That is how we are situated. All is lost !
The Falkenstein alone remains ours, and we are reduced to three hundred men. Now the question is,
shall we go on to the end? I have already told you
that I dread to bear alone such a responsibility. So
long as it concerned defending the road to the Donon, there was no doubt about it: every man belongs to his country. But this road is lost. We
should need ten thousand men to retake it; and at
this very moment the enemy is entering Lorraine.
Come, what is to be done?"

"We must go on to the end," said Jérome.

"Yes, yes !" cried the others.

"Is that your opinion, Catherine?"

"Certainly," exclaimed the old dame, whose
features expressed an inflexible tenacity.

Then Hullin, in a firmer tone, explained his plan:
—" The Falkenstein is our point of retreat. It is
our arsenal ; it is there that we have our ammunition ; the enemy knows it ; he will attempt an attack on that side, therefore all of us here present
must make an effort to defend it, so that the whole
country may see us and say, ' Catherine Lefèvre,
Jérome, Materne and his boys, Hullin, and Doctor
Lorquin are there. They will not lay down their
arms.' This idea will give fresh courage to all man-
ly hearts. Besides, Piorette will remain in the
woods ; his troops will grow more numerous day by
day : the country will be filled with Cossacks and
marauders of every description ; when the enemy's
army shall have entered Lorraine I will signal to
Piorette; he will throw himself between the Donon and the highway, so that all the laggers behind
scattered over the mountains will be caught as in a
trap. We shall also be able to profit by favorable
chances to carry off the convoys of the Germans, to
harass their reserves, and, if fortune aids us, as we
must hope it will, and all these ' kaiserlichs ' are
beaten in Lorraine by our army, then we can cut off
their retreat."

Everybody got up, and Hullin going into the
kitchen, pronounced this simple address to the
mountaineers :—" My friends, we have decided

that we must push our resistance to the end. Nevertheless, every one is free to do as he likes ; to lay down his arms and return to his village ; but let those who wish to revenge themselves join us ; they will share our last morsel of bread and our last cartridge."

Colon, the old wood-floater, arose and said, " Hullin, we are all with thee ; we began to fight together, and so will we finish."

" Yes, yes ! " they all shouted.

" Have you all decided? Well, listen. Jérome's brother will take the command."

" My brother is dead," interrupted Jérome; " he lies on the slopes of the Grosmann."

There was a moment's pause ; then in a loud voice Hullin continued : " Colon, thou wilt take the command of all those that remain, with the exception of the men who formed Catherine Lefèvre's escort, and whom I shall keep with me. Thou wilt go and rejoin Piorette in the valley of Blanru, passing by the ' Two Rivers.' "

" And the ammunition? " said Marc Divès.

" I have brought up my wagon-load," said Jérome; " Colon can use it."

" Let the dray be loaded," said Catherine ; " the Cossacks are coming, and will pillage everything. Our men must not leave empty-handed ; let them

take away the cows, oxen, and calves—everything:
it will be so much gained on the enemy."

Five minutes later the farm was being ransacked;
the dray was loaded with hams, smoked meats, and
bread ; the cattle were led out of the stables, the
horses harnessed to the great wagon, and soon the
convoy began its march, Robin at the head, blowing
on his horn, with the partisans behind pushing at
the wheels.   When it had disappeared in the road,
and silence had succeeded to all the noise, Catherine
turning round, beheld Hullin behind her.

"Well, Catherine," said he, "all is finished !
We are now going to make our way up there."

Frantz, Kasper, and those of the escort, with
Marc Divès and Materne, all armed, were waiting
in the kitchen.

"Duchêne," said the good woman, "go down
to the village ; you must not be ill-treated by the
enemy on my account."

The old servant shook his white head, and, with
his eyes full of tears, replied :—" I may as well die
here, Madame Lefèvre.   It is nearly fifty years
since I came to the farm.   Do not make me leave ;
it would be the death of me."

"Do as you like, my poor Duchêne," replied
Catherine, softly; " here are the keys of the house."

And the poor old man sat down in the chimney-corner, on a settee, with fixed eyes and half-open mouth, as though lost in some painful reverie.

Then began the journey to the Falkenstein. Marc Divès, on horseback, sword in hand, formed the rear-guard. Frantz and Hullin watched the plateau to the left ; Kasper and Jérome the valley to the right : Materne and the men of the escort surrounded the women. It was a singular sight. Before the cottages of the village of Charmes, on the door-steps, at the windows and loopholes, ap-peared the faces of young and old, looking at the flight of Mother Lefèvre; nor did their evil tongues spare her :—" Ah ! they are turned out at last," cried some ; " another time, do not meddle with what does not concern you."

Others reflected with a loud voice, that Catherine had been rich long enough, and that every one should have his turn at poverty. As for the indus-try, wisdom, kind-heartedness, and all the virtues of the old farm-wife, or Jean-Claude's patriotism, or the courage of Jérome and the three Maternes, the disinterested motives of Doctor Lorquin or Marc Divès's self-sacrifice, nobody ever mentioned them ; for were they not vanquished?

CHAPTER XXII

AT the end of the valley of Bouleaux, two gun-shots from the village of Charmes, to the left, the little troop began slowly to ascend the path to the' old " burg." Hullin, remembering how he had taken the same road when he went to buy powder of Marc Divès, could not help feeling very sad. Then, notwithstanding his journey to Phalsbourg, the spectacle of the wounded from Leipzig and Hanau, and the account given by the old sergeant, he did not despair or doubt of the success of the defence. Now all was lost ; the enemy were descending into Lorraine, and the mountaineers were retreating. Marc Divès rode by the side of the wall in the snow ; his horse, apparently accustomed to this journey, neighed loudly. The smuggler turned from time to time to look back on the plateau of Bois-de-Chênes. Suddenly he exclaimed, " Look! here come the Cossacks! "

They all halted to look.   They were already high
up on the mountain, above the village and farm
of Bois-de-Chênes.   The morning mists were giving
way to the gray light of the winter's day, and, on
the hill-side could be distinguished the forms of several Cossacks, with their heads raised, and pistols
pointed, stealthily approaching the old farm-house.
They were scattered after the manner of sharp-
shooters, as if they feared a surprise.   A few minutes later more appeared, ascending the valley of
Houx, then still more, all in the same attitude, upright in their stirrups, in order to see as far as possible.   The first, having passed by the farm and .
observing nothing threatening, waved their lances
and returned half way back.   Whereupon the others galloped up at full speed like a flock of crows
when they have sighted their prey.   In a few minutes the farm was surrounded and the door opened.
In another moment the windows were smashed, and
the furniture, mattresses, and linen, thrown outside.   Catherine calmly looked on at the pillage.
She said nothing for some time ; but, on seeing Yégof, whom she had not perceived before, strike
Duchêne with the butt-end of his lance, and push
him out of the farm, she could not restrain a cry of
indignation.

"The wretch ! Could any one be cowardly

enough to strike a poor old man unable to defend himself. Ah ! brigand, if I only held thee ! "

" Come along, Catherine," said Jean-Claude ; " that's enough ; what is the use of gazing at such a spectacle any longer? "

" You are right," said the old mistress ; " let us go on, or I shall be tempted to go back and revenge myself."

On approaching the red rocks, incrusted with large white and black pebbles, overhanging the precipice like the arches of an immense cathedral, Louise and Catherine stopped in ecstasy. The magnificent view of the streams of Lorraine, and the blue ribbon of the Rhine to their right, with the distant woods and valleys, filled them with joy, and the old dame said piously, " Jean-Claude, He who created these rocks, and formed these valleys, forests, heaths, and mosses, He will render to us the justice we merit."

As they were gazing thus on the rugged precipices, Marc led his horse into a cavern close by, and, returning, began to climb up before them, saying, " Take care, or you may slip ! "

At the same time he pointed to the blue precipice on their right, with pine-trees at the bottom. Everybody then relapsed into silence till the terrace was reached, where the arch commenced. There

they breathed more freely. In the middle of the
passage were the smugglers Brenn, Pfeifer, and
Joubac, with their long gray mantles and black hats,
sitting round a fire. Marc Divès said to them,
"Here we are ! The 'kaiserlichs' are masters.
Zimmer was killed last night. Is Hexe-Baizel up
there?"

"Yes," replied Brenn ; "she is making cartridges."

"They may be of use," said Marc. "Keep your
eyes open, and if any come up fire on them."

The Maternes halted at the corner of the rock; and
these three sturdy men, with their powerful muscular
limbs, their hats pushed back, and carbines on their
shoulders, offered a curious spectacle in the blue
mists of the abyss. Old Materne was pointing with
outstretched hand to a small white speck in the distance, almost hidden in the midst of the pines. "Do
you recognize that, my boys?" said he ; and they
all three peered through their half-closed eyes.

"It is our house," replied Kasper.

"Poor Margrédel ! " rejoined the old hunter,
after a short pause ; "how uneasy she must have
been these last eight days? What prayers does she
not offer up for us to Saint-Odile?"

At that moment Marc Divès, who was walking on
in front, uttered an exclamation of surprise.

"Mother Lefèvre," said he, stopping short, "the Cossacks are burning your farm."

Catherine received the tidings very calmly, and advanced to the edge of the terrace, Louise and Jean-Claude following. At the bottom of the abyss was a great white cloud, through which could be seen a bright spark, as it were, on the side of Bois-de-Chênes—that was all ; but at intervals, when the wind blew strong, the flames shot up, the two high black gables, the hay-loft, the small stables burned brightly, then all disappeared once more.

"It is nearly finished," said Hullin, in a low voice.

"Yes," replied Catherine ; "there are the labor and trouble of forty years vanishing in smoke ; but they cannot burn my good land, nor the great meadow of Eichmath. We will begin our work over again. Gaspard and Louise will repair it all. I regret nothing I have done."

A quarter of an hour later thousands of sparks arose, and the building crumbled to the ground. The black gables alone remained standing. They continued to ascend the path. As they were ascending the higher terrace, they heard the sharp voice of Hexe-Baizel.

"Is it thou, Catherine?" she cried. "Ah, I never thought thou wouldst have come to see me in my wretched hole."

THERE GO UP IN SMOKE FORTY YEARS OF TOIL AND TROUBLE.

Baizel and Catherine Lefèvre had been at school together in former days, therefore they used the third person when speaking.

"Nor I neither," replied the old farm-mistress. "All the same, Baizel—one is glad to find in misfortune an old companion of one's childhood."

Baizel seemed touched by her words.

"All that is here, Catherine, is thine," she exclaimed; "everything!"

She pointed to her miserable stool, the furze broom, and the five or six fagots on the hearth. Catherine looked on a few moments in silence, and then said : "It is not grand, but it is solid ; at least, they will not be able to burn down thy house."

"No, they will not burn it," said Hexe-Baizel, laughing ; "they would need all the wood of the province of Dabo even to warm it a little. Ha ! ha ! ha !"

After so many fatigues, the partisans stood in need of repose. They all placed their guns against the wall, and lay down on the ground to sleep, Marc Divès having opened the second cavern to them, where they at least were sheltered. Marc then went out with Hullin to examine their position.

CHAPTER XXIII

On the rock of the Falkenstein, high up in the clouds, stands a tower, somewhat sunken at its base. This tower, overgrown with brambles, hawthorn, and bilberries, is as old as the mountain ; neither the French, Germans, nor Swedes have destroyed it. The stone and cement are so solidly combined that not even a fragment can be detached from it. · It looks gloomy and mysterious, carrying one back to ancient times, beyond the memory of man.

At that time of the year when the wild-geese migrated in flocks, Marc Divès, when he had nothing better to do, used to await them hidden in the tower, and sometimes at nightfall, when the flocks came through the fogs flying in large circles before resting, he would bring down two or three, much to the satisfaction of Hexe-Baizel, who was always very willing to put them on a spit. Often, too, in the autumn, Marc laid traps in the bushes,

286

where he caught thrushes.   The old tower also
served him as a wood-house.

Divès, perceiving that his wood, covered with
snow and soaked by rain, gave more smoke than
light, had covered in the old tower with a roof of
planks.   With reference to this occasion, the smuggler related a curious story.   He pretended that,
on laying the rafters, he had discovered, at the bottom of a fissure, a snow-white owl, blind and feeble,
but supplied with quantities of bats and field-mice.
He therefore called it the " grandmother of the
country," as he supposed that all the birds came to
feed it on account of its extreme old age.

Toward the close of the day, the partisans posted
round the rock saw the white uniforms appearing
in the neighboring gorges.   They poured in on all
sides in large numbers, thereby clearly showing
their determination to blockade the Falkenstein.
Perceiving this, Marc Divès became more thoughtful.   " If they surround us," said he, " we shall
not be able to procure food, and shall have to surrender or die of hunger."

The enemy's staff on horseback could be clearly
distinguished, halting round the fountain of the
village of Charmes.   There also stood a tall chief
with a large paunch, who was contemplating the
rock through a telescope.   Behind him was Yégof,

whom from time to time he turned round to question. The women and children formed a circle beyond them, apparently highly delighted, and five or six Cossacks pranced about. The smuggler could not contain himself any longer, and, taking Hullin aside, "Look," said he, "at that long line of shakos gliding along the Sarre, and at the others who are scaling the valley on this side like hares ; they are ' kaiserlichs,' aren't they? Well, what are they going to do, Jean-Claude? "

" They are going to surround the mountain, that is clear. How many are there, dost thou think? "

"From three to four thousand men, without counting those who are walking over the country. Well, what can Piorette do against this pack of vagabonds with three hundred men? I ask thee frankly, Hullin."

" He can do nothing," replied the worthy man, simply. " The Germans know that our ammunition is on the Falkenstein ; they dread an insurrection after they enter Lorraine, and wish to insure their rear. The enemy's general knows that we cannot be taken by mere force, he is deciding to reduce us by hunger. All that is true, Marc ; but we are men : we will do our duty—we will die here ! "

There was a short silence; Marc Divès frowned, and did not seem at all convinced.

"We will die !" he replied, scratching his head. "I do not see why we should die at all ; it is not our intention to die : too many people would be gratified by it."

"What wouldst thou do?" said Hullin, dryly. "Wouldst thou surrender?"

"Surrender !" exclaimed the smuggler. "Dost thou take me for a coward?"

"Then explain thyself."

"This evening I start for Phalsbourg. I risk my skin in crossing the enemy's lines ; but I like that better than folding my arms here, and perishing with hunger. I will enter the town on the first 'sortie,' or I will endeavor to climb one of the gates. The commandant, Meunier, knows me. I have sold him tobacco for three years. Like thyself, he has gone through the campaigns of Italy and Egypt. Well, I will explain everything to him. I shall see Gaspard Lefèvre. I will so arrange that they will give us, perhaps, a company. Dost thou see, Jean-Claude, that the uniform alone would save us? All the brave men who remain will join Piorette ; and in any case we shall be delivered. That is my idea. What dost thou think of it?"

He looked at Hullin, whose gloomy, fixed expression made him uneasy.

"Dost thou not think that a chance?"

19

"It is an idea," said Jean-Claude at last. "I do not oppose it." And, looking full in the smuggler's face, "Swear to me to do thy best to enter the town."

"I will swear nothing," replied Marc, whose brown cheeks were covered with a flush. "I leave all my possessions here, my wife, my comrades, Catherine Lefèvre, and thee, my oldest friend! If I do not return, I shall be a traitor; but if I return, Jean-Claude, thou shalt explain what thou meanest by thy demand: we will settle this little affair between us."

"Marc," said Hullin, "forgive me! I have suffered much these last days. I was wrong. Misfortune makes one distrustful. Give me thy hand. Go! Save us, save Catherine, save my child! I say so now: our only resource is in thee."

Hullin's voice faltered. Divès relented; but he rejoined: "All the same, Hullin, thou shouldst not have said that to me at such a time. Never let us speak of it again. I will leave my skin on the way, or return to deliver you. This evening, when darkness sets in, I will leave. The 'kaiserlichs' surround the mountain already; but no matter, I have a good horse, and, besides, I have always been lucky."

By six o'clock the highest peaks were hid in dark-

ness.   Hundreds of fires, sparkling in the depths of
the gorges, announced that the Germans were preparing their repasts.

Marc Divès felt his way down the narrow path.
Hullin listened for a few seconds to the retreating
steps of his comrade, then walked anxiously toward
the old tower, where their head-quarters were established.   He lifted the thick woollen covering
which closed the owl's-nest, and perceived Catherine, Louise, and the others crouching round a small
fire.   The old farm-mistress sat on an oak log, her
hands clasped round her knees, watching the flames
fixedly, with compressed lips.   Louise leant dreamily against the wall.   Jérome stood behind Catherine, his hands crossed on his stick, his otter-skin
cap touching the mouldy roof.   All were sad and
discouraged.   Hexe-Baizel, who was lifting the
lid of a kettle, and Doctor Lorquin, who was
scratching the softer parts of the old wall with
the point of his sabre, alone preserved their usual
expression.

" Here we are," said the doctor, " returned to
the days of the Triboques.   These walls are more
than two thousand years old.   A great deal of water must have flowed from the heights of the Falkenstein and Grosmann to the Sarre and Rhine since
a fire was last kindled in this tower."

" Yes," replied Catherine, as though awaking
from a dream ; " and many besides ourselves have
suffered cold, hunger, and misery here.   Who knew
of it?   No one.   And one, or two, or three hundred years hence, others, perhaps, will again come
for shelter to this place.   They will find, as we have,
the wall cold, and the earth damp ; they will make
a fire ; they will look as we look ; and they will say,
like us, ' Who suffered here before ourselves? Why
did they suffer?   They must have been pursued and
hunted, like ourselves, to be obliged to come and
hide in this wretched hole.'   And they will think
of past times; and no one will reply."

Jean-Claude came up to them. , The old dame,
raising her head, and looking at him, said, " Well !
we are blockaded ; the enemy wants to subdue us
by famine."

" True, Catherine," replied Hullin; " but I did
not expect that.   I felt certain of a sudden attack;
but the ' kaiserlichs ' have not gained all yet.
Divès has just left for Phalsbourg.   He knows the
commandant of the place; and if they will only
send a few hundred men to our help——"

" Do not count on that," interrupted the old
woman.   " Marc may be taken or killed by the
Germans: and, if not, and suppose he manages to
cross their lines, how will he be able to enter Phals-

bourg? You well know that the town is besieged by the Russians."

Then everybody relapsed into silence. Hexe-Baizel brought up the soup, and they sat in a circle round the smoking bowl.

CHAPTER XXIV

A FLAG OF TRUCE

CATHERINE LEFÈVRE came out of the ancient ruin about seven in the morning; Louise and Hexe-Baizel were still asleep; but broad daylight, the clear light of the high regions, was already penetrating the abysses. In the depths, through the azure, the woods, valleys, and rocks could be clearly traced, like the mosses and pebbles of a lake beneath the blue crystal water. Not a breath disturbed the air; and Catherine, gazing over this grand spectacle, felt a calmness and tranquillity beyond even that which comes of sleep. "What are our miseries of a day," thought she, "our uneasinesses and our sufferings? Why pester heaven with our moans? why fear the future? All this lasts but a second; our sighs are of no more avail than the chirp of the grasshopper in autumn; and do its cries prevent winter from coming? Must not time pursue its course, and everything die to be renewed?"

Thus thought the old dame, and she had no longer any fears for the future. She had been thus musing for a few instants, when suddenly a hum of voices struck her ears: she turned, and saw Hullin with the three smugglers, talking seriously together on the other side of the plateau. They were engaged in a grave discussion, and had not noticed her. Catherine approached closer to them, and heard the following conversation:—

"Then you do not think it possible for any one to get down either side?"

"No, Jean-Claude, it is quite impossible," replied Brenn; "those brigands know the country thoroughly well: all the paths are guarded. Hold, look along the paths of that stream: we never dreamt of observing it even; well! they are defending that now. And over there, on the passage of the Rothstein, a path only for a goat, which is not trodden once in ten years—thou canst see a bayonet sparkle behind the rock, canst thou not? And that nearer path along which I have slipped with my bags for these eight years past without meeting a single gendarme, they occupy that also: the devil certainly must have showed them all the defiles."

"Yes," exclaimed Joubac, "if the devil has nothing to do with it, at least Yégof has!"

"But," continued Hullin, "it seems to me that three or four men might, if they liked, push through one of those posts."

"No, those posts lean one on the other; at the first shot one would have a whole regiment upon one's shoulders," replied Brenn. "Besides, supposing one had the luck to get through, how could one return with provisions? My opinion is, that it is impossible."

There was a pause.

"After that," said Joubac, "if Hullin likes we will try all the same."

"We will try what?" said Brenn. "To break our legs in escaping ourselves, and leave the others in the trap. I don't mind; if any others go, I will too. But as for pretending to return with provisions, it is impossible. Come, Joubac, by which way art thou going, and by which way wilt thou return? If thou knowest of a passage, tell me. For twenty years I have scoured the mountain with Marc. I know all the paths and roads ten leagues round, and I see no other way but through the sky!"

Hullin turned round at that moment and saw Mother Lefèvre, close behind, listening attentively.

"What! were you there, Catherine?" said he. "Our affairs are taking a bad turn."

"Yes, I heard; there is no means of renewing our provisions."

"Our provisions!" said Brenn with a queer laugh. "Are you aware, Mother Lefèvre, for how long we have them?"

"Why, for a fortnight," replied the old dame.

"For a week," said the smuggler, shaking out the ashes from his pipe.

"It is true," said Hullin, "Marc Divès and myself thought they would attack the Falkenstein; we never imagined the enemy would blockade it like a fortress. We have been deceived!"

"And what is to be done?" said Catherine, turning pale.

"We are going to put everybody on half rations. If, in a fortnight, Marc does not return we shall have nothing left—then we shall see."

So saying, Hullin, Catherine, and the smugglers, with bowed heads, took the path to the breach again. As they were coming down the slope, thirty feet below them they perceived Materne. He was climbing breathlessly among the ruins, and clutched hold of the bushes to help him along faster.

"Well," shouted Jean-Claude to him; "what is the matter, old fellow?"

"Ah! there thou art. I was coming to find thee; one of the enemy's officers has come forward

on the wall of the old ' burg' with a little white
flag; he looks as though he had something to say
to us."

Hullin advanced immediately to the edge of
the rock, and saw a German officer standing on the
wall, and awaiting a signal to mount. He was
about two gun-shots distant; farther behind five
or six soldiers were stationed with their arms
shouldered. After having inspected this group,
Jean-Claude turned and said: " It is a flag of truce.
He comes no doubt to summon us to surrender."

" Fire upon them! " cried Catherine; " it is all
we have to say."

All the others appeared of the same advice, excepting Hullin, who, without making any reply
descended to the terrace, where the rest of the partisans were assembled.

" My children," said he, " the enemy sends us
a flag of truce. We do not know what he wants
of us. I suppose it is to order us to lay down our
arms; but it may possibly be something else.
Frantz and Kasper will go to meet him; they must
blindfold the officer and lead him here."

No objection being made, Materne's sons shouldered their carbines and walked away under the
lofty arch. About ten minutes later, the two red-
haired hunters reached the officer; there was a rapid

conference between them, after which all three began to climb to the Falkenstein. By degrees, as
the party ascended, the uniform of the officer and his
face could be distinguished: he was a thin man,
with light brown hair, well made, and determined-
looking. At the foot of the rock Frantz and Kasper blindfolded him, and soon the sound of their
steps under the arch could be heard.

Jean-Claude going toward them, himself un-
bound the handkerchief, saying, " You desire to
communicate something to me, sir; I am listening."

The partisans stood about fifteen paces away.
Catherine Lefèvre, the foremost among them,
frowned; her bony, angular face, long beaked nose,
her three or four tresses of gray hair, falling down
over her temples and hollow cheek-bones, her compressed lips, and the fixity of her gaze, appeared
at first to rivet the attention of the German officer.
Next to her stood Louise, with her sweet pale face.
Jérome, with his long tawny beard, draped in his
horse-hair tunic, and Materne, leaning on his short
carbine, and the others around him completed the
group.

The officer himself was the object of particular
attention. One could see in him, his attitude, fine
sunburnt features, clear gray eyes, handsome mus-

tache, in the elegance of his limbs, hardened by the labors of war, a member of an aristocratic race: he combined the old soldier and the man of the world, the warrior and the diplomatist.

This reciprocal inspection being finished, the bearer of the flag of truce said, in good French, " I have the honor of addressing the Commandant Hullin? "

" Yes, sir," replied Jean-Claude.

And seeing the other gazing hesitatingly around the circle, he continued, " Speak loud, sir, so that everybody may hear you. When honor and the country are in question all are concerned in France; the women are interested as well as ourselves. Have you any proposition to make me, and from whom? "

" From the General Commander-in-chief. Here is my commission."

" Good; we are listening to you, sir."

Then the officer, raising his voice, said in a resolute tone: " Permit me first, commandant, to remark that you have fulfilled your duty splendidly: you have called forth the esteem of your enemies."

" In the matter of duty," replied Hullin, " we have all done our best."

" Yes," added Catherine, dryly, " and since our enemies esteem us on that account, well, they will esteem us still more in eight or fifteen days, for we have not reached the end of the war yet. You will live to see more of us."

The officer turned his head, and looked with astonishment at the savage energy in the old woman's face.

" They are noble sentiments," he retorted, after an instant's silence: " but humanity has its rights, and to squander blood uselessly is returning evil for evil."

" Then why do you come into our country?" cried Catherine sharply. " Go away, and we will let you alone. You make war like brigands: you steal, pillage, and burn. You all deserve to be hanged. And to set a good example, you personally ought to be hurled over that rock."

The officer turned pale, for the old woman seemed quite capable of carrying out her threat; however he soon regained his composure, and replied calmly: " I am aware that the Cossacks have set fire to the farm in front of this rock. They are pillagers, such as are to be found in the rear of every army, and this isolated act proves nothing against the discipline of our troops. The French soldiers did the same in Germany, and particularly in the Tyrol; not content with pillaging and burning the villages, they mercilessly shot all mountaineers suspected of having taken up arms for the defence of their country. We might make reprisals, and should be justified in doing so; but .we are not barbarians, we can understand that patriotism is noble and grand, even in its most ill-advised acts. Besides, we are not making war on the French people, but on the Emperor Napoleon. And the general, on learning the conduct of the Cossacks, has publicly punished this act of Vandalism; more, he has decided that an indemnity shall be accorded to the proprietor of the farm."

"I will not receive anything from you," Catherine hastily interrupted; "I will keep my injustice and revenge myself."

The officer understanding by the accent of the old woman's voice that he could make no impression upon her, and feeling that it was even dangerous for him to reply, turned toward Hullin, and said: "I am ordered, commandant, to offer you the honors of war if you will consent to give up this position. You have no provisions, we know that. In a few days you will be obliged to lay down your arms. The esteem felt for you by our general has alone caused him to make you honorable conditions. A longer resistance would be useless. We are masters of the Donon, our battalions are entering Lorraine; the campaign will not be concluded here, therefore you have no interest in defending such a position. We wish to spare you the horrors of famine on this barren rock. Come, commandant, decide."

Hullin turned toward the partisans and said to them: "You have heard? I refuse; but I will submit if everybody accepts the propositions of the enemy."

"We refuse, all of us," said Jérome.

"Yes, all," replied the others.

Catherine Lefèvre, who had looked inflexible till then, regarded Louise and seemed touched; she took her by the arm, and turning toward the officer, said to him: "We have a child with us; is there no means by which we could send her to one of our relations at Saverne?"

Hardly had Louise heard these words, than throwing herself into Hullin's arms with fear, she cried out: "No, no, I will remain with you, Papa Jean-Claude; I will die with you."

"Well," said Hullin; "go tell your general what you have seen: tell him that the Falkenstein will be ours till death! Kasper, Frantz, reconduct the truce-bearer."

The officer appeared to hesitate, but as he opened his mouth to speak, Catherine, pale with rage, exclaimed, "Begone! you have not yet gained all the advantages you think. It is that brigand Yé-

gof who has told you that we have no provisions;
but we have for two months, and by that time our
army will have exterminated you all. Traitors will
not always have the best of it: bad luck to you."

Seeing she was becoming more and more excit-
ed, the officer thought it best to take his departure:
he turned to his guides, who put the bandages over
his eyes, and conducted him to the foot of the Falkenstein.

The instructions which Hullin had given concerning the provisions were executed on the same
day, and each received his half ration. A sentry was
placed before Hexe-Baizel's cavern, where the food
was kept; the door was barricaded, and Jean-
Claude decided that the distributions should be
made in the presence of all, so as to prevent any injustice; but all these precautions were destined to
fail in preserving the unfortunate people from the
horrors of famine.

CHAPTER XXV

" BATTLE OF THE ROCKS "

FOR three days they had been entirely without
food on the Falkenstein, and Divès had given no
signs of life. How often, during those long days
of agony, did the mountaineers turn their eyes toward Phalsbourg!—how often had they listened,
fancying they could hear the smuggler's step, while
the vague murmur of the wind alone filled the
space!

The nineteenth day since the arrival of the partisans on the Falkenstein was passed amidst all the
tortures of hunger. They no longer spoke; they
remained crouched on the earth, with pinched faces,
and lost in endless reveries. Sometimes they
watched each other with sparkling eyes, as though
about to devour one another, then relapsed into
sullen calm.

Occasionally Yégof's raven, flying from crag to
crag, would approach this place of misfortune.
Then old Materne would take aim with his rifle,

but the ill-omened bird would immediately take flight with dismal croakings, and the old hunter's arm fell helpless by his side. And as though the exhaustion of hunger was not enough to fill the measure of so much misery, the poor creatures only opened their mouths to accuse and menace one another.

"Do not touch me," cried Hexe-Baizel, in a shrill voice to those who looked at her—"do not look at me, or I will bite you!"

Louise was delirious; her great blue eyes, instead of living objects, saw only shadows flit across the plateau, touching the tops of the bushes, and resting on the old tower.

"Here is food!" she said. Then the others became enraged with the poor child, crying out with fury, that she was mocking them, and bidding her beware.

Jérome alone remained perfectly calm; but the great quantity of snow he had swallowed to appease the pangs of ravenous hunger, had inundated his whole body and bony face with a cold sweat. To appease the cravings of his stomach, Doctor Lorquin had bound a handkerchief round his loins, and tightened it more and more. He was seated with his back against the tower, and his eyes closed, though he now and then opened them to say, " We have reached the first—the second—the third stage. One more day, and all will be over!"

He then began to declaim about the Druids, Odin, Brahma, Pythagoras, quoting Latin and Greek, and announcing the near transformation of the people of Harberg into wolves, foxes, and animals of all sorts. "For myself," he exclaimed, "I will be a lion! I will eat fifteen pounds of beef every day!"

Then renewing his discourse:—"No, I will be a man. I will preach peace, brotherhood, justice. Ah, my friends, we suffer for our own faults. What have we done with the other side of the Rhine for the last ten years? With what right did we set up masters over those peoples? Why did we not exchange our ideas, our sentiments, the produce of our arts and of our industry with theirs? Why did we not approach them like brothers, in place of wishing to subject them to us? We should have been well received. What must they not have suffered, those unhappy people, during those ten years of violence and rapine! Now they are avenged, and it is just! May the malediction of heaven fall on the miserable wretches who get up divisions among peoples in order to oppress them!"

After these moments of excitement he would fall exhausted against the wall of the tower, and murmur—"Some bread; oh, only a morsel of bread!"

Materne's two sons, crouched in the brushwood, their carbines at their shoulders, seemed to expect the passage of some game which never arrived. Their ceaseless watching alone sustained their expiring strength.

Others, bent double with pain, were shivering with cold, and yet were burning with fever: they reproached Jean-Claude with having brought them to the Falkenstein.

Hullin, with a superhuman force of character, still went and came, observing what took place in the neighboring valleys, but without saying anything.

Occasionally he would advance to the edge of the rock, and with his massive jaws clinched and shining eyes, looked at Yégof, seated before a large fire, on the plains of Bois-de-Chênes, in the midst of a band of Cossacks. Since the arrival of the Germans in the valley of the Charmes, the madman had never quitted his post, but appeared to be watching the agony of his victims.

Such was the position of these unfortunate people beneath the open heaven.

In the gloom of a prison the torture of hunger is doubtless frightful, but in the broad light of

FOR THREE DAYS PROVISIONS HAD COMPLETELY FAILED.

day, in the eyes of a whole country, in face of all
the resources of nature, its sufferings are beyond
all description.

At the close of the nineteenth day, between four
and five o'clock in the afternoon, the weather was
gloomy; large gray clouds rose behind the snowy
summit of the Grosmann; the red sun, like a ball
of fire, threw a few last rays into the misty horizon.
The silence on the rock was unbroken. Louise no
longer gave signs of life; Kasper and Frantz remained among the bushes immovable as stones;
Catherine Lefèvre, crouching on the earth, her
skinny arms clasped round her pointed knees, with
hard, rigid features, her hair hanging over her
clammy cheeks, looked like some old sibyl seated
in the heather. She had ceased speaking. That
evening, Hullin, Jérome, old Materne, and Doctor
Lorquin gathered themselves around the old farm-
mistress to die. They were silent, and the last rays
of twilight fell upon the wretched group. To the
right, behind a jutting rock, a few German watchfires sparkled in the abyss. Suddenly the old dame,
rousing from her dreams, began to murmur some
unintelligible words.

"Divès is coming," said she, in a low voice.
"I see him. He goes out from the door to the
right of the arsenal. Gaspard follows him,
and——"

Then she began to count.

"Two hundred and fifty men," she exclaimed; "National Guards and soldiers. They cross the ditch; they mount behind the demilune. Gaspard is speaking with Marc. What does he say?"

She appeared to listen.

"Let us . hurry!—yes, hurry! Time flies! There they are on the glacis!"

There was a long pause; then the old woman suddenly arose, with outstretched arms and hair on end, and screamed aloud in a terrible voice:— "Courage! Kill, kill! Ah, ah!" And she fell down heavily.

This fearful cry awoke them all; it would have aroused the dead. The besieged seemed born anew. Something was abroad. Was it hope, life, a spirit? I know not; but all rose up on their hands and knees, like wild beasts, holding their breath to hear. Louise even moved softly and lifted her head; Frantz and Kasper dragged themselves along; and, strange to say, Hullin, turning his eyes toward Phalsbourg, thought he saw through the darkness the flashes of a fusillade announcing a sortie.

Catherine had resumed her first appearance; but her cheeks, before still and pale as those of a corpse, trembled now. The others listened as though their salvation hung on her lips. A quarter of an hour nearly had passed, when the old dame slowly re-commenced:—"They have passed the enemy's lines; they are running toward Lutzelbourg. I see them! Gaspard and Divès are before, with Des-marets, Ulrich, Weber, and our friends of the town. They come! they come!"

She again became silent. Long did they listen; but the vision was gone. Seconds followed seconds slowly like centuries. At length, Hexe-Baizel, in an angry voice, began to say:—"She is mad! She saw nothing! Marc, I know him: he is making fun of us. What does it matter to him if we perish? So long as he has his bottle and tobacco and can smoke his pipe in peace by the fireside, all the rest is nothing. Ah, the wretch!"

Then all relapsed into silence, and the unhap-py creatures, reanimated for an instant by hope of a speedy deliverance, again fell into despair.

"It is a dream," thought they; "Hexe-Baizel is right: we are condemned to die of hunger."

While this was going on night arrived. When the moon rose behind the high pine-trees, and lit up the gloomy group, Hullin alone kept watch, in spite of his raging fever. Far off—very far off in the gorges—he heard the voices of the German sen-tries; "Wer da? Wer da?" the rounds of the pa-trols in the woods; the shrill neighing of the horses

at the picket, and the shouts of their keepers.
Toward midnight the worthy fellow fell asleep like
the rest. When he awoke, the clock of the village
of Charmes struck four. At the sound of the distant chimes, Hullin shook off his drowsiness, and
he opened his eyes. As he gazed unconsciously into
the darkness, trying to collect his thoughts, the
vague glimmer of a torch passed before his eyes.
A feeling of dread came over him, and he said to
himself:—" Am I mad? The night is dark, and
I see torches! "

Nevertheless, the flame reappeared; he looked
at it, then raised himself quickly, resting his con-
tracted face for a second in his hand. At length,
hazarding one more look, he distinctly saw a fire on
the Giromani, on the other side of Blanru—a fire
which swept the heavens with its purple wings,
causing the shadows of the pines to dance on the
snow. Recalling to himself that this signal had
been agreed upon between him and Piorette to announce an attack, he trembled from head to foot,
his face streamed with perspiration, and, walking
in the dark, groping like a blind man with his
hands outstretched, he stammered,—" Catherine,
Louise, Jérome." But no one answered. Still
groping about, thinking he was walking while he
did not make a step, the unfortunate man fell down,

exclaiming, "My children! Catherine! they come! We are saved!"

A vague sound immediately arose. One would have said that the dead were awaking. There was a shrill laugh: it was Hexe-Baizel, gone mad from her sufferings.

Then Catherine exclaimed: "Hullin! Hullin! who spoke?"

Jean-Claude, recovering from his emotion, said, in firmer tones: "Jérome, Catherine, Materne, and the others, are you dead? Do you not see that fire down there, in the direction of Blanru? It is Piorette, who is coming to our assistance."

At the same instant, a deep boom rolled along the gorges of the Jägerthal, like the rumbling of a storm. The summoning trumpet of the Judgment could not have produced a greater effect on the besieged: they suddenly awoke.

"It is Piorette! it is Marc!" cried broken, harsh voices, such as might have belonged to skeletons; "they are coming to our aid!"

And all the wretched creatures tried to rise: some sobbed; but they had no longer any tears to shed. A second report brought them upright.

"They are firing in detachments," said Hullin. "Ours are doing so too. We have soldiers in lines! France forever!"

"Yes," replied Jérome. "Mother Catherine was right; the Phalsbourgers are coming to our assistance; they are descending the hills of the Sarre; and there is Piorette, who is now attacking by Blanru."

Indeed, the fusillade now began to resound on both sides at once, toward the plateau of Bois-de-Chênes and the heights of Kilbèri.

The two chiefs embraced; and, as they groped along in the dark night, seeking to reach the edge of the rock, suddenly Materne cried out, "Take care, the precipice is near!"

They stopped short and looked down; but nothing was to be seen: a current of cold air ascending from the abyss alone warned them of the danger. The peaks and gorges round were all plunged in darkness. On the hill-sides in front the flashes of the fusillade passed like lightning, illuminating now an old oak, now the heather, or the black outline of some rock; and groups of men were coming and going, as though in the midst of a conflagration. Two thousand feet below, in the depth of the gorge, could be heard dull sounds of galloping horses, and the clamors of command. Now, the shout of a mountaineer hailing another was prolonged from peak to peak, and arose to the Falkenstein like a sigh.

"It is Marc!" said Hullin; "it is Marc's voice!"

"Yes, it is Marc, who bids us have courage," replied Jérome.

The others looked around them with outstretched necks, their hands grasping the rock. The fusillade continued with a vivacity that betrayed the fury of the battle; but nothing could be seen. Oh! how they wished to take part in this supreme struggle! With what ardor would they not have thrown themselves into the fire! The fear of being abandoned once more, of seeing by daylight their defenders retreating, rendered them speechless with terror.

Day began to dawn; the pale light arose behind the black summits, and began to illumine the gloomy valleys, and soon the fog of the abyss turned to silvery mists. Hullin, looking across the openings of these clouds, at length made out the position. The Germans had lost the heights of Valtin, and the plain of Bois-de-Chênes. They were massed in the valley of Charmes, at the foot of the Falkenstein, so as to obtain shelter from their adversaries' fire. Piorette, master of Bois-de-Chênes, had thrown out outworks in front of the rock, on the side of the descent to Charmes. He was pacing to and fro, his pipe in his mouth, and

carbine slung across his shoulders; and the blue
axes of the wood-cutters glistened in the rising sun.
On the left of the village, toward Valtin, in the
midst of the furze, Marc Divès, on a small black
horse, with a long tail, his blade by his side, pointed to the ruins and the sledge road; while an infantry officer and a few National Guards were listening to him. Gaspard Lefèvre stood alone, in
front of the group, leaning on his gun; and, on the
summit of the hill, by the wood, two or three hundred men were keeping watch.

The sight of the small number of their defenders
caused the hearts of the besieged to grow fearful;
all the more so, as the Germans were seven or eight
times superior in numbers, and had already begun
to form columns of attack, to regain the positions
they had lost. Horsemen were conveying on all
sides the general's orders, and the bayonets began
to defile.

"It is all over," said Hullin to Jérome. "What
are five or six hundred men to do against four thousand in line of battle? The Phalsbourgers will return to their houses and say, 'We have done our
duty.' And Piorette will be crushed."

The others thought so too; and their despair was
brought to a climax when they suddenly saw a long
file of Cossacks riding furiously along the valley

of Charmes, with Yégof the madman galloping like
the wind at their head, his beard, horse's tail, dog-
skin, and red hair floating wildly in the air. He
looked up at the rock, and brandished his lance
above his head. Reaching the bottom of the valley,
he made at once for the enemy's staff, and coming
up to the general, he indicated by gestures the other
side of the plateau of Bois-de-Chênes.

"Ah, the brigand!" shouted Hullin. "See,
he tells them that Piorette has no outworks
on that side, that they must go round the mountain."

In fact, a column began immediately to march
in that direction, while another went toward the
outworks to mask the movement of the first.

"Materne," cried Jean-Claude, "is there no
means of sending a ball into the madman?"

The old hunter shook his head.

"No," said he, "it is impossible; he is out of
range."

Just then, Catherine Lefèvre gave a wild scream
like a hawk.

"Crush them, crush them, as they did at the
Blutfeld!"

And the old woman, an instant before so feeble,
threw herself on a mass of rock, lifted it with both
hands, advanced, with her streaming gray hair, bent

over to the edge of the abyss, and the rock dashed through the space beneath.

A terrible crash resounded below, pieces of pine flew out on all sides, the great stone rebounded a hundred feet away, and descending the steep slope with fresh impulse, struck Yégof, and crushed him at the feet of the enemy's general. This was but the work of a few seconds.

Catherine, upright on the edge of the rock laughed with a rattling sound, which seemed as though it would never end.

The others, as though all animated with new life, precipitated themselves on the ruins of the old castle, shouting: " Slay them! slay them! Crush them as at the Blutfeld! "

It is impossible to imagine a more terrible scene. These beings, at death's very door, lean and haggard as skeletons, found strength for the carnage. They no longer stumbled, they trembled no more; each one lifted his stone and threw it down the precipice, then returned to take another, without even looking to see what was passing below.

Imagine the stupor of the " kaiserlichs " at this deluge of ruins and rocks. All had turned at the sound of the stones bounding above through the bushes and clumps of trees. At first they stopped as though petrified; but looking higher up, and

seeing more and more stones descending, and above it all the spectres coming and going, lifting their arms, and continually discharging fresh burdens—seeing their comrades crushed, fifteen or twenty at a time, an immense cry went up from the valley of Charmes to the Falkenstein, and, notwithstanding the fusillade which they kept up on every side, the Germans scampered away to escape this fearful death.

In the thickest of the rout, the enemy's general contrived to rally a battalion, and descend slowly toward the village.

There was something grand and dignified about this man, so calm in the midst of disaster. He turned from time to time with a gloomy look to watch the bounding rocks, which made ghastly havoc in his columns.

Jean-Claude observed him, and, notwithstanding the intoxication of his triumph and the certitude of having escaped famine, the old soldier could not suppress a feeling of admiration.

"Look," said he to Jérome, "he acts as he did on returning from the Donon and Grosmann: he is the last to retire, and yields only bit by bit. There are, indeed, brave fellows in every country!"

Marc Divès and Piorette, the witnesses of this stroke of fortune, then descended into the midst of the fir-trees, to try and cut off the retreat of the enemy. But the battalion, reduced to half its strength, formed into square behind the village of Charmes, and slowly ascended the valley of the Sarre, stopping sometimes, like a wounded boar who turns to look at the huntsmen, whenever Piorette's men or those of Phalsbourg tried to press too nearly upon them.

Thus terminated the great battle of the Falkenstein, known in the mountains under the name of the Battle of the Rocks.

CHAPTER XXVI

CONCLUSION

THE combat was hardly over, when, toward eight o'clock, Marc Divès, Gaspard, and about thirty mountaineers, laden with provisions, ascended the Falkenstein. What a spectacle awaited them! The besieged, stretched on the earth, appeared to be dead. It seemed useless to shake them, to cry into their ears; "Jean-Claude! Catherine? Jérome!" There came no reply. Gaspard Lefèvre, seeing his mother and Louise immovable, with clinched teeth, told Marc, that if they did not return to life, he would blow out his brains with his gun. Marc replied that each man must do as he liked; but for his part he should not do likewise on Hexe-Baizel's account. At length old Colon, having laid his burden down on a stone, Kasper Materne opened his eyes, and seeing the provisions, his teeth began to chatter like those of a fox pursued by the hounds.

They immediately understood the meaning of

this symptom; and Marc Divès, going from one to the other, passed his gourd under their noses, which sufficed to bring them to. They wanted to drink its contents all up at once; but Doctor Lorquin, notwithstanding his condition, had still enough sense to warn Marc not to allow them to do so, and the slightest action of choking would be fatal to them. Each one, therefore, only received a morsel of bread, an egg, and a glass of wine, which wonderfully revived their spirits; then Catherine, Louise, and the others, were laid on sledges and were brought down to the village.

It is impossible to describe the enthusiasm and joy of their friends when they saw them return, leaner than Lazarus when he rose from his grave. They gazed at one another, and embraced, and the process was repeated on the arrival of every newcomer from Abreschwiller, Dagsburg, St. Quirin, or elsewhere.

Marc Divès was obliged to relate more than twenty times the story of his journey to Phalsbourg. The brave smuggler had had no luck. After having miraculously escaped from the balls of the "kaiserlichs," he got into the valley of Spartzprod, and fell into the midst of a band of Cossacks, who ransacked him from top to toe. He had been compelled to wander for two weeks around the Russian posts which surrounded the town, exposed to the continual fire of their sentries, and running endless risks of being taken as a spy, before being able to get into the town. Then the commandant, Meunier, at first refused to give any succor, assigning the weakness of his garrison as an excuse, and only at the pressing petitions of the towns-folk at length consented to detach two companies. Listening to his recital, the mountaineers gave vent to their admiration of Marc's courage and perseverance in the midst of danger.

"Well," replied the tall smuggler good-humoredly to those who thus congratulated him, "I have only done my duty; could I have allowed my comrades to perish? I well knew it would not be easy; those rascally Cossacks are sharper than the customs' folks; they sent you a league off like crows; but all the same, we have outwitted them."

Five or six days later everybody was on the alert; Captain Vidal, from Phalsbourg, had left twenty-five men to guard the powder; Gaspard Lefèvre was of the number, and the sturdy fellow went down every morning to the village. The allies had all passed into Lorraine, and were no longer seen in Alsace, except around the fortresses. Soon after came the news of the victories of Champ-Aubert and Montmirail; but a great misfortune was at hand; for the allies, notwithstanding the heroism of our army and the genius of the Emperor, entered Paris.

It was a terrible shock to Jean-Claude and Catherine, Materne, Jérome and all the mountaineers; but the history of these events does not belong to this tale. It has already been related by others.

Peace having been made, the farm of Bois-de-Chênes was rebuilt in the spring; the wood-cutters, the shoemakers, masons, wood-floaters, and all the workmen of the district, lent a hand in the work.

Toward the same time, the army having been disbanded, Gaspard cut off his mustaches and his marriage with Louise took place.

On the day of the wedding all the combatants of the Falkenstein and Donon came to the farm, where they were received with open doors and windows. Each brought his present to the newly married pair; Jérome, small shoes for Louise; Materne and his sons, a black cock, the most loving of birds, as all know; and Divès, packets of smuggled tobacco for Gaspard; and Doctor Lorquin a fine set of baby-linen. Tables were spread out, even in the granaries and sheds. How much wine, bread, meat, and tarts was consumed I cannot say; but what I am sure of is, that Jean-Claude, who had been low-spirited ever since the entry of the allies

into Paris, revived on that day, and sang the old
song of his youth as cheerfully as when he shoul
dered his gun and set out for Valmy, Jemmapes
and Fleurus. The echoes of the Falkenstein re
peated in the distance that old patriotic song; the
grandest and noblest that has ever been heard by
man. Catherine Lefèvre kept time on the table
with the handle of her knife; and if it be true, as
many say, that the dead come to listen when they
are spoken of, our departed friends must have been
happy, and " The King of Diamonds " have fumed
in his red beard.

Toward midnight, Hullin arose, and addressing
the newly married pair, said: " You will have fine
children; I will jump them on my knees, I will
teach them my old song, and then I shall go to rejoin my old comrades! "

So saying he embraced Louise, and arm in arm
with Marc Divès and Jérome, descended to his cottage, followed by the rest, who sang together the
fine old song. A more beautiful night was never
seen: numberless stars shone out in the dark blue
sky; the shrubs on the hill-side, where so many
brave fellows had found a grave, quivered slightly
in the breeze. Every one felt happy and softened;
they shook hands on the threshold of the small
house, and wished each other " good-night," and

departed, to the right and to the left, to their different villages.

"Good-night, Materne, Jérome, Divès, Piorette —good-night!" cried Jean-Claude.

His old friends turned back, waving their hats, and said to themselves: "There are some days when one is very happy on the earth. Ah, if there were never any plagues, or wars, or famines; if men would but agree to love and help each other; if they would but live in peace together, what a paradise this world would be!"